"Dinah, it's okay to look.

"Hell, I've been doing more than looking since we arrived here. I've been thinking, too."

The heat started deep inside her, at that secret place no one had ever penetrated . . . except this man. "Thinking?" Her voice sounded more like a croak.

"About us."

"There is no us," she quickly informed him.

"Not yet," he agreed. "Maybe never. But there is something. I feel it. You feel it—"

"No."

"Yes," he said softly, insistently. "But we're rational human beings. We don't have to act on our impulses."

She didn't feel very rational right then. She was being consumed from within—the fire inside and the one in his eyes. "Of course not. I, uh, need to go outside, get some fresh air." She had a feeling this was going to be a long night. A long, cold night. . . .

Dear Reader,

Welcome to Silhouette *Special Edition* . . . welcome to romance.

Last year I requested your opinions on the books that we publish. Thank you for the many thoughtful comments. For the next couple of months, I'd like to share quotes with you from those letters. This seems very appropriate while we are in the midst of our THAT SPECIAL WOMAN! promotion. Each one of our readers is a very *special* woman, as heroic as the heroines in our books.

This month, our THAT SPECIAL WOMAN! is Kelley McCormick, a woman who takes the trip of a lifetime and meets the man of her dreams. You'll meet Kelley and her Prince Charming in *Grand Prize Winner!* by Tracy Sinclair.

Also in store for you this month is *The Way of a Man,* the third book in Laurie Paige's WILD RIVER TRILOGY. And not to be missed are terrific books from other favorite authors—Kathleen Eagle, Pamela Toth, Victoria Pade and Judith Bowen.

I hope you enjoy this book, and all of the stories to come!

Sincerely,

Tara Gavin
Senior Editor

QUOTE OF THE MONTH:

"I enjoy characters I can relate to—female characters who are wonderful people packaged in very ordinary coverings and men who see beyond looks and who are willing to work at a relationship. I enjoy stories of couples who stick with each other and work through difficult times. Thank you, Special Edition, for the many, many hours of enjoyment."

—M. Greenleaf, Maryland

LAURIE PAIGE

THE WAY OF A MAN

SPECIAL EDITION®

Published by Silhouette Books
America's Publisher of Contemporary Romance

To the men and women of the National Forest Service at Butte Falls and the Rogue River National Forest, for their unfailing courtesy in answering questions and sharing information.

 SILHOUETTE BOOKS

ISBN 0-373-09849-9

THE WAY OF A MAN

Copyright © 1993 by Olivia M. Hall

This edition published by arrangement with Harlequin Enterprises B. V.

® and TM are trademarks of Harlequin Enterprises B. V., used under license. Trademarks indicated with ® are registered in the United States Patent and Trademark Office, the Canadian Trade Marks Office and in other countries.

Printed in U.S.A.

Books by Laurie Paige

LAURIE PAIGE

reports that life after a certain age (thirty-something and then some) keeps getting rosier. She was recently presented with the *Affaire de Coeur* Readers' Choice Silver Pen award for favorite contemporary author. Laurie gives the credit—and thanks!—to her romance readers, who are the most wonderful, loyal people in the world. She also just had another super event— the birth of her first grandchild, a boy. "Definitely hero material!"

"There be three things which are too wonderful
for me, yea, four which I know not:

The way of an eagle in the air;
The way of a serpent upon a rock;
The way of a ship in the midst of the sea;
And the way of a man with a maid."

Proverbs 30: 18–19
King James Bible

Chapter One

Dinah St. Cloud opened the door of the split-log cabin and peered out into the darkness. The road was deserted. A block down the street, she could see the lights of the town—one thoroughfare and a couple of side streets.

Most of the lights gleamed from the local watering hole, which was a small restaurant with a bar and dance area in the adjoining room. From the forest service cabin where she was staying, she could hear the band belting out a lively country-pop tune. Saturday night was in full swing, she surmised.

Where the heck was Paul? she questioned the empty road. He was supposed to have been there to pick her up ten minutes ago.

She slammed the door, then shivered as a rush of cold air swirled around her. Spring had not yet arrived on this first Saturday in April in southern Oregon.

But it was more than the temperature that chilled her. She was wary of seeing Paul again.

When she'd left Minnesota, her home state, two years ago, she'd thought that would be the end of it . . . of them. And so it had been. This meeting was strictly business . . . assuming he showed up for it.

Wrapping her arms across her chest, she considered her mixed emotions. The memories returned, as fresh and strong as if it had been yesterday since she'd last seen him.

During the year they'd worked together—he'd been the expert consultant who flew in, checked their progress, advised them on what to do next, then left—she'd been attracted to him as they discussed forest growth and reclamation projects. Then, in the fall and winter, they'd worked on a huge logging operation. He'd been in camp constantly, right up until Christmas.

She pulled her arms tight against the pain that suddenly filled her chest. She shouldn't have gotten mixed up with him, a man as handsome as a Greek god.

Pacing across the narrow room, she summoned her anger to still the remembered hurt and the present knowledge that he obviously didn't consider her important enough to be on time for this particular outing, although that wasn't like the man she'd known.

Paul had observed the niceties of polite society—always on time, always considerate, always charming. And always that touch of cynical humor.

It wasn't until the latter was turned on her that she'd realized how it could stab right to the heart.

She pushed the thought aside. She was over it now. Going to the window, she peered out at the road. Nothing.

If he thought she'd wait around for him for hours, then jump to his bidding when he crooked a finger, he was in for a surprise. She wasn't the same person she'd been in their mutual past, either.

A tremor ran over her.

She wasn't.

Paul hadn't been her first experience with the fickleness of the male half of the population. While a junior in college, she'd fallen for Carl, a man with a handsome face and charming manner, and had learned a hard and bitter lesson as a result.

She'd been doubly cautious when she'd first met Paul, worried that she had some fatal flaw that drew her to good-looking but shallow men of the playboy type.

But Paul had been different. He was intelligent, a success in his field and interested in the same things she was. There had been a quietness in him. She'd sensed the deeper man within while they'd worked together. Gradually she'd come to trust him.

And to love him.

It was hard to admit she'd been wrong a second time. She'd been older and wiser by three years since her encounter with the college heartthrob. When she met Paul, she'd just gotten out of graduate school with her master's degree in botany. She'd thought she was a lot smarter than she'd been before.

Live and learn, as they say. She finally had.

She walked the rough plank floor of the one-room cabin, uneasy about the evening ahead and angry that someone she hadn't seen in two years could affect her this way. If she could have gotten out of the assignment, she would have.

Her lips suddenly tingled with an intensity that made her gasp. She could almost feel the pressure of a firm male mouth on hers, kissing her, tantalizing her with his surprising gentleness, then pressing deeper....

Paul had shown her the difference between a callous boy's kiss and the caress of an experienced, confident man. With him, she'd learned the difference between infatuation and love. He'd shown her passion and made her long for completion in his arms.

For months after she'd left, she'd awakened from strange, tormenting dreams she couldn't exactly recall, knowing they had involved Paul. For a second, she experienced it again—the aching fire deep inside her, the hot longing to feel those lips on hers.

Thank God she'd realized the truth about his feelings before things had gone too far. Before they had made love.

After passing the exams and being certified as an arborist, she'd taken a position with the National Forest Service and moved west. When she left Minnesota, she'd assumed she would never see Paul McPherson, *heartthrob extraordinaire*, again, but here she was, waiting for him, as nervous as she'd been on their first date after the Christmas kiss that had started the whole conflagration.

She sighed shakily and wished he wouldn't show up.

The flash of lights across the front windows stopped her restless pacing and started a distinct pounding in her chest. There was another saying...one about bad pennies always turning up. Right, but was the bad penny Paul or herself? she mused, adopting his cynical brand of humor.

She went to the door. Yes, it was Paul.

He swung out of the truck—one of those four-wheel utility vehicles with rear seats that could be let down to produce extra cargo space...or a bed.

Another unexpected riot of emotion hit her. That worried her. She had to stay in control. She was a woman with a job to do, not a silly child caught up in the wonder of first love.

Calming herself, she studied him as he paused by the truck. In the pale glow of the April moon, his bronzed good looks were altered to shades of silver and pewter. He seemed suddenly remote and self-contained, like those tight-lipped sheriffs in Western novels who refuse to need anyone lest they appear vulnerable.

A silly notion. She knew him to be a laughing, teasing devil of a man, tall and lean and filled with a sardonic humor toward life. Even when he'd accused her of "buttering him up" in order to advance her career, he'd found it amusing.

He'd been surprised at her anger resulting from the accusation, and he hadn't believed her denial. Instead, he'd given his attractive grin and shrugged her protests aside. He'd chucked her under the chin and asked if it really mattered in the grand scheme of things since women had been using men for their own reasons since Day One.

"After all," he'd mocked, "Eve had wanted Adam to eat the apple, too, so he could take the fall with her."

"You hate women," she'd said slowly, trying to understand.

"Not at all," he'd assured her. "After all, we men get the pleasure of your...um...company." He'd kissed her lightly.

That had been the moment she'd realized he couldn't possibly love her as she loved him. If he'd loved her, he would have felt the same wrenching pain she did, and he'd have been devastated by what he saw as a betrayal of that love. Instead, he'd merely laughed.

Yes, she'd learned. Paul McPherson wasn't a man to be taken seriously...nor lightly, she added as he approached the cabin.

Her heart upped its tempo until her blood rushed through her body at a frantic speed. She saw him raise his hand to knock; then he spied her standing three feet away, watching him through the window next to the door.

For a moment—the strangest moment—they stared at each other as if... as if they were kindred souls separated by an invisible and insurmountable barrier.

Regret curled through her, leaving her filled with a yearning for something she couldn't name. She summoned all her willpower to force a calmness that was far from secure.

He dropped his hand to the latch and opened the door without waiting for an invitation.

"Hello, Dinah," he said. His mellow baritone seemed to thrum right through her, setting off vibrations deep inside.

She waited for him to add "Is there anyone finah?" as he used to do, but he didn't. His eyes roamed her face almost intently, as if he'd been wondering if she would look the same.

The silence stretched. She realized it was her turn to speak. She did so with an effort. "Hello, Paul. Do come in." She was pleased that her voice was an echo of his—coolly amused, with no overt emotion, which was hardly how she felt.

He had always had an unsettling effect on her—confusing her and filling her with an achy, impossible longing. She couldn't seem to control her reactions to him at all.

The fact that his expression was clear-eyed and candid didn't help, either. It was part of his appeal. The heartthrob in college had presented the same earnest countenance to the world.

Another tremor of unease ran through her. She stifled it. *Show no fear.*

That was her motto. A woman who worked around loggers, fire fighters, woodsmen and such couldn't afford to disclose any personal weaknesses.

"Thanks." He stepped inside and closed the door against the cold spring wind.

He wore a dark suit and tie with a blue shirt that was almost a match for his blue eyes. In the lamplight, his flesh tones became bronzed again. The contrast of those sky-blue eyes against his tanned skin and dark hair was incredibly alluring.

Dressed in evening clothes, he looked every inch the suave, cosmopolitan man rather than the authority on land management she knew him to be. His book on the subject was required reading for college students in the natural sciences.

He was, she saw, as handsome as she'd remembered, as sure of himself and his charm as he was of the rising of the sun each morning. It seemed unfair that he should be unchanged.

"We meet again," he said, a slow smile curving his attractive lips. He was apparently amused at her silent appraisal. He'd always delighted in teasing her about her reactions to him and his come-hither teasing. She'd never quite known how to take him.

When he stepped one foot closer, she instinctively stepped one foot back. She had to look up to meet his gaze. At six-three, he was four inches taller than her own five feet eleven inches.

He'd once suggested to her, during that madly intoxicating month together after the Christmas party, that they could probably produce a good-sized basketball team. "If we were so minded," he'd added, a devilish "dare you" glint in his eyes.

She'd waited, hiding her love for him and the uncertainty he engendered in her behind her laughter, but her face had warmed into an excited blush. Seeing that, he'd teased her more. He was as incorrigible as he was handsome.

Handsome is as handsome does.

She'd thought his words were a promise to their future. She'd thought he'd really meant them. She was humiliated all over again at how naive she'd been.

"Yes," she finally replied, holding a cool edge. There was something she had to get straightened out right off the bat. "In the future, I would appreciate it if you would arrange appointments directly with *me* instead of first consulting my supervisor."

He studied her for a second, then shrugged. "It seemed simpler that way. I didn't know how to reach you."

And never bothered to find out. She kept the thought in, but used it as a reminder to her troublesome heart to calm down. "My supervisor should have told you to call me."

He started to say something, then changed his mind. Instead, he watched her, his eyes seemingly fathoms deep, as if his thoughts were profound . . . which was probably the result he wanted, part of his charm-'em-till-they-fall-at-your-feet technique.

Yet, in spite of her common sense, his gaze made her achingly aware of being a woman. *A lonely woman.* The thought came to her with startling clarity as if someone had whispered it in her ear.

This get-together was business, she reminded herself. She was attending in order to meet the local ranchers whose land was included, along with the Rogue River National Forest, in her project: Wildlife Rehabilitation in Logged versus Old-Growth Forest. This and the yew tree study were her and Paul's only involvement.

But when he smiled at her, warmth poured over her, making her think of summer. She realized she was staring at him.

Stop it, she warned her too-active imagination. It was a darned cold night in April, and they had a birthday party to attend and a long way to go to get there.

"We'd better go," he said, picking up on her thoughts. "I'm ready."

She grabbed her parka and pulled it around her shoulders. Although she wore a sensible wool pantsuit with a long-sleeved ruby-red satin blouse, the temperature was supposed to drop into the low forties before morning. Not that she intended to stay out that late, of course, but it paid to think ahead, in case they had car trouble.

A picture of them stranded together for the night in some dark and lonely place darted into her mind. She turned toward the door, baffled by the unhappy longing that rose in her.

Life could be so difficult and confusing. She didn't know what she wanted from it anymore. At any rate, this wasn't the time to go off the philosophical deep end. She had to keep her wits about her in dealing with Paul.

He put his hand on her waist as they went out into the night. After he closed the door behind them, she locked the cabin and dropped the key in her purse. Their actions seemed like those of people on a date. She moved away from his touch.

Grasping her elbow, he helped her off the tiny stoop to the ground and held on to her—much to her annoyance—until she was safely installed in his truck. She was hardly fragile.

"Thank you," she muttered, sure that he was deliberately provoking her with his touch.

"You're welcome." He gave her a keen glance before closing the door and getting in on the driver's side. He started up. They rode in silence until he left the small town behind.

"How was your trip?" he asked.

"Fine. No problems. One of the men from the forest service office in Butte Falls met me. He gave me a tour of the area before bringing me up to the cabin."

"Good. He told you about the yew trees we've found?"

"Yes." Taxol, a compound in yew bark, had been found to have cancer-fighting properties. "He said . . ." She hesitated, then blurted out, "He said a man named McPherson had requested my help on the job."

"Yes, my cousin," Paul said. "When he and I talked to the forest service supervisor, I saw your name on the roster of botanists. I mentioned I had worked with you before. Keegan liked the idea of having someone we knew on the project."

"Oh."

"I thought it sounded like a good idea, too." At her quick glance, he asked, "Does that surprise you?"

She caught the sardonically amused undertone and lifted her chin, although he couldn't see the reaction. "Frankly, yes."

"I like to work with people who are good at what they do," he went on. *As I am* was the implied last part of that statement.

She tried to decide if there was a covert message in it for her. Did he think they would pick up where they'd left off? She'd never be that foolish again. "Thank you."

"I think," he added.

"I beg your pardon?"

"Thank you, I think," he reiterated. "You're not really sure you want this assignment, even though it's a plum in many ways."

Heat crept into her face as he put her earlier misgivings into words. "That's not true. Studying the effects of logging on the spotted owl and other wildlife, as well as bark regrowth of the yew trees, is very important.''

It was just that she didn't want to work with *him*. Naturally, she didn't say that.

Again he read her mind. ''You needn't worry. Our dealings will be strictly business. I'll control my wilder impulses,'' he said, so softly she wasn't sure she'd heard him correctly. It took only a glance at him and she knew that she had.

His face looked harsher, purer in its lines, in the faint light from the dash. *Devil's angel*, she thought inanely. A man sent by Satan to plague women with his looks and charm . . . and the skill of his mouth on a woman's lips.

The silence seemed to close around her. A tremor started deep within, like distant thunder—low and vibrant, striking a clashing chord in her, reminding her how vulnerable she was when it came to him. She cleared her throat and sought an answer.

''I'm not worried at all,'' she informed him, gathering the tattered cloak of her dignity around her, the only defense she could muster against the memory of her ill-advised love and his attractive presence. It was mortifying to realize she was still susceptible to him after all this time.

''Besides, our involvement was years ago,'' she quickly added, as if time had all but erased the memory from her mind.

He flicked her a quick look before turning back to the dark ribbon of highway. ''Two years, four months. Christmas.''

''Mistletoe,'' she murmured, remembering the evening when Paul had caught her coming through the doorway.

He'd kissed her relentlessly. Hungrily. Deeply.

When they'd drawn apart to the hoots and calls of the other men, both had known the delicate balance between them, carefully maintained for months, had been over-turned.

The memory of that kiss returned, sharp and clear—every teasing nuance at the start of it, every ardent demand at the end of it. And the memory of Paul's voice...

"Dinah," he'd whispered.

For the first time, she'd seen uncertainty in his eyes. It had struck a note inside some quiet, secret place in her soul. Then the men's laughter had intruded.

But the distance between them had disappeared. For the next few weeks, they'd seen each other every night, their kisses becoming longer, their embraces less easy to break.

When she'd passed her arborist certification exams, Paul had taken her out to celebrate. Returning to her place, she'd spoken of her coming interview to join the National Forest Service and had asked him for a recommendation.

That had been the moment of truth. For a second, she'd glimpsed a bitter fury in his eyes, then it was gone, so fast she'd never been sure afterward if that was what she'd witnessed.

"You're a cool one," he'd said, then laughed. "Sure, I'll give you a recommendation. But you didn't have to butter me up with kisses to get it. I'd have done it based on your ability."

She still couldn't believe he'd thought that of her and yet had embraced her so passionately she'd felt her heart would stop from the wonder of it. Hurt and disbelieving, his cynicism had killed the dreams she'd harbored of their future together and destroyed the illusions she'd cherished regarding his love.

She'd rejected his letter of recommendation and retreated behind the barrier of ice that had surrounded her heart in that instant. She'd never wanted to see him again, but she had had no choice. Fortunately, she'd gotten the new position and was able to leave shortly thereafter.

During her time left on the logging project, she'd avoided him whenever possible and been coolly polite when she couldn't. She'd taken care to treat him no differently than she did the loggers she'd worked around as she performed her study.

He'd seemed puzzled by her attitude. The final proof of his lack of feelings for her was the fact that he'd let her leave without a word, although later she'd found out he'd sent the letter to the forest service office regarding her ability as an arborist in spite of her refusal to send it herself.

The humiliation of their affair, if one could call it that, washed over her—her naiveté about the meaning of his kisses, her assumptions about their future. How could she have been such a fool? In college, she'd excused herself due to lack of experience. With Paul, she'd had only herself to blame for getting hurt. He would never know how difficult it was to face him again, knowing how ridiculous she'd been.

Her lips tingled suddenly, and she felt hot and troubled. "I could have driven out to the ranch. You could have sent me a map," she said, needing to distract her thoughts.

"No," he said. "It's too far and too easy to miss landmarks in the dark. I didn't mind driving in."

"I could have waited to meet your cousins. I mean, tomorrow would be soon enough, and more official, rather than their birthday party." She didn't know if she was arguing with him or herself.

It seemed portentous for her to be in this vehicle with him, driving through these dark country roads to God-knew-where for a party with people she didn't know. It's only Paul, the Lothario of the north woods, she reminded herself.

The loggers had delighted in telling her stories of Paul's conquests. She should have listened to the cautious voice inside her, instead of reading more into him and his feelings than was there. She wouldn't make that mistake this time. She moved closer to the door, putting as much space as possible between them.

"Chill out. I'm not going to attack you." He spoke into the darkness, his eyes straight ahead. She couldn't read his mood, but he sounded impatient with her.

"I never thought you were." A shiver ran over her. She hugged the parka closer around her.

Show no fear.

It would be a mistake to let this man know he shook her to her very foundation. No, not really, she told herself sharply. She was overreacting. Breathing deeply, she forced her muscles to relax, realizing at that moment how edgy she'd become.

The only saving grace to the whole episode between them was the fact that they hadn't made love. To have been totally intimate, then to have to work with him again, realizing it had been merely a fling for him, would have been too much. At least she'd been saved that indignity.

To be truthful, Paul hadn't pushed beyond what she'd been ready to give. He'd been surprisingly patient. In fact, he'd realized she was a virgin. When she'd admitted she was, he'd looked thoughtful and mentioned it no more.

She wondered, since he thought she was going with him for her own gain, why he hadn't taken advantage of her response to his caresses? While she'd been hesitant, she doubted she would have refused if he'd really wanted her, she'd been so in love with him.

Forget it, she advised sternly. The past was water over the dam. Upon joining the forest service and leaving Minnesota, she'd been immediately transferred to northern California as she'd requested. Now here she was, in southern Oregon, driving through the dark with her nemesis. Life could take strange turns. This one might prove dangerous as well as maddening.

A chill ran down her neck, and she frowned in annoyance. These wild sweeps of imagination wouldn't do. She prided herself on being a practical person, not the foolish dreamer she'd once been. She'd never fall under the spell of his charm again. She'd never fall in love again, not with him, not with anyone.

In a few minutes, they turned off the blacktop onto a gravel road. She exhaled in relief. They must be close to the ranch.

"A half hour more and we'll be there," he said, again seeming to read her thoughts.

The time stretched into forever. The gravel crunched under the tires with a steady noise. At last she had to ask, "Why did you mention to your cousin that we'd worked together?"

"Why wouldn't I? You're a good worker, and your supervisor thought we'd make a good team."

"Team?" She stared at him as if the word were new to her.

"My cousins have hired me as their consultant for the areas of old-growth trees on their land. We'll work together on the national forest stuff." He gave the sardonic chuckle she'd once found so attractive.

It sounded so logical. Why did she feel as if it were some diabolical plot to make her life miserable? She shook her head slightly at her misgivings. There was nothing to worry about as long as she kept her mind on the job at hand.

"If you think you can bear it," he added.

"I'm sure I can if you can," she replied coolly.

Dinah saw two driveways branching off to the right. Paul turned into the second of them. In a moment, they arrived at a large Victorian house, its windows glowing like jewels against the dark hills outlined in silver by the pale moon.

It seemed unreal. She felt that she'd been transported to the set of some Gothic movie. Was she the naive heroine stepping blindly into danger? And who was the hero of this story?

Chapter Two

Paul swore silently as he went around the truck and opened the door for Dinah. Her manner irritated him. She was one woman he couldn't figure out. Worse, she was the only woman he'd ever met that he couldn't forget. He'd wanted her with a driving, insistent passion when they'd first met. Seeing her tonight, he discovered that longing hadn't changed one iota.

"Watch your step," he cautioned when she swung both legs out of the truck and slipped gracefully to the ground.

It wasn't at all necessary, but he caught her at the waist to steady her anyway. The clean smell of her hair, the scent of her light but enticing perfume, wafted under his nose.

She looked up at him, her face solemn. A shafting desire to crush her in his arms the way he once had, her mouth hot and moving under his, flashed through him. He restrained the impulse.

At one time in their mutual past, he would have leaned down and stolen a quick kiss, then laughed about it. Not now, not with this Dinah. There had been a point where she'd changed.

The Dinah he'd known had been reserved. The one who had emerged after their brief affair had been cold. She was more so now, he saw. A man was likely to get frostbite if he reached beyond the barricade of icicles that surrounded her.

The same sensation he'd experienced when they'd locked gazes through the window at the cabin returned to him. He had a sense of distance, yet there was a connection, as if an invisible thread of fate bound them together and drew them toward each other.

A sudden weariness with the whole crazy man-woman thing hit him. There was, or had been, lust between them, maybe more, but in the grand scheme of things, what the hell did it matter?

It didn't.

The lessons of the past came back to haunt him. He understood exactly how fleeting the passions of the heart could be. His fiancée—the woman who was supposed to have loved him forever, the woman who had accepted his ring, thus indicating she'd stick with him for richer, for poorer, in sickness and in health—hadn't made it past the first tough patch, a car crash that had landed him in the hospital, seriously injured.

At the time he'd needed her most, the person he'd trusted above all others had headed for the nearest exit, leaving his ring and him behind. So much for eternal love.

After that, there had been other women. Women who had wanted to be seen with him, the handsome scholar, the wealthy author, as if he were some kind of trophy. Women who'd wanted him in their beds for a night's fun and games. None of them had ever looked for the man inside.

The automobile accident had happened a year before he'd met Dinah. He'd recovered, both from his injuries and from his broken heart by then.

During the time they'd worked together, she'd impressed him with her dedication, her lack of subterfuge—he'd been wrong there—and the absolute fairness she displayed in her dealings with others. He had liked her way with the loggers, her modest reserve and quick humor. Then they had kissed.

There had been fire and passion and other things between them. It had almost made him believe in the softer emotions again. Almost. A man who didn't learn from his past was a fool.

He'd caught on quick enough when Dinah had requested a letter of recommendation from him to go with her application to the forest service. She'd buttered him up until she got what she wanted from him, giving him her wild, sweet kisses....

He cursed as he realized just what that line of thinking was doing to him, physically and mentally. Why had he expected Dinah to be different from any other woman?

However, he had to hand it to her—she was the most confusing, most exasperating woman he'd ever met. After he'd agreed to do what she wanted, she'd done an about-face, accused him of doubting her integrity and rejected the recommendation.

Figure that one out.

He glanced toward the soft, welcoming light glowing in the windows of the house and again felt the prickly thorn of envy at his cousins' good fortune. They'd lucked out. They'd found women who loved them, not a face or a body or a help to their careers.

He dismissed the thought with a shrug. What did it matter? Pitted against the grand scheme of life, what was one man's dream?

"Come on. We'd better get in before we freeze." He rushed his companion—he knew better than to think of her as his date—toward the ornate door with the fanlight of etched glass above the paneled oak.

He noticed she'd left the bulky parka in the truck. So, she wasn't without vanity, even dressed in her neat black suit and sensible low-heeled pumps. In that sneaky way the mind sometimes operates, he was swept back in time to the Christmas party.

She'd worn a dress—black, high-necked and dignified. Her hair had been pulled into a severe chignon, giving her face a haunting loveliness that had appealed to him.

Her looks weren't classically beautiful, he acknowledged. Striking perhaps, although she could be very off-putting with her razor glances that sliced right through a man, keeping all but the bravest at a distance.

At the Christmas party, when she'd stopped in the doorway and gazed around in her friendly but nontouchable manner, he hadn't been able to resist the temptation. He'd kissed her under the mistletoe.

He'd been stunned by the experience . . . the incredible softness of her lips under his . . . the tiny gasp she'd given when she'd realized his intent . . . the way she'd felt in his arms, fitting him perfectly as if they'd been made for each other.

Right now, she looked like a glacier, but he knew, underneath that outer composure, there existed an ebony-haired Venus with a heart of fire. Upon seeing her tonight, he'd experienced an overpowering need to find that fire again . . . to warm himself in her flames . . .

He cursed silently and pushed the fantasy furiously from his mind. At the front door, he didn't pause, but ushered her inside to the laughter and safety of others.

The soft light of pink-globed hurricane lamps cast interesting hollows in her face, turning her tawny complexion to dusky rose.

A little Spanish mixed with that cool English blood. Fire and ice. The combination every man dreams of finding in his woman.

Yeah, right.

However much he might fantasize about a woman, of having a special one all for himself, he'd never expose that much of himself to a female again. They wanted only what they could get from a man, and only so long as it was easy for them.

"You want to leave your jacket here?" he asked.

"Yes. Thank you," she added when he helped her take it off.

He hung the black wool jacket in the coat closet, then hooked her hand over his arm to guide her into the living room. To his surprise, she moved closer. He felt a slight tremor run over her. Was the ice maiden nervous?

"Paul!" His cousin's wife, Beth McPherson, came over to welcome them. "And this must be the tree expert. Hi, I'm so glad you're here in time for the annual bash. You'll get to meet the other ranchers who are in on the forest study."

Dinah saw a lovely woman in a red silk dress with hair as black as her own. The woman had eyes the color of green glass, though, instead of black like hers. Her hostess had a perfect figure and wore an exquisite necklace of emeralds. Her smile was without pretense. Dinah found herself smiling back.

"Beth, Dinah. Dinah, Beth. Beth is married to one of my cousins, I forget which one," Paul explained with his usual humor and dodged a swat from his pretty cousin-in-law. "Where's your better half?"

"He and Kerrigan are arguing with Elmer. Elmer's ranch is the next place south of us," she said to Dinah. "Their topic is natural forest versus pasture. You two are just in time to settle the dispute. Let me direct you to the refreshments first. You'll want something to fortify yourself before tackling them."

Dinah shot a quick look at Paul. He pressed his arm to his side, giving her hand a reassuring squeeze. She dropped her hold on him, realizing she was clinging like some recluse at her first outing in years.

Actually, it was her first party in a long time, other than family get-togethers. Since Christmas two years ago, in fact.

In the dining room, Beth introduced Dinah to Rachel, who was also married to one of Paul's cousins.

"We're so glad you could come," Rachel said, her manner quieter than the other woman's, but just as friendly. She was a blonde with wonderful golden-brown eyes. "What would you like? We have champagne...oh, and a delicious hot rum punch. Would you like to try it?"

"Yes, thank you. That sounds delightful."

With cups of steaming punch in hand, Beth led them off in search of the two male cousins Paul had mentioned on the phone earlier that day.

Dinah had been surprised when the telephone at the cabin had rung ten minutes after she'd arrived. Somehow she'd known who it was before she'd picked up the receiver.

When his pleasant baritone had come through the receiver, a frisson had rushed down her arms and over her scalp. He had the most sensuous manner of speaking, as if his voice carried a verbal caress . . . as if that were what he was thinking about while he spoke.

She should have turned down the party invitation right then, she told herself. Except her supervisor had requested that she attend and meet the ranchers in a friendly setting. While she'd known Paul was advising the forest service, she hadn't realized he was so deeply involved in the projects.

"This is my husband, Keegan," Beth said, introducing the host. "This is his twin, Kerrigan."

Dinah looked from one brother to the other. She glanced at Paul, who was a couple of inches taller than his cousins, and back at the brothers. They weren't identical twins, but they were close enough in looks to be easily confused.

Each of the three men, taken individually, was a classic—tall, muscular, dark hair, light eyes ranging from blue to gray, a dollop of humor in those eyes as they witnessed her reaction, obvious keen intelligence and more than a trace of stubbornness in the jaw. As a group, they were overwhelming.

The world wasn't ready for that much ideal masculinity in the raw, she thought. A picture of Paul came to her, standing in the woods, his head raised in the alert manner of a wild stag, his lean, powerful body clothed only by nature. . . .

Heat flooded her face as she pushed the image away. "I'm happy to meet you. I hope you'll forgive me if I get you mixed up."

"Happens all the time," one of the twins said. "I don't understand it myself. I'm so much better-looking than Keegan. Of course, against Paul, neither of us stands a chance."

Rachel joined them while they were laughing. Kerrigan, the one who'd spoken, dropped an arm over his wife's shoulders in loving familiarity.

"It's hard to tell who's the most conceited in this bunch," she said in mock disgust, "but it isn't the women."

After the men protested this statement, Keegan turned toward the table. "Let's go have some food. I hope we have tacos."

"Tacos! Rachel and I slaved all day to make exotic dishes and he wants tacos." Beth elbowed her husband, then ducked when he reached for her, his eyes narrowed.

Dinah felt herself relaxing in the company of the genial couples and the other ranchers at the party. While they filled plates with various tidbits and found a place to sit, she learned that Beth and Keegan lived in the Victorian mansion and that Rachel and Kerrigan had a modern ranch house a short distance away through the woods.

After eating, their host and hostess circulated while the other couple introduced them to the ranchers, who wanted advice on increasing the productivity of their land. That was Paul's area of expertise. Dinah listened while they talked.

By midnight, most of the older people and young couples who had baby-sitters had left. Someone turned off the background music and put dance records on the stereo. A space was cleared in the living room, the lights dimmed. Several people began to dance.

"Come on," Paul said, taking her hand.

"Good night," she said to the local game warden. Instead of preparing to depart as she'd expected, Paul escorted her into the living room and took her into his arms.

She stumbled slightly in surprise before joining the rhythmic movement of his tall form to the slow, romantic music. Even though they seemed to flow into the same steps naturally, she couldn't control the stiffness in her limbs as he pulled her closer.

"Relax," he growled next to her ear. "I'm not planning to bite you tonight."

She pulled out of his arms. He stopped dancing and studied her with a thoughtful gaze. Dinah tried to hide her turmoil. He was merely being amusing, but she didn't need his taunting to remind her how inept she was at reading men's natures.

"It was just a joke," he said after a tense fifteen seconds.

"Yes, sorry," she said, forcing a modicum of a smile. She didn't feel up to the pretense the evening demanded.

"Easy," he murmured, soothing her. He drew her back into his arms, slowly, carefully, as if she were fragile and might shatter at a harsh touch. "I'll watch what I say in the future."

She felt ridiculous. It had been a long time since she'd reacted like that to a chance remark. With this man, she wanted to be in complete control of her emotions.

After the song ended, she glanced around at the crowd that remained. Mostly singles, she realized. They were dancing as closely as possible, their arms locked around each other in tight embraces. She looked away.

"I think it's time I was getting back. I want to read over some reports first thing in the morning."

"Tomorrow's Sunday," he reminded her.

"Aren't we allowed to read on Sunday?" She smiled at him, her tone cool, amused, controlled once more.

"Only the comics," he replied in the same vein. "I'd planned to invite you out for a drive tomorrow, to check over the territory. Rachel wants you to have supper at her house tomorrow night. I told her you'd be there."

32 *THE WAY OF A MAN*

Dinah was dismayed. An instinct for self-preservation told her she should stay as far away from Paul as possible. "Please don't make commitments for me. I can handle my own schedule."

He shrugged. "So tell her you can't come if you have other, more important plans."

She glared at him. He knew she didn't have any plans at all. The thought of being cooped up in the cabin all day or of hiking around the country roads by herself didn't appeal to her, either. Besides, she had a job to do. "I suppose I can go."

"Good. I'll pick you up at ten."

"Ten? In the morning? Isn't that a little early for supper?"

"Yes, but first we're going to explore. You need to be thoroughly familiar with the area. I'll bring lunch." Without giving her time to consider this, he turned her toward the dining room. "I'm hungry again. Let's eat before we go."

She reluctantly followed him to the table.

Paul was aware of Dinah's hesitation before she acquiesced. They selected food and found seats. He was irritated and intrigued all over again by her, just as he'd been when they'd first met and her cool disdain had presented a challenge he couldn't ignore. That kiss under the mistletoe had shown her facade of indifference for what it was—an out-and-out pretense.

What was with her anyway?

She'd gotten what she wanted from him. He'd given her a glowing recommendation. It had been an honest one, he admitted.

Dinah was one of the best workers he'd ever met. Her intelligence was keen, the working of her mind logical.

Look at how she'd played him just right to get what she wanted.

After that first second, it hadn't bothered him, just as long as he knew whose rules they were playing by. Then she'd gone all cold on him, as if he'd mortally insulted her.

"I would never butter anyone up by... by using passion... like a... as if I..." She'd opened the door to her apartment, her face as unreadable as carved marble. "Keep your recommendation. I don't need it!" And she'd stepped inside and closed the door in his face.

She'd gotten the position she'd wanted and left and never looked back as far as he knew. Fine, but she needn't pretend to be the untouchable ice maiden. He knew she wasn't.

Even as he thought of her coldness, his body heated. While they'd danced, he'd fantasized about taking her to that primitive little cabin where she was staying and being invited inside. There, he'd reawaken the fire in her....

A hot shaft of longing hit him. She was an irresistible lure to a highly masculine part of him that was difficult to control, but perhaps it would be better to keep his distance. Frostbite was painful.

"Hi," a voice said to his left when he finished the last bite of the midnight snack. He recognized the woman smiling down at him. He'd met her at the diner in town.

"Sita," he said, pulling the name out of his subconscious. He was good with names. It was part of his charm, he admitted cynically. Women liked to be remembered. He stood. "Join us."

"Um, no. I was... um... wondering if you'd like to dance."

He glanced at Dinah. The flash of her eyes when she met his gaze indicated emotion, then it was gone. "Go ahead. I'll finish my crab dip before it gets cold."

Damn but she irritated him with her cooler-than-thou ways.

"Sure," he said and led Sita to the dancing area. He looked over his partner's shoulder to find Dinah watching. He gave her a slow, deliberately sexy smile and pulled Sita closer.

"Good," his partner said and giggled.

He saw Sita watching a tall, lanky cowboy propping up the wall between two windows. "Ah," he said. "I think I'm being used."

Sita looked slightly ashamed. "Do you mind? I've been trying to make that man notice me for years. This year is his absolutely very last chance," she declared.

Paul laughed with her. "Nah, I don't mind, not as long as I get to hold a beautiful woman in my arms." He twirled her around, found she could follow his steps and led her into an intricate dance that had everyone gazing at them with envy.

Dancing was another thing he did well that women loved. Besides his pretty face and good memory. And perhaps his money now that he was wealthy. And his contacts in government and business.

Ah, hell, what had brought those thoughts on? One glance to the side told him. Dinah sat on the love seat, primly eating her snack. He felt suddenly tired.

"Come on," he said when the number ended, managing to stop beside the silent cowboy with the lonely eyes. Paul could identify with the feeling. He gave a silent curse, then smiled. "Here. Take her off my hands," he pleaded. "I've got to get back to my woman before she runs off with someone else."

"Oh, that was a big help," Sita grumped. She threw herself at the cowboy. "Hank, save me from this Casanova."

Startled, Hank caught her in his arms. She sighed up at him soulfully, then winked at Paul.

With a wave, Paul went back to Dinah. His irritation with her aloofness—as if there was no undercurrent of passion between them—grew. "Come on. I'll take you home."

She caught the vibes. "I'm sure I can find a ride with someone else if it isn't convenient for you."

"Forget it," he said flatly. Hunger, impatient and forceful, prompted him to want to take her to a deserted glen and kiss the devil out of her until she melted for him.

There was, he realized, a certain delicate madness in him tonight. It wouldn't take much to tip the scale. One look into her flashing eyes and he tamped the hunger into submission. She, too, seemed ready for a fight ... or for making love.

"Let's go," he said, abruptly wanting to be done with the evening ... and with her. Just why the hell *had* he mentioned their past working connection to his cousin?

Dinah clamped her lips together. He was the most irritating person she'd ever met. It was impossible to stay on an even keel around him, he was so moody. And men said women were contrary!

She marched down the hall, burningly aware of him right behind her. He got her jacket out of the closet and slipped it on her.

"Are you leaving already?" Rachel called out.

"Yes, Cinderella's glass slipper is pinching."

Dinah shot Paul a furious look, then smiled at Rachel. "I really need to go over my supplies tomorrow."

"Be sure and come to supper," Rachel invited. "Paul did tell you, didn't he?"

"Yes."

"Wonderful. We'll look forward to having you. Kerrigan wants to show you the aerial maps of the ranch." She turned to Paul. "Be here around six. We'll make it an early evening."

"Fine," he said.

Kerrigan joined them. "I just had a brilliant idea. Why don't you stay out here instead of in town?" he asked Dinah. "Rachel and Beth love company, and it would be more convenient to use the ranch as your home base rather than the town cabin."

Dinah couldn't think of anything to say. His reasoning was logical, yet she wasn't sure it would be best for her peace of mind. Paul was staying at the ranch house, too.

She noticed he was staying stubbornly silent on the subject, a trait not at all like him.

"Do," Rachel said in her quiet, friendly way, her eyes warm and golden in the soft light. "I'd love to have you."

In view of their friendliness, Dinah couldn't refuse. "That would be very nice, if you're sure I won't be in the way."

"Heavens, not at all," Rachel assured her. "I suspect you and Paul will be in the mountains most of the time, anyway. You two can come in and shower and sleep in a real bed once in a while."

"Now that's an offer I can't refuse," Paul murmured wickedly.

Dinah ignored the innuendo. She knew Rachel didn't realize she'd made it sound as if Paul and herself would be doing those things together. Naturally, Paul had picked up on it.

"Well, we'd better be going," she said firmly, taking Paul by the arm and heading out the door.

"Hey, the lady wants to be alone with me. What can I say?" he called back, acting the part of a hapless male.

His cousins laughed while Dinah fumed. "Must you be so... so... blatant?" she demanded when they were in the truck.

Paul started the engine and eased into gear. They drove off into the darkness. "Didn't you want to be alone with me?" he asked, a tinge of false innocence, a trace of mock hurt in his voice.

The wounded hero act.

She heaved a loud sigh to let him know how much his teasing irritated her. "Hardly."

"Don't tell my cousins," he cajoled. "They're walking around on rosy clouds and want everyone else to join them. They probably think they're helping Cupid by throwing us together."

"Really—" she began.

"Lighten up," he cut her off, his tone suddenly hard. "You seem to think I've grown fangs since the last time we met, but I've never left a mark on a woman."

Dinah glared at him in the dim light of the dash.

"Yet," he added.

Although, Paul admitted with grim satisfaction, there was a first time for everything. Perhaps he'd better lighten up himself, he decided in the lengthening silence. He drove on into the night, not another car on the road, just the two of them. He felt he could drive for eternity.

He ran a hand through his hair and heard the crackle of static electricity caused by the cold, dry air. He adjusted the controls on the heater, and warm air poured into the truck. By the time he turned on to the paved road, they were cozy.

Glancing at his companion, he saw that while she sat with her customary straight back, her head lolled slightly to the side and her lashes had dropped over her eyes. A feeling went through him, like a fist clenching deep in his gut.

He remembered how stiff she'd been in his arms when they'd danced earlier. He also remembered how it was to kiss her and feel her melt against him. At one time, she hadn't been so standoffish as she'd been tonight.

An unusual experience for him, he mused without false modesty. Women had been falling all over themselves over him since his earliest memories. He'd learned to cope by answering their flirting glances with flattery and a laugh, keeping it light.

Occasionally, things had progressed beyond a smile and a kiss. He'd made sure everyone knew the rules there, too— that it wasn't serious. He liked to leave 'em laughing. And a pleasant time was had by all, one might say.

But Dinah had never fallen at his feet. In the midst of their wildest kisses, he'd sensed a reserve in her and hadn't pushed for more. Instead, he'd waited. He just didn't know for what.

Fatigue washed over him. The fist clenched tighter, causing a strange pain. For just a second, he felt tired of it all. And envious of his cousins.

Well, hell, he should be tired. He'd been up since dawn, riding the ranch, feeling the ease that came to a man when he sat on a piece of good horseflesh and surveyed the land, watching it prosper for the families who lived there and worked it. His cousins had been fortunate in their choice of land and in their women. What normal man wouldn't be envious?

A yawn overtook him. It was—he peered at the clock— almost two in the morning. No wonder he was beat.

Dinah stirred, then slumped into the comfortable seat, her head slipping farther to the side. One thing—she'd never lied to him. She'd never vowed undying love and later walked out on him. She'd simply asked for what she wanted, rejected it when he'd agreed to give it and *then* walked out.

A smile, involuntary and filled with an odd gentleness, kicked up the corners of his mouth. On an impulse, he reached over and tucked her coat collar around her neck. She looked pale in the dim light, but her skin was warm. And soft.

He stroked along her cheek, then quickly moved his hand back to the steering wheel as heat spiraled deep inside, adding to the fire already burning there. A man could get used to touching her real fast. But he wouldn't make that mistake again. He'd almost believed the soft, uncertain promise in her eyes. He'd almost trusted her. Almost.

They arrived in town. He drove down Main Street. Not a soul disturbed the stillness, other than the two of them. When he stopped at the cabin, Dinah sat up.

"Are we home?" she asked in a sleep-thickened voice.

He experienced a distinctive tightening in the nether regions. "Yeah. Your place," he added to distinguish it from *his* place, which sure as hell wasn't in the dark, empty cabin alone with her. He jumped out and came around the truck.

She had already gotten out when he reached her. He took her arm when they stepped onto the tiny stoop. She couldn't get the key fitted into the dead bolt. He took it from her and wrenched open the door.

Warm air, still fragrant from her perfume and bath powder, wafted over them from the interior like a lover's breath. When she smiled up at him, her lashes at half mast over those dark, obsidian eyes, he was lost.

"Ah, hell," he muttered. "In for a penny, in for a pound."

Chapter Three

Dinah was totally unprepared for Paul's strange remark. When she forced her eyes open to thank him for the evening, she saw his head dip toward hers. Of its own volition her mouth shaped itself for the kiss.

His lips settled on hers with a gentleness that surprised her. His were the softest lips imaginable, giving the softest caresses all over her mouth as if he couldn't stop himself from touching and tasting her.

For a long, mind-drugged minute, that was all she could think of—how gentle his kiss was, with no mocking humor or fierce demand she didn't have to repel. For a minute...then she realized what was happening.

"Stop it," she said, pushing against his chest.

He stepped back immediately. She saw him take three deep breaths, like a man making up for oxygen shortage after hard exercise. Then he watched her, his thoughts hidden behind the facade of his handsome face.

"I . . . you had no right," she began, her voice trembly.

Or was the kiss her fault? Had she asked for Paul's kiss when she'd paused on the threshold and looked at him, feeling like someone in a dream? For just a minute, she'd fantasized they were on a real date.

"I mean . . . I didn't mean to lead you on—" she started over.

His short bark of laughter interrupted her. "You didn't. It just seemed like the natural thing to do there for a minute."

"Well, don't do it in the future," she said, ignoring her own shaken state. She didn't want to quarrel. After all, they had to work together for the next four months, so she had to set limits.

"Yeah, sorry," he said, seemingly distracted by his own internal musings.

She saw his eyes sweep the cabin when she flicked on the inside light. He paused for a moment, his mood dark and unreadable; then he smiled with a great deal of irony. She tried to follow the direction of his gaze to find what was amusing.

There were only two bunks on the wall next to the bathroom door, a table and bench that was also a storage locker and a couple of pine chairs. A tiny kitchen formed its own alcove to the right.

A lightening of the atmosphere was called for. She managed a smile. "That's all right. I'm sure a kiss is par for the night for someone like you, but personally I prefer to keep business separate from my—" She stopped, realizing where that line was leading her.

"From your love life?" he asked, his sardonic grin tugging at the finely molded corners of his mouth. "Don't worry. I won't forget our association is strictly business this time. I guess the kiss was an afterthought from the party.

You know, good food, good company, a perfect moon and a friendly kiss."

She felt foolish for overreacting. "Yes, well, good night."

After stepping inside, she closed and locked the door securely after her. It was a full thirty seconds after that before she heard his steps on the gravel, then the truck crank up and leave.

Her sigh of relief was cut short by the sudden surge in her heartbeat when she turned and glanced at the bunk bed where she'd already spread her down sleeping bag and pillow.

I've never left a mark on a woman... yet.

She had a feeling those words were going to haunt her for what was left of the night... along with that unexpectedly tender kiss.

"But I'm supposed to have a truck of my own," Dinah protested into the telephone. She squinted against the golden rays streaming in the kitchen windows and poured a cup of coffee.

"No problem. I spoke to McPherson this morning. The ranch can provide transportation. Good idea—staying with them. Saves us some money." Her supervisor chuckled, obviously delighted.

She realized there was no use arguing, but she persisted, anyway. "I'd still feel better with my own wheels. Paul can't be expected to drive me everywhere—"

"Talk to him. I'm sure you can work it out. Well, I have a call on the other line. I'll see you in a couple of weeks if not longer."

The line went dead. Dinah hung up the phone with a little bang. Without a car, she was at Paul's mercy....

His truck pulled into the narrow parking space in front of the rustic cabin. Speak of the devil, she thought waspishly. Yet, her heart leaped to a foolish staccato when he climbed out and came to the door. He always had an effect on her. It was maddening.

When he knocked, she was ready for him. She opened the door, her poise intact, prepared to ignore any taunting remarks about the past or last night.

She hadn't counted on the sun, though.

Its cool morning rays danced over the landscape, striking flashes of color in dewdrops, backlighting the trees to brilliance, but what she noticed, what grabbed her attention and wouldn't let go, was the effect of the sun on Paul.

It illuminated him, turning his masculine good looks into a creation of beauty by a master painter.

His dark hair glowed with warm highlights. His skin looked gilded in an alloy of bronze and gold. His eyes were like pieces of sky with stardust glittering in them. He was primal man, a work of nature perfect in its form.

"Good morning." He gave her his insouciant smile.

She swallowed against the sudden emotion that filled her throat and stepped back. "Good morning. Come in. I'm almost ready." Her voice was husky. She cleared it impatiently and frowned, alarmed by her uncontrollable response.

Paul's smile disappeared as he stepped over the threshold. What the hell did he do this time to annoy her? he wondered.

The usual, he answered the question with a cynical retort. He breathed. Apparently that act offended her. Of course she no longer needed to be friendly toward him. She'd gotten the job she'd wanted. Now she made her own rules.

What really got to him was the fact that her attitude bothered him so much. She kept him off balance. One minute, he found himself trying to prove to her that he was one of the good guys. The next, he wanted to show her just how low-down and dirty he could get in the cold war between them.

He tried to decide if she detested him because she was innocent of the subterfuge he'd accused her of or because she was guilty and didn't like the fact that he'd seen through her.

For a moment, he wondered what he was doing there, but looking at her closed expression, he knew. She was a challenge he couldn't ignore. Simple.

As he'd figured, he'd spent a restless night, his body hungry and unsatisfied after that one kiss. He glanced toward the bunk bed. His body hardened at once. Hellfire, he'd never wanted a woman the way he wanted this one. It was enough to make a preacher cuss.

"All present and accounted for," she declared. She picked up her parka and small case with one hand, a large duffel and her sleeping bag with the other. "Ready."

"I'll take that." He reached for the duffel. For a second, they had a tug of war, but he was determined. She finally let go.

He had to laugh at the twinge of triumph that darted through him. Score one for our side, he silently jeered.

She gave him one of her drop-dead glances.

Briefly, he wondered why she was really so cold toward him. Someday he'd ask. When he was feeling masochistic. He had no doubt she'd tell him in terms unflattering to the male half of the human race. As she'd done after their breakup.

He followed her out, watching the way her jeans clung to her delectable rear. She was tall and lithe, all her curves

THE WAY OF A MAN 45

fitting his in just the right places. That she was also intelligent, not without a sense of humor and a damned good worker only added to the allure and the puzzle that was Dinah St. Cloud.

He put her luggage in the back of the truck while she locked the cabin. She hid the key in a chink above the lintel.

"That should keep out everyone under the age of ten," he called out.

She shrugged. "That's where I was told to put it. Someone from the Butte Falls office will be by later to pick it up." She climbed in the truck without another word.

Paul got in and slammed the door. Easy, he cautioned himself. He swung out onto Main Street and headed for town a block away. At the diner, he pulled into a parking space. "Sita's fixed a lunch for us. How about a doughnut and coffee?"

"Fine."

"Don't swoon with excitement," he advised dryly.

When he returned, carrying two sacks and two cups of coffee, she was sitting as straight and stiff as a statue on her side of the truck.

"Help," he said when she didn't move.

She leaned across the seat and opened the driver's door. He handed her a cup of coffee and dropped the two bags between them. Once he was strapped into his seat again, he opened the smaller one and handed her an apple fritter, still warm from the oven.

"Thank you," she said.

He did a slow burn. If she didn't thaw out soon, he was going to start a fight to warm her up. Maybe kiss her.

"Who put a knot in your tail already this morning?" he asked in a strictly friendly tone.

That got a response. She whipped her head around and glared at him. "It's none—" She stopped as if regretting the show of anger.

"None of my business?" he asked, wanting to taunt her a little. "Well, I was just wondering if it was me, or if something else had tweaked you off."

She didn't answer until she'd taken a careful sip of coffee. He noticed she hadn't taken a bite of the treat. He crunched into his and wished it was her neck.

Cool it, he ordered. Just because she turned him on and he didn't do the same for her was no cause to get nasty. So she didn't consider him God's gift. Most women did.

Since Dinah had protested she didn't want a man for his looks, his money or his connections, he wondered what she did want. He knew she wasn't totally immune to the man-woman attraction. Like it or not, she'd responded to him.

The thought helped ease some of the frustration he felt with the ice maiden beside him. He paused and considered his own reactions. What did he want from a woman?

Not a damned thing, other than a bit of companionship on occasion. His fiancée had taught him a valuable lesson about the gentler sex and their idea of love. She hadn't been able to face a lifetime with his battered face.

Too bad she hadn't stuck around. The doctors, after seven operations, had put him back together with no scars on the outside. They'd rebuilt his nose and cheekbones by working through his mouth and nostrils. It had taken a year—

Dinah's voice startled him out of his thoughts when she finally spoke. "I was annoyed because I'd been promised a vehicle, then I was told there wasn't one available. Without asking me, you and my supervisor arranged for my transportation. I like to be consulted when I'm involved. I could have brought my own car from California."

"The local ranger said you'd been working in the Mount Shasta area. Do you like it there?"

"Yes."

"You didn't know I had relatives here in southern Oregon, did you?" he asked on a sudden hunch. "Or that I would be staying at the ranch on this job?"

"No."

"Else you wouldn't have taken the assignment, right?" At her frowning glance, he knew he read her right.

"Maybe," she answered coolly.

He remembered the kisses they'd shared. She hadn't been so cool then. First she'd been startled, then she'd been urgent and hot. And so had he.

"Where are we going?" she asked when he stayed on the highway instead of turning off at the county road to the ranches.

"Crater Lake. Have you seen it yet?"

"No."

"I figured you hadn't. People never go see the sights around their stomping grounds. Since it's close, they assume they'll do it later. Only they rarely do."

"I didn't realize you were so deep into human nature." She didn't bother to hide the mocking tone.

She licked her fingers, and he realized she'd eaten the fritter. He polished off the last of his with a silent curse. Dinah kept him off center like no other woman he had ever met.

When she looked at him, he flashed her a smile, hoping to thaw her out a little. She blinked, hesitated, then smiled back. A person would think she limited her smiles to one a day the way she thought it over before returning the innocent gesture.

"There's a crumb of sugar at the side of your mouth," he said.

Just as he reached over to remove it, she flicked her tongue out to wipe it off. His skin sizzled at the contact of that moist, warm touch. He went into instant and full arousal.

He bit back a gasp at the painful pressure of confinement. He needed to get out of his clothes...fast. Or he could touch Dinah and wait for the frostbite to take effect.

Cursing to himself, he tried to understand his own reactions. Usually with women, he could take 'em or leave 'em, but with Dinah, he was as mixed up as an adolescent.

At times, he wanted to crush her to him and smother her with his passion until she responded, until her blood rushed as wild and rampant as his did; at others, he simply wanted to hold her, to know her as a person and to be known in the same way.

And the fact remained—he wanted her with a relentless need that drove him to goad her for not feeling the same way.

There had been moments when she had seemed driven by the same need. He frowned and gave up trying to figure out the chemistry between them. To hell with it!

Dinah couldn't help but be aware of Paul's problem. Signals seemed to fly in the air between them, alerting her to his every nuance. It was maddening. When she was around him, she felt trapped by something she couldn't name, drawn toward some vortex of danger that was inevitable.

A tremor of apprehension shook her.

She looked out the side window while he shifted in the seat as if uncomfortable. It was another example of the human male's uncontrollable appetites, she reminded herself virtuously, denying the heat that coursed through her own body. She was positive she'd done nothing to arouse his desire.

She took a peek at herself. Plain jeans, not too tight. Sensible walking boots with ankle-high tops. A loose sweatshirt over a turtleneck of yellow knitted cotton. Her faithful old red parka slung over her shoulders. There just wasn't a sexy thread on her.

However, she had to admit, it was rather a heady feeling to be the object of a man's intense passion. It was exciting and unnerving and made for an unpredictable relationship.

What relationship? she asked herself, mocking the thought of any such thing between her and Paul McPherson.

Sighing, she watched the countryside as they followed the road to Crater Lake. Snow lay in glittering banks and swells among the fir and pine trees. It often lasted into June if shaded from the sun. As they neared the lake, the piles pushed up by the snowplow grew deeper.

"Do you have a warm hat?" Paul asked when they arrived.

"Uh-huh." She retrieved a knitted toboggan hat from her pocket and pulled it down until it covered her ears. After putting her arms in the sleeves, she zipped her parka to the neck, and climbed out.

Paul joined her, taking her arm to guide her to a lookout point over the lake. The snowbank beside the observation shed was twice her height. The wind off the lake was freezing cold. She estimated the chill factor at zero degrees.

Paul opened the door to the tiny shelter, and they went inside. With the door cutting the flow of wind, they could stand at the open front and get a panoramic view of the lake.

"How high are we?" she asked, clasping her arms across herself to keep her warmth in.

"Close to eight thousand feet, I think. That's Wizard Island in the lake. Its peak is nearly seven thousand feet. That other little jut of land to the right is called Phantom Ship."

"Yes, it looks like a sailing ship." She surveyed the cliffs, crags and ridges that surrounded the lake. The rocks and bluffs were of volcanic origin, carved by wind and weather.

"Crater Lake is the deepest lake in the country. Can you imagine the size of the volcano that once was here before it blew its top?" Paul murmured near her ear.

He stood close behind her, his body helping hers retain its warmth in the open shelter. A shiver rushed over her, and she felt tight and achy inside. His hands touched her shoulders. He waited for a moment, but her throat had closed. She said nothing.

With exquisitely gentle motions, he encircled her shoulders, enclosing her within his protective embrace. His arms crossed her chest right below her throat, well above her breasts, which became heavy and tight. A warning pinged through her. *Danger*.

The buffed leather of his jacket brushed her chin. She suppressed an urge to rub against it and absorb the texture and scent of the soft leather. He smelled of balsam mixed with a trace of horse and saddle, as if he'd been riding in the woods lately.

When he leaned his face over her shoulder and started naming the bluffs that rimmed the lake, she turned her head slightly toward his cheek. The after-shave he wore was spicy. She inhaled deeply, unable to stop. He was so terribly...male.

And at the moment, she felt so terribly female.

He stopped speaking. They stood there in a taut silence while threads of some gossamer substance wound around them... around and around and around... until she felt totally ensnared.

His cheek lightly pressed her temple. Tendrils of feeling—fear or something else—rose in her. She had to move, to say something and break this strange spell. She had to get away.

She was saved from having to protest by the arrival of a group of tourists, laughing and pushing their way into the tiny building.

"Let's go," Paul muttered, his face inscrutable.

They drove the thirty-five-mile loop around the lake and hiked to one of the vantage points. There, sheltered from the wind by a rocky outcropping, they ate club sandwiches piled high with ham and turkey and bacon and shared an insulated jug of coffee.

"The land is so rugged and wild-looking." She gestured to the miles and miles of lava rock and sparse vegetation. To the west, evergreen trees hugged the skyline. "You'd never believe that five hundred species of wildflowers grow in this park, would you?"

"No."

His voice was deeper, with a quietness in the tone that touched her soul. She looked into his eyes. Their color seemed deeper, too, taking the hues of the lake and the sky into their lighter blue depths, deepening the silvery striations that joined the pupil to the darker rim of the iris.

She looked away with an effort. To fall under this man's spell again would be worse than foolish. She forced herself to remember the lesson she'd learned about men like him.

He hadn't been serious about them, but she had. He hadn't trusted her, but she'd trusted him. He thought she'd been out for what she could get. She'd thought they were in love.

Paul was cynical about women. Perhaps handsome men had things too easy. When the rewards of life came without effort, they weren't valued. Love became a game...a charade.

Unlike the jerk in college, who'd tried to force her when she didn't succumb to his charm, Paul hadn't had to do more than kiss her into yielding. Had he been waiting for her total submission, for a declaration of love, before going further?

Thank God she hadn't given him that satisfaction. While she'd known how she felt about him, she'd been shy about saying it first, especially since she was sure he was used to women falling at his feet like burnt tree snags in a high wind.

She gazed into the distance and judged her own reactions to Paul. She wished she hadn't been one of those foolish women who'd fallen for him, but the fact was, she had.

Whenever Paul had kissed her, wildfire had erupted in her, burning right down to some secret place that had never before been reached. The memory of those kisses still bothered her.

"We'd better get back," she said all at once, jumping to her feet. Aware of Paul's quizzical glance, she stuffed sandwich wrappers into the bag and shook out the remaining drops of coffee in her cup. She was anxious to get to the ranch and other people, back to reality.

They made the return trip in almost total silence. It was late afternoon when they arrived at the ranch.

"Lovely," she murmured, hardly conscious that she'd spoken aloud as they drove down the row of budding cottonwoods and alders that lined the creek.

Evergreens formed a woods on the other side of the gravel ranch road. The trees opened into a clearing that contained a lovely wood-and-stone home and multiple stables and other buildings, forming three sides of a large quadrangle.

Rachel was on the wide covered deck at the front of the house. She waved to them, obviously pleased at their arrival.

"I'm so glad you're here," she called as they approached the deck. "There's a bad storm on the way. It's supposed to snow."

Dinah looked at the sky. It was fairly clear, but if one looked closely, dark clouds lurked on the horizon miles away, but she knew how fast that could change.

"That will slow our survey," Paul said. "I'd wanted to get started with on-site observations by the end of the month."

"You can do aerial surveys when it clears," Rachel advised. "Did you enjoy your outing?" She glanced from one to the other.

Paul turned to Dinah. "I did. Did you?"

The directness of his question startled her. She remembered his arms around her during those oddly tense moments in the snow shelter. "Yes." Her voice held the tiniest quaver, but Paul picked right up on it.

"Don't be so enthusiastic," he said in a stage whisper. "They'll wonder what else we did besides picnic."

His smile teased, but his eyes reminded her of those river-polished agates she'd loved as a child—beautiful, perfectly formed, but cool and hard.

Rachel flicked a strand of honey-colored hair out of her eyes as a gust of wind bore down on them. "There's a foal about to be born. Throw your stuff in the bedroom and come out to the stable if you feel like it. Otherwise, I'll see you in the house in a little while." She smiled and dashed across the gravel driveway to the open door of the stable.

"Go on." Paul slipped her case from her hand. "I'll take your stuff in."

"Uh, I'll go in now, too."

She followed him inside. They went through the modern kitchen into a short hall and up six steps into the bedroom wing. A reading alcove was attractively situated between two rooms on the left. Three doors opened off the right side. He led her to the last one.

The bedroom had an old-fashioned spool bed, a piecrust lamp table and a rocking chair. A large window with a padded window seat afforded a view of the valley and the hills beyond.

"The bathroom is through there," Paul offered. He set her case on the chair and laid her duffel on the floor. "This is the closet." He opened the door and flicked on a light. "You want to go see the grand event?"

"Yes, if you mean the birth."

He nodded. "I'll meet you on the deck in five minutes." He walked out and closed the door behind him.

Dinah laid her heavy coat on the bed. Going into the bathroom, she found it had two doors. A closet or another bedroom? Just to be sure, she opened the other door cautiously. It was a bedroom. Paul's bedroom, she corrected.

He was stripping out of his T-shirt. He tossed it aside, picked up a sweatshirt and turned to find her standing there staring like a rube at a circus. He draped the sweatshirt over his shoulders and faced her, his hands resting on his hips, his powerful chest gleaming like bronze in the radiant beams of the setting sun.

"Yes?"

Heat hit her like a flash fire, curling up her middle and lodging behind her breasts. "I thought maybe this was a closet."

"No, it's my room. We'll have to share the bath."

"Oh."

"Is that a problem?" He lifted one dark eyebrow, which gave him a look of diabolical sophistication.

"Not at all." Very carefully, as if she'd disturbed a jungle beast, she closed the door, freshened up, then conscientiously made sure she'd released the lock before exiting through her room.

A minute later, she joined him on the deck. Together, they walked to the long, narrow stable. The building was warm inside. Horses filled several stalls. Rachel and a couple of men were gathered at the back of the building. She and Paul joined them.

"We have a colt," Rachel announced. On the railing in front of her, she held a toddler so he could see the proceedings.

"Hey, Kelly," Paul said. "How's it going, old man?"

"Aul," the boy cried, grinning at Paul. He pointed toward the stall.

"A fine colt," Paul said. He introduced Dinah to his small cousin, who smiled at her, then turned back to the stall.

Paul let Dinah stand in front of him at the railing. Again she was aware of his sturdy warmth behind her. She remembered how smooth his chest and torso had looked. She wondered how the diamond-shaped patch of black hair just below his throat felt in contrast. She jerked her thoughts back to the present.

Two men worked with the mare. She seemed to be having trouble, but Dinah wasn't sure what it was. Rachel's husband pulled on a long plastic glove that covered his whole arm. After examining the mare, he said the other one wasn't turned correctly.

"There's another?" Rachel questioned.

"Yes." Kerrigan worked for several minutes. "Hank, you want to give it a try?"

The quiet cowboy nodded. After pulling on a glove, he took Kerrigan's place with the mare. Several tense minutes passed. The new colt tried to nurse, but Kerrigan shooed it away.

"Got it," Hank said. He pulled his hand free, bringing the forefeet of the foal with him.

Kerrigan grabbed one of the tiny hooves. He and Hank helped the horse birth the smaller foal. "A filly," Hank said.

Dinah released the breath she'd been unconsciously holding. At the same moment, she realized she was leaning against Paul, his body perfectly fitted to hers so that she felt his chest, his stomach and his hard thighs all at once. His arms were braced on each side of hers, his hands beside hers on the railing.

"Nice job," he said, his voice dropping to that deeper, quieter register that sent funny little cascades of electricity along her neck. She leaned forward against the railing.

"Heavens, I've got to finish supper. Come in as soon as you can, darling," Rachel requested.

Paul stepped to the side and lifted Kelly, placing him over his head and onto his shoulders. "Dinah and I will take care of this scamp for you."

"Thanks." Rachel shot him a smile, poked her son playfully in the ribs and headed for the house.

"Come on. We'll give you the grand tour." Paul, holding Kelly steady, turned to Dinah. "That was Queenie, the prize mare."

"Eenie. Aul," Kelly echoed.

Dinah smiled up at him. He grinned back. A drool of saliva slipped from his lower lip and landed on Paul's forehead. Paul reached up and swiped it off on the sleeve of his sweatshirt.

"This job isn't without its perils," he commented drolly, but with an indulgent smile.

She was entranced. Paul, the heartthrob of the entire western United States, was wonderful with children. It was obvious Kelly trusted him completely and had done this before. The child clicked his tongue, grabbed a handful of dark hair and ordered his cousin to, "Go, Aul."

Dinah couldn't help but laugh. When Paul pivoted so he could see her, she smiled approvingly at him. He paused, as if startled, then he gave her his slow, devastating grin. Her insides rioted.

She calmed down when she remembered another proverb about handsome rogues—the one about them being able to charm candy away from a baby. Paul had the gift—in spades.

Chapter Four

Dinah walked beside Paul and the child he carried while they examined each building of the ranch complex. Paul called the area surrounding the house "the homeplace."

There was a bunkhouse with individual rooms off a long hall, plus a common lounge and kitchen for the men. Two small houses tucked into wooded lots were for married men and their families.

Looking at the activities on the ranch, Dinah sensed the thread of life stretching back into the past and forward to the future. There was a connectedness about it all, a sense of lives touching lives. She envied Paul's cousins. And Paul, she admitted. She felt outside the mainstream of life.

"It all looks so new and fresh," she commented as they headed for the kitchen. "So cared for."

"It is. The twins used to compete in rodeos and used their winnings to turn their operation into a model ranch.

They're not afraid to try new methods, to be innovators. Of course some of the other ranchers think they're crazy."

"Like Elmer?"

Paul gave her an appraising glance, then laughed. "You got it. He's hard to convince."

"I noticed his views on intensive grazing last night. They weren't very favorable."

She felt Paul's gaze on her mouth. Icy-hot tingles ran over her lips and down her throat to lodge in her chest. He could make her feel things with just a glance.

"If a man hasn't tried it, he shouldn't knock it," he said, his voice going deeper while his eyes devoured her.

Dinah dropped back a step, her heart pounding. Somehow she felt she'd lost the thread of the conversation. Or was she imagining that seductive, hungry need in him?

"Eat," Kelly said.

"Sure, pal. We're headed that way."

Paul led the way to the broad wooden deck. Troubled, Dinah followed the man and child. Through the windows, Dinah could see Rachel moving around the kitchen. Their hostess beamed when they tramped inside.

"Wash up," she called. "It's ready."

In a few minutes, the four adults were seated around an oak table in the kitchen. Kelly was in a highchair between his mom and dad. The meal was casual—oven-barbecued chicken, baked beans, a plate of fresh veggies and a hot loaf of pumpernickel bread.

Paul buttered a slice of bread. When Kelly pointed and waved his arms, Paul tore off a piece and gave it to him. The boy munched happily, making quiet sounds to himself.

"He's darling," Dinah said. "How old is he?"

"Thirteen months," Rachel answered. "And into everything. I don't know what I'd do if there weren't ten other people on the ranch willing to take him off my hands during the day.''

"It's better for him to be outside. He's got a lot of ranching to learn." Kerrigan grinned at his wife's groan. He added beans to the child's plate.

Kelly scooped up one and stuck it into his mouth. When he saw Dinah watching him, he gave her a big smile. The bean dropped out. He looked surprised.

The adults chuckled.

Paul helped himself to chicken and passed the platter to Dinah. "Kelly hasn't learned the art of flirting and eating at the same time. You'd better give him a few lessons," he advised his cousin. "Can't have him taking a woman to dinner and dropping food in his lap every time he smiles at her."

"You can handle the flirting part," Kerrigan said. "My wife doesn't let me look at girls anymore."

That drew another laugh.

Dinah found her envy growing as the evening progressed. The three adults were so obviously fond of one another and at ease together. She thought Kelly was one lucky little boy to be brought up in that atmosphere of warm camaraderie.

Briefly, she wondered what her life would have been like if her parents had been younger, or at least not so strict. They had both taught at the local high school, her father in the chemistry department, her mother in biology. They'd required hours of study from her and perfect test scores. She'd moved two grades ahead of her classmates, but it had been a lonely triumph, she realized now. She'd had friends but never a boyfriend.

An unexpected sting of tears caused her to keep her eyes on her plate for a moment or two. A longing grabbed hold of her and wouldn't let go. She didn't even know what it was that she longed for, only that it was acute and it hurt.

Certainly Rachel had a family life to be desired, as far as Dinah could tell. What would it be like to have someone, a special someone, to share life with? Was that what the achy feeling inside was all about?

It was a startling revelation, and one that worried her.

There was a natural attraction between men and women. The force of life demanded it. If she ever met the right man, it would all work out, she assured herself. She hoped.

A shadow of doubt rippled through her. She was twenty-five, would be twenty-six in August. She'd never met anyone who turned her inside out...

Her eyes went to Paul against her will.

Not him. She wanted more than sex and a casual good time. Perhaps her flaw was to demand more than life could ever deliver. How did a person get over that? "You said your parents were retired. Where are they living now?" Rachel asked.

Dinah brought her wandering thoughts under control. "In Arizona. It's better for Dad's arthritis and Mom's allergies. I burn up when I visit them, but I don't perspire."

"That desert wind takes the moisture right out of you," Paul agreed, coming out of his own spell of introspection. "It's easy to become dehydrated without realizing it. A person can miss a lot of things in life without realizing it's passing them by," he added, his gaze flicking over the group around the table.

"Sounds like you've been doing some serious thinking on the subject," his cousin said.

Paul shrugged, then smiled, his mood changing. "Nah, that was a philosophical quip. Women love men who wax philosophical. Didn't you know that?"

"No."

"Well, no wonder it took you so long to land a wife."

Dinah laughed with the others at Paul's teasing. She studied the two men covertly while she ate. Kerrigan was probably thirty-four or five. Paul was thirty-one. Almost six years older than she was. And three times as experienced.

Paul was so vibrant, so full of pure male energy. He could teach a woman all she needed to know about life. She wanted to touch him, to make the connection with life that she longed for.... What was she thinking! She brought herself under control.

When the baby started smearing more food on his face than into his mouth, his mother cleaned him up and put him on the floor to play. He headed for the cabinets and opened a drawer.

"His drawer," Rachel explained.

Dinah saw it was filled with safe kitchen things for him to play with—plastic cups and measuring spoons, tart pans and wooden spoons. The adults finished. While the men went into the family room—Paul scooped Kelly into his arms and carried him off—she and Rachel cleared the table and stored the dishes in the dishwasher.

"Paul is so good with Kelly and the other children at the ranch." Rachel closed the pantry door and squirted lotion on her hands. She held the bottle out to Dinah, who did the same.

Rubbing the scented lotion in, they went into the family room, which was separated from the office by a glass-fronted case. Dinah paused to admire the rodeo trophies. Paul came over to her.

"Always regretted I never took up rodeoing. Women love a champion." His sardonic smile was in place.

"You don't need any more attractions," Dinah said without thinking. She was annoyed with herself as she realized she'd all but blurted out that she found him alluring.

"Hmm, then you do think I have some qualities of my own that a woman might like?"

At the amused challenge in his eyes, she was sure he was taunting her about her past response to him. "I'm sure you're quite aware of each and every charm you possess. And of a woman's reaction to all of them."

"Would you like coffee now?" Rachel called.

"Yes," Paul answered for both of them. "And how about some of that chocolate cake you had in the oven before I left this morning? Any of that left?"

Rachel gave him a mock frown. "That was going to be a surprise. Nothing is a secret around here."

"Oh, one or two things might be," her husband disagreed. He gave her a warm smile, secretive and special.

Dinah felt the tiny hairs on her neck prickle.

"Oh, that." Rachel waved a hand airily. "I think everyone knows we're expecting a brother or sister for Kelly this winter."

Dinah offered her congratulations after Paul did. Again a funny tightening ran through her.

"All the ranch hands have been pretending not to notice when I suddenly turn and run for the bathroom," Rachel continued drolly. "But I went to the doctor Friday, and it's official. Guess who I ran into coming out?"

"Who?" Kerrigan asked.

"Beth."

Paul and his cousin laughed uproariously.

"Well, heck, it's about time Keegan was caught up in the joys of parenthood." Kerrigan was plainly delighted. "I'll finally get to grouse at him when he's late getting started after being up all night with a crying baby."

"Don't say I told. They might want to keep it their secret for a while." She exchanged a glance with her husband.

Dinah wondered at the special feeling between them and how a person ever found it. Was it just blind luck? Her wary attitude might prevent her from recognizing the real thing when she met the right man. Perhaps a person had to take a chance.

After an hour, Rachel and Kerrigan went to put their son to bed. Dinah looked up to find Paul studying her, a half smile on his lips. For a second, his expression was...tender?

Seeing her watching him, his smile widened. "A half dozen would be enough for a basketball team," he said.

His tone seemed to mock the deep longing she felt. It was as if he'd been aware of her troubling thoughts all evening and was laughing at her. Embarrassed, she went on the defensive. "You might not like all those sleepless nights."

"There are other things to do beside sleep."

And he'd be very skillful at doing them. The thought came to her before she could suppress it.

He shrugged in his nonchalant way at her stiff silence. "It was just a suggestion." Then he had the gall to laugh when she tried to put him in his place with a repressive glare.

Really!

Dinah woke to the sounds of the shower running in the bathroom. She snuggled under the covers and watched the raindrops hitting the windows with icy splatters. The storm had come in during the wee hours of the morning. It had woken her up.

Heat built in her as she recalled slipping out of bed and going to the window. A tree branch had hit against the house when the wind gusted around the corner. A soft knock at the bathroom door had startled her.

"Yes?" she'd answered.

Paul had entered her room. "I thought I heard you stirring. It's just a branch. I'll trim it back in the morning."

"That's all right. It doesn't really bother me. I wanted to make sure it wasn't going to hit a window and break it."

"It won't." He'd paused. "You want a cup of hot chocolate?"

The faint glow of the night-light in the bathroom had backlit his tall, powerful body. He'd slipped into pants, but had worn no shirt. His feet had been bare, which seemed to make him curiously vulnerable. She'd felt that way, too.

What would have happened if she'd accepted? she wondered, stretching and yawning. She hadn't, although she was honest enough to admit she had been tempted.

If she had, would Paul have kissed her?

She remembered his lips on hers, the kisses that were demanding, others that were enticing. Each time he'd kissed her, including the other night at the cabin, something had flared into existence inside her.

She worried over this admission. Paul McPherson wasn't a candidate for a long-term relationship. He was a breaker of hearts. She'd do well to remember that instead of what his lips had felt like, caressing hers....

The lock snicked on her bathroom door, and she heard Paul's door open and close. She jumped up, tossed off the football jersey she'd worn to bed and headed for the shower.

When she opened the door, the mingled scent of Paul's shampoo and cologne enfolded her like a warm embrace.

She stopped dead-still as tingles shot from her head to her toes. It was almost as if he were in here with her.

Taking a deep breath, she proceeded with her shower. When she returned to her room, she found a cup of coffee and a small glass of orange juice on the piecrust table.

She drank the juice while dressing in the only good slacks and sweater outfit she'd brought with her. After drying her hair and adding pink lip gloss to her mouth, she picked up the empty glass and half-empty cup and headed for the kitchen.

Paul stepped into the hall when she did.

"Hi. Do I have you to thank for the juice and coffee?" she asked, determinedly holding on to the brisk cheer she'd shown toward men after she'd left Minnesota.

"I brought them, yes."

"Thanks."

"Don't mention it." He gave her a sideways glance. "Do you sleep in that football shirt?"

"Yes."

A slow smile spread over his face. "Red. Who'd have thought it?" He shook his head in mock wonder.

His amusement rubbed her the wrong way. "Maybe there're lots of things you don't know about me."

He shot her a glance. "I'm willing to learn."

They entered the kitchen before she could come up with a response to his comment. Rachel and Kerrigan were there, reading the Sunday paper. Their hostess laid the paper aside and started breakfast. Dinah offered to help and was put to work cooking bacon in the microwave.

Soon pancakes, sausage and bacon were placed on the table in heaping platters. "Who cooks for the men?" Dinah asked, taking her place at the round table.

"Wills," Kerrigan said. "He's a retired rodeo clown."

She sensed a story. Upon probing, she discovered the brothers had found the old man pretty far down on his luck. They'd brought him home, dried him out and given him a job.

"Between them, Wills and Rachel keep a tight hand on the reins around the homeplace," Kerrigan complained soulfully.

Rachel wasn't impressed. "This place needed a firm hand."

A cry from the back of the house announced Kelly's awakening. Paul got to his feet before Rachel. "I'll get him."

"He'll be soaking wet," she warned.

"I'll change him."

To Dinah's amazement, he disappeared down the hall. In fifteen minutes, he was back, the child in his arms. Kelly had evidently been washed and changed expertly. He wore red rompers and a striped T-shirt. The McPhersons were men of many talents.

He gurgled with joy upon seeing the others. "Eat," he said.

"He's going to be as big as a house," Rachel declared. She prepared him a plate of pancakes, cut into bite-sized pieces, and served it with fruit chunks.

Dinah studied Paul in surreptitious side glances.

"What?" he asked, having noticed her looking at him.

"You're very good with children." Her voice was husky. "For a bachelor."

"Paul loves kids." Rachel gave her son a drink of milk. "He's even better than Keegan with them."

"Hey, what about me?" Kerrigan demanded. "Who changed all those diapers and got up in the middle of the night—"

"All the McPherson men are wonderful with children," Rachel amended.

"Da-dee," Kelly said and offered up a bite of his meal to his father.

"Thanks, son." Kerrigan took the bite. "Have one of mine."

Dinah felt her throat close for a second. Again, that restless yearning washed over her. She wished she'd been raised in a home like this. Not that her parents hadn't loved her or that she didn't appreciate them, but they'd been so solemn and stiff, as if they didn't quite know what to do with this child who'd been given to them so unexpectedly late in life.

After the meal, the men insisted on cleaning up the kitchen. Then they all went into the office. Kerrigan pulled out maps of the ranch and spread them on the floor. Rachel took Kelly into the family room and played ball with him while Dinah and the two men studied the aerial photographs.

Her shoulder brushed Paul's when he leaned over to point out a rounded peak. "There's a channel for spring runoff from this high point. I believe we could dynamite the low ridge and bring the water to this pond on the Triple R."

Kerrigan nodded. "Sounds like a good idea. Talk to Keegan about it. See what he thinks."

"I'll look at the land around there as soon as Dinah and I are able to get in and set up camp."

"Be careful. One of the men saw some tire tracks on that old logging road through the gulch earlier in the month. He said it looked like whoever had been there had got stuck and had to dig out. Guess they left after that."

"Probably a hunter," Paul suggested.

"Whatever, it's illegal. Keep an eye out when you're up there. It's pretty rugged country. You'll be isolated while you study the yew trees." Kerrigan turned to Dinah. "Did Paul tell you we found a big patch of yew trees at the northern edge of the property?"

"Yes. The forest service office had a report on it. They want me to conduct a bark regrowth study for them."

"How does that work?" Paul asked.

"I'm going to strip the bark in patches and see how long it takes to recover. If the taxol found in the bark is as good at fighting cancer as is currently thought, then we might have a new industry come from this."

Paul nodded. "And it might give the loggers an occupation with a brighter future."

"Right." Dinah leaned over the photographs. "Explain each area to me. These look like a mixture of pine and aspen."

They discussed the land and the areas of old-growth forest the rest of the morning. After a lunch of pot roast, Rachel put Kelly down for his nap, then she and Kerrigan went to their room.

Dinah felt restless. She would have liked a walk, but the weather was uncertain. Standing at the window of the family room, she debated finding a book in the reading alcove or chancing a walk along the gravel road. At least it wouldn't be muddy, and if she got caught in a downpour, so what? Her parka would shed the water until she could get back to the house.

"Let's go to the stable and look at the foals." Paul came up behind her and peered out the window.

"I'd like that," she agreed. "I'll get my coat."

In a few minutes, they were ready. They walked across the wet gravel. From the bunkhouse came the sounds of someone playing a guitar and singing a mournful tune.

"Hank," Paul explained. "He writes songs."

"Has he gotten any published?"

"Not that I know of."

They went into the warm, quiet stable. A horse nickered as they passed a stall. Paul stopped and rubbed its ears. They walked on to the back stall. There, the mare and her two babies were lying in the straw, cuddled close to each other.

Life touching life, drawing nourishment from each contact.

Dinah felt the tightening in her chest. That was what she wanted—the mysterious, pervasive connection with life that seemed to flow in the air here on the ranch.

Again a glimmer of an earlier, ridiculous notion flickered into her mind—that Paul could teach her all she needed to know so she could find that connection to life. She stole a glance at him.

He was watching her.

His eyes seemed dark and moody in the dimness of the stable. There was no humor in his expression. She couldn't tell what he was thinking, but he stared at her relentlessly.

He was most likely thinking of something unrelated to them and didn't realize he was staring at her. She watched the scene in the stall and tried not to think of him. It was hopeless.

The heat of his gaze seemed to make her face glow. She put a hand up to her cheek. Her skin felt hot. Risking a quick look at him, she saw his attention still on her. His lips parted slightly, his chest lifting as he drew a deep breath.

She wanted to be cuddled against that strong chest the way he'd done with Rachel's child. The memory of his kiss at the cabin returned. It hadn't been like the other kisses they'd shared two years ago. Instead of teasing and hungry, it had been strangely tender... an asking, not a taking.

It had haunted her ever since, adding to her restless longing. She stared at his mouth and wondered if he would be a gentle or a demanding lover.

Paul heaved the breath out of his lungs. He leaned closer to Dinah. "If you continue to look at me like that, I won't be responsible for the outcome," he warned, his voice coming out harsher than he'd intended.

She blinked up at him, her eyes dark and mysterious with thoughts he couldn't read. However, he didn't have to be a genius to know what was on her mind. A woman didn't give a man that come-on stare unless she was sensuously interested.

Her face closed instantly. "I don't know what you're talking about." She was back to her haughty air.

"Let me put it in plain English—you're asking to be kissed."

She puffed up like an offended society matron. "I am not!"

"Like hell," he snarled. "Then if a man dares take you up on it, you act like an outraged virgin. What's with you, Dinah? I never took you for a tease."

The word was like a slap in the face. Dinah was horrified, insulted and torn between denial and the fear that what he said was true. "I . . . I'm not."

"Then it must be me. I'm getting my signals crossed. That's never happened before that I can recall."

She couldn't say a word.

"I've apologized for the kiss at the cabin. I promise I won't overstep the boundaries in the future. There, is that enough assurance for you, or do you want it written in blood?"

It occurred to her to tell him she might not want him to control his impulses at all. As quickly as the thought came, she pushed it away. She had to show some sense.

"Dammit, say something!"

"I believe you," she said with difficulty.

He swung away from her. The mare raised her head and watched them as if wary of the quarreling humans.

Dinah knew she should let it drop, but guilt ate at her. Her innate honesty wouldn't let him take all the blame. "I did...I was thinking about...about kissing...about your kiss."

He pivoted slowly as she spoke, his expression closed and controlled. A puzzled frown nicked a line between his dark eyebrows.

"I didn't realize it showed," she finished. "I'm sorry."

His face softened. "Well," he said.

She had to smile. "Paul McPherson, the great Casanova of the western world, speechless."

His wry grimace was at himself. "You keep a man off center, Ms. St. Cloud. I've never had that problem with a woman before."

"It's probably good for you." Keep it light. That was the way to handle the situation between them until she could sit down and have a long, reasonable talk with herself.

"It's damned hard on the ego, that's what it is. Last night and then just now—well, I wasn't certain whether you wanted me or you didn't." He cocked one eyebrow and studied her. "You were thinking about the kiss, huh?"

"Yes."

"The one at the cabin or past ones?"

She wasn't sure she wanted to confess that much, but she could tell by the determined gleam in his eyes that he wouldn't let it go until he had satisfied his curiosity...or his male ego. She tried to be truthful yet cautious in her answer. "Well, mostly the one at the cabin. It was different."

"How?"

She shrugged and wished she'd kept her mouth shut.

"How was it different?" he insisted on knowing.

She felt they were on dangerous ground. They were completely alone in the dim stable. The gloom gave the interior an intimate quality that could induce a person into confessing more than was good for her. "It just was. Really, it doesn't matter."

He persisted. "To me, it does."

She heaved an exasperated breath. "Well, it was tender. The others, the ones in the past were more...demanding."

"Demanding?"

"Like the one under the mistletoe that time. It started out teasing. You wanted a response from me and were determined to get it. Then it became hungry...demanding."

"You responded," he said.

"Yes. That was years ago—"

"Two years isn't so long," he corrected. He gave her an intent perusal like a scientist figuring out a new theory. Paul could be very single-minded when he was curious about something.

"We're here on business," she reminded him, trying to regain ground she felt she'd lost by her admission. "Nothing else."

He chuckled. "Nothing? That's like telling the sun not to shine. I look at you and..." He let the thought trail away.

"Paul," she began sternly.

"Shh," he said, pointing to the sleeping foals. He turned Dinah toward the broad corridor between the stalls. They walked along the row of horses, pausing to inspect some of them.

Dinah worried about their conversation. Paul knew she was attracted to him. A blind man could tell that, and Paul wasn't obtuse where women were concerned. She'd have to be careful, of him and her own wild impulses. She'd stay on guard and not give him a chance to get close. She wouldn't be foolish again.

She studied him, trying to figure out his attitude, but he only looked at her with a thoughtful expression. She realized she was staring at him and glanced away.

"It's all right," he murmured. "I know how things stand now. I won't think you're asking for a kiss when you look at me with those black velvet eyes. I'll wait until you ask next time."

She roused from her musing and briskly headed for the stable door, needing the cool air on her face. "Ha. That'll be the day."

"Yeah," he taunted, but lightly. "I can hardly wait."

They took a walk along the lane, then returned to the house. He settled in the family room and picked up the paper.

"I think I'll take a nap," she decided.

"See you later," he called.

Once in her room and lying on the bed, a knitted afghan over her, she couldn't sleep. Their brief contretemps in the stable circled around and around in her mind.

She thought of Paul's lips on hers. There was a gentleness in him that surprised her. She would like to know that gentleness for herself, to experience it firsthand.

I'll wait until you ask.

She wanted to ask. She wanted him to teach her about making love. She wanted to know the fulfillment of being a total woman. She wanted to touch life....

Chapter Five

Reason returned. After dismissing the notion for the crazy idea that it was, Dinah tossed restlessly for thirty minutes. When the rain started again, she got up. She'd read the rest of the reports from the forestry office this afternoon.

Taking them with her, she went to the family room. Paul was there, lying on the sofa, boots off, his hands propped behind his head while he stared at the fire.

She stopped at the doorway, not sure whether to proceed or not. He turned his head and saw her. They watched each other warily, like ancient enemies who'd met again after many years.

It reminded her of the night they'd stared at each other through the cabin window as if an abyss separated them. Sometimes it seemed he held the secret to her inner self and she had to find it before she could understand herself.

The future opened before her—dark and uncertain. A chill of foreboding washed over her. She knew better than to get involved with a man like Paul, yet she sensed there was something she must do, something unresolved between them that she must get out of the way before she could get on with her life.

Yearning, swift and inexplicable, knifed through her. What was it about him that made her so restless and angry?

Angry?

Yes, but angry with him, herself, or life in general, she didn't know. She sighed and walked forward.

"I didn't mean to disturb you. I thought I'd read over the rest of the reports," she said.

He sat up.

"No, no, don't get up," she murmured. "I can read in my room just as well—"

"Don't go."

The low-drawled request stopped her in the act of rushing off. Electric currents darted through every cell in her body at the husky cadence of his voice. She detected an undertone whose emotion she couldn't decipher. Longing? Need? Whatever it was, she could hear no humor or amusement in it.

While she hesitated, he observed her solemnly, then he stood, and the tension fled. He smiled in his usual manner while adding a log to the fire. "The temperature dropped this afternoon. I thought a fire would be nice." He closed the fire screen. "Here, take this chair. The light is good."

He flicked on the lamp and adjusted it for her when she sat down. "Thank you."

She felt awkward around him. With his knowledge of women, she was sure he could sense the uncertainty he caused in her. Around men like him, a woman would be wise to be on guard at all times.

She read while he lounged on the sofa. To her surprise, he went to sleep. As the fire burned lower, he wrapped his arms across his chest as if he was cold. On tiptoe, she built up the fire and laid a knitted afghan over him.

He stirred only slightly, turning his head and brushing his lips over her hand when she tucked the afghan around his neck.

She returned to the chair, her hand burning. Staring into the dancing flames, listening to the wind and rain pelt the snug house, she wondered what it would be like to live with a man day after day. There were so many things to share if two people liked and respected each other.

It came to her that her parents were like that.

She stared into the leaping flames and contemplated the last thought. It was true, she realized. Her mother and father were very much alike—both highly intelligent and dedicated to the ideals and importance of teaching—they had spent their lives in mutual endeavor. She recalled all the quiet evenings at her home, studying while they discussed their day and their lesson plans. They'd consulted with each other constantly on ways to improve their teaching methods. And tried those methods out on her. She had strived to be a model pupil for them.

Hadn't she? A small doubt entered her mind.

She considered. Yes, but there had been times when she'd been rambunctious. They'd always been so gentle in their reprimands. Feeling like a goose among swans, she'd immediately lowered her voice and controlled her excited gestures.

Rebelling against teaching, she'd chosen botany and a life in the outdoors rather than the world of academia that they'd wanted for her. They hadn't been able to curb her love of nature.

She looked at the tall, handsome man lying on the sofa. Paul, too, loved the great outdoors, she reflected. He was a man with intriguing characteristics.

He stirred, then opened his eyes. Seeing her watching him, he stayed where he was, his eyes returning her gaze as unbidden thoughts sprang to life within her. Tension arced between them.

She felt the heat…and the longing. In him as well as her. He wanted her…passionately, hungrily. She could sense it.

If she asked, he would come to her. She had only to let him know. She looked away, her heart pounding, while emotions too turbulent to be named whirled through her.

"Did you get your reports finished?" he asked.

She nodded, unable to speak. This was part of his charm, she told herself—the penetrating stare that indicated she was the only woman in the world as far as he was concerned.

But it touched a chord in her. And set it to humming. She'd have to be careful around him. She wasn't young and idealistic anymore. She wouldn't fall for a handsome face again.

When the rest of the family joined her and Paul, they chatted, then the men put on slickers and did the outdoor chores. Later that evening, after a casual supper, the two couples played cards until bedtime. She and Paul were partners. They won the game.

The rain had let up during the night and Tuesday dawned bright as fresh-laundered sheets. Dinah learned the roads were too wet to travel. She was disgruntled. Tired of being inside, she wanted the freedom of the outdoors.

"How do you feel about riding?" Paul asked. He came into the office where she was reading and poured fresh coffee into her cup.

"Where?" she asked, her wariness about being alone with him surfacing unintentionally.

His lazy smile disappeared. Anger flicked through his eyes. "I said I'd wait until asked," he reminded her savagely.

His temper prodded hers. "What if you're never asked?"

"Then it'll never happen," he told her coolly. "This thing between us . . . nothing will come of it. If that's what you want."

"There is no—" She stopped at his sardonic expression. She couldn't get the lie past her lips. Instead, she asked, "Where are we riding to?"

"To look at the yew trees. We can go across country on horses and save a lot of time. We can also scout out the area where we'll pitch camp when the weather improves."

She looked at the logging requests she was reviewing. They could wait. "All right," she said, giving him a composed smile.

While she changed into old jeans, a thermal top, sweater and hiking boots, he volunteered to pack a lunch and saddle the horses. Pulling on her parka, she joined him at the stable.

Rachel and the baby were there, talking to an old cowboy who was introduced to Dinah as Wills.

Rachel watched Paul and Dinah prepare to leave with envy in her eyes. "I love the woods. There's a pair of eagles who nest on our land at the east boundary, where Sky Creek runs into the Rogue River. I've studied them for the past two years. I don't think I'll be able to this year, though." She smiled at her son.

Paul tightened the cinch on a saddle. He stuck a rifle into a leather scabbard on one horse. "Too bad our work is in the northern sector. We could check them for you."

"Kerrigan is going to take me over later this month. Beth and Keegan said they'd keep the monster for a long weekend. I've only left him a couple of times overnight."

"All the ranch hands will keep on eye on him," Paul predicted. "And also take turns walking the floor with him in case he cries for his mommy all night."

That brought a smile to Rachel's face. Dinah realized how astute Paul was to understand the other woman's fears and to bring them into the open. He'd also reassured her that she'd be missed by her son.

A warm feeling spread through Dinah. Paul could be so thoughtful. That, too, was part of his charm.

"Ready?" he asked.

She nodded. He cupped his hands and tossed her into the saddle. The gelding pranced, ready for a run. She held him to a walk as she turned him toward the stable door.

"Watch your head," Paul called out. He swung up on another gelding, a big, red horse also eager for an outing.

Dinah lifted her face to the sun when they were outside. Its radiant heat soaked into her skin like a lover's caress.

"Here," Paul said. He handed her a billed cap. "Did you remember to wear sunscreen? We'll be going across open meadow for more than an hour before we reach the hills."

"Yes." She pulled the cap low over her forehead to keep the sun out of her eyes.

The gelding shook his head and snorted impatiently.

"How do you feel about a run?" Paul asked.

"Love it!" She spurred her mount and took off.

She heard Paul give a shout behind her, then the sound of hooves coming up on her left. She stretched out over the neck of the dark brown gelding. He increased his pace until it felt as if they were flying. From the corner of her eye, she caught sight of the red horse, pushing to close the distance between them.

Excitement pounded through her. The *dum-da-da-dum* of the galloping horses sang in her blood and echoed in her ears. She laughed and urged the brown to greater effort, faster and faster.

Paul and his mount caught up, and the horses raced neck and neck across the smooth pasture. Cattle stopped grazing and stared at them curiously. A crow flew up and cawed at them in irritation.

On and on they ran. There was no one in the world but them, racing through the sunlight on a perfect spring morning. As their mounts tired, the race slowed, first to a canter, then a trot, and finally the two horses walked, side by side, excess energy spent.

"That was wonderful," she exclaimed.

The blood still pumped riotously through her. When she glanced at her companion, he was watching her, his expression curiously taut and unsmiling, unlike his usual teasing manner.

He didn't seem to realize he was watching her, his gaze intent, like a predator studying its prey. With a little shake of his head, he came out of his introspection, saw her eyes on him and smiled suddenly, dazzling her.

"You're a fine rider," he said.

"Thanks. You, too." She felt a trifle self-conscious after her exuberant display. She rarely allowed childish enthusiasms to have free rein, but it had felt so good to let go. "What happened to those big Belgian horses you worked with in Minnesota? Do you still have them?"

"Yes. They're at my farm in Tennessee."

She was surprised. "I didn't know you had a farm."

He gave her a sardonic grin. "Maybe there're things about me that you don't know."

"Touché," she said, conceding him a point in their battle.

Battle? Sort of. There seemed to be an ongoing skirmish between them whenever they were together.

"Come on. We'll let the horses drink and have a rest." He led the way to a tiny creek at the edge of the meadow.

There, they sat under a river alder and ate the Danish rolls he'd brought and shared a spot of coffee.

"Here, you go first," he invited. "I forgot to bring a cup. There's only the top on the insulated bottle. Do you mind drinking from it?"

"No, that's fine."

But her lips tingled when she took a drink and handed the top back to him. She gazed out over the verdant meadow. The homeplace shimmered in the distance like a hazy Utopia amid the fresh green of the pastures. She wished she could stay there forever.

Life, she thought, filled with the now-familiar longing. The ranch oozed life, not repressed and refined the way it was at her home, but free and full and overflowing...

"We'd better go," Paul said, standing all at once as if he were tired of being idle.

She nodded. When he held a hand out to her, she took it and let him pull her upright. With the ripple of muscle under his shirt, she became acutely aware of the life force that radiated from him like the energy-giving warmth of the sun.

Feeling vulnerable to that force, she tried to step away too quickly, went a little off balance and bumped into him. Her breath caught at the contact, but he stepped back at once.

He studied her with a frown on his handsome face. "Sometimes you forget yourself and loosen up," he said slowly, as if thinking aloud. "Then you clench up again. Like now, when we touched."

"It was just reaction," she said quickly.

"Yeah," was all he said.

They rode on up into the hills, finally coming to a long, sloped ledge that led to the top of a high ridge. They angled along it, climbing steadily for an hour. She caught glimpses of the valley below through the trees. It was a beautiful vista.

Her soul took flight, and she imagined what it would be like to be the first woman to traverse this mountain. She looked at Paul's broad back, dauntlessly leading the way, and smiled.

First man. First woman.

No wonder she was having so much trouble around him. Her head was full of romantic nonsense. Living at the ranch, seeing the interplay between the other two couples, had brought it on.

Someday she'd meet the man meant for her. He'd be a solid person, dependable and trustworthy, not someone like Paul.

Handsome men were spoiled. They demanded too much and got their way by using their looks and charm. They thought they had a right to any woman they desired, and that no woman would refuse them.

The college heartthrob had thought she'd been joking when she'd refused to give in to his demands. Then he'd gotten angry and accused her of wasting his time. A faint tremor of remembered fright ran through her. A lucky, unplanned blow to his nose had stopped the struggle between them.

Paul wasn't like that, but he was more dangerous to her heart. With him, she wanted to experience all of life.

As they rode out on the long, narrow ridge that formed the spine of the mountain, she let the horse pick its way over the rocks, lost in her fantasy. After going down into a dip between two ridges, called a saddle by her guide, Paul pulled up.

"This is where I want to check the water for Keegan. We're on the Triple R now, which belongs to Beth and Keegan. The Sky Eagle Ranch belongs equally to both families. The national forest land begins over there, at that highest peak." He pointed out the boundary.

"Where did we leave Sky Eagle land?" she asked, fixing landmarks in her mind.

"At the beginning of the ledge."

They dismounted, tied the horses to low branches of a tree in a patch of grama grass and explored the area. A tiny creek, which ran part of the year, seeped from a rock face and descended in a rocky channel, winding its way to a shallow basin where it pooled, stagnant and murky, useful mainly to mosquitoes.

Dinah had to admire Paul's expertise in his field. He knew right away that the creek could easily be rerouted to the west, thus providing additional water to a pond on the high pasture.

They examined the creek and terrain around it carefully, then traced the new path Paul wanted it to follow. They found another channel filled with spring runoff a short distance around the hill on the western slope.

"Perfect," Paul announced. "Less than a hundred feet of digging will direct the runoff over here from the basin. That'll flush the pool and keep the water flowing."

A further check convinced them that this was the best course. Going back to the top of the ridge, Paul indicated it was time for lunch. He pointed out a boulder with a larger one behind it for a backrest. She sat down, surprised at the advanced hour.

The parka was too hot. She pulled it off and folded it into a pad for a seat.

"Boulder hard?" Paul inquired. He laid out their lunch.

"Very. Also the saddle." She rested her head on the rock.

He chuckled. "It takes a while to get used to roughing it again. We'll be using horses a lot in this country."

"Somehow I suspected that."

The easy camaraderie lasted throughout the meal. It wasn't until Paul found a comfortable niche near her among the boulders and stretched his long legs out in front of him that she realized how isolated they were. She couldn't even see the ranch buildings from here.

But this was nice. Paul was a safe companion. He'd promised.

She closed her eyes.

"Dinah."

She blinked awake.

Paul leaned over her, his eyes concerned. A warm place grew in her. "Are you all right?" he asked.

She sat up abruptly, remembering where they were. For a moment, she'd been trapped in a dream in which they were two exiles, driven from their homes and looking for a place of their own. She cleared her throat. "Yes, of course."

"You were sleeping so soundly."

"I . . . I didn't sleep very well last night."

He nodded. "I heard you. You were restless. You read for a long time after you went to bed."

She stared at him. "How did you know that? Were you spying on me?" she demanded.

He stood and stepped away from her, the clean lines of his face becoming hard and cold. "Hardly. I was observing the stars after everyone had gone to bed. I saw your light come on, stay on for about an hour, then go off again. I assumed you were too restless to sleep and were reading the reports you seem to carry around with you all the time."

Embarrassed by her melodramatic accusation, she rose and brushed the back of her jeans off. "Sorry, I didn't mean to sound like a..." A what? Harridan? Prude? "Like an old maid wishing that someone would be interested enough to spy on her."

He looked surprised at her self-mocking appraisal. She laughed. After a minute, he joined in. "You are totally unpredictable," he murmured, shaking his head.

She thought the conversation needed a change of topic. "Is it time to go?"

"Yes. We have a short but rugged ride over to the yew trees." He picked up his coat and headed out.

The ride was brief as promised, but it wound around a boulder field, down into a steep ravine and angled up the other side on a trail that was actually a twelve-inch ledge.

Dinah carefully refrained from looking down into the gorge and thinking about a misplaced hoof. Instead, she gazed at Paul's back and thought about her dream.

She wondered if dreaming of them exploring a new world together reflected her insane desire to ask him to be her guide in exploring the sensual part of life. The world of the senses would be no novelty to him, but it would be for her.

Heat flamed in her even thinking about broaching the subject to him. He'd probably laugh at her. That was a daunting thought. She couldn't bear to come across as the shy, uncertain virgin in the eyes of someone as cosmopolitan as he was.

Sighing, she turned the ridiculous musing off and concentrated on staying perfectly still in the saddle while the gelding picked its way up the bluff. She was relieved when they reached the top.

The yew trees were a quarter mile from there. Paul left the horses ground-hitched by tossing the reins over their heads and letting them trail along the ground. The geldings immediately began cropping the short sprigs of grass.

"This way," he said.

She followed him through the woods. Under the canopy of the other trees, they found the low-growing yews.

"Oh, dear," she said.

Paul was more articulate. He cursed eloquently as he examined the site.

Thieves had stripped the trees of their bark by girdling the lower trunk close to the ground, then ripping strips off in an upward direction as far as the culprits could reach. The trees would die from the maltreatment. While she studied the damage to the yews, Paul examined the ground.

"Two men," he said. "Three horses. Probably one was a packhorse for the bark. They were in a hurry and not too careful. They left some big pieces of bark. Let's see which direction they went." He headed off through the woods.

Dinah stayed on his heels. Watching him find the trail was a lesson in the art of tracking. He was an expert at it.

Thirty minutes later, they came to an old logging road. She could see the imprint of truck tires in the damp earth.

"Just missed them," Paul announced. He glanced at her with a frown. "They were in there this morning. The rain would have washed out the tracks if they'd come earlier."

"Maybe they were the ones your cousins warned us about, the ones who were here before. What will they do with the bark?"

"Try to sell it to a contractor who supplies the research department of a drug company." He shook his head. "The fools. As if a reputable supplier would deal with scum off the street. Unless they have contacts with renegade companies who are interested, their trip was for nothing."

"And they'll have wasted the trees," she said.

He nodded in disgust. "Well, we may as well start back."

As they turned to retrace their steps, an eerie scream vibrated through the forest. Dinah froze. Even her heart seemed to stop as the sound resonated off the rocky bluffs and echoed through the trees. The hair rose on the back of her neck.

Before the sound died away, another shriek followed it, this one behind them...and closer. She gasped in fright and spun around to see what new danger stalked them.

Paul laid an arm across her shoulders. "Easy," he whispered next to her ear. "Just a couple of cougars."

"Only two?" she asked, not bothering to hide the irony as the piercing cry lowered into a menacing snarl. She wished they were on the horses and riding out of there. Paul hadn't even brought the rifle attached to his saddle.

The snarl was answered by an enraged scream from the other mountain cat. Dinah's mouth went dry at the fury in it. Two males, she thought, having a territorial dispute.

She dimly remembered that the big cats couldn't meow, but they could purr...or screech to high heaven like something dying. Great thought. She hoped she and Paul didn't end up as minced meat in the middle of the quarrel.

"Will they fight?" she asked. A tremor rushed through her as the snarly cat responded to the continuing challenge of the other.

Paul pulled her closer. His big hands stroked up and down her back. "Don't be frightened," he murmured, his lips against her hair. "All that screaming isn't fighting."

Dinah looked up at him, shocked. He seemed rather amused by the whole thing. Didn't he have any sense of survival?

"A male and female," he explained.

The outraged cries from the cats rose to a crescendo. The memory of warding off an enraged male returned to her, and she clung to Paul instinctively. Strange, in his arms she'd always felt secure. Only her own feelings had alarmed her.

"Will he . . . will he kill her?" she asked anxiously.

Paul stared at her, a puzzled smile on his face. He touched the tear that clung to her lower lashes, then rubbed the moisture between his fingers. "No," he said, quite gently, as if he were dealing with a child. "He's courting her."

It took a second for the information to sink in. When it did, Dinah felt her face suffuse with heat as blood rushed to her head.

Courting!

She must have sounded like an idiot, worrying over the fate of the female. A last scream echoed through the forest, then all was silent. No birdcalls. No whisper of a breeze. Nothing.

The hair rose on her neck again. The silence was as eerie as the death-defying shrieks had been.

"We'd better get a move on," Paul said. He released her and led the way through the deep woods to the bluff and the trail where they'd left their mounts.

Dinah paced along behind him, keeping a sharp lookout over her shoulder for attacks from behind. Then she remembered that cats liked to leap on their victims from high places. She added the overhead branches to her list of possible dangers. After stumbling and nearly falling twice, she gave up and concentrated on keeping up with her escort.

Right before they reached the opening in the trees, the high-pitched snarls started up again. It sounded as if both cats were directly in front of them.

Paul muttered one distinct expletive. Looking around, he grabbed a big stick and ran forward. Dinah desperately looked for one, too. Spotting a thick branch beside the trail in a clump of poison oak, she ignored the poison shrub and grabbed the stick. Any weapon was better than none.

She almost ran into Paul when he stopped behind a big tree. She peered out around him. A cougar stood on the path ahead, right at the edge of the bluff. From the size of its head, Dinah assumed it was the male.

Before they could decide what to do, the tawny cat sprang forward. The next sound she heard was the screams of their horses.

Paul cursed again. "Stay here."

He dashed out onto the ledge. She followed, unwilling to let him face the danger alone.

The cat paused, ready to spring from a boulder, looked over his shoulder at them, then bounded into the woods.

Their horses galloped wildly down the ridge trail, across the ravine and disappeared up the trail on the other side. For a minute, all she could hear was the sound of their fading hoof beats. Then all was quiet.

She glanced around, her heart pounding loudly in her ears. They were alone, without food or weapons or horses...only them. And two courting cougars roaming wild in the woods.

Chapter Six

"What do we do now?" Dinah asked. She was proud of the calm she displayed.

"Walk," he replied. "How do you feel about hiking?"

"What's the alternative?"

"Spending the night in the woods. Someone will look for us come morning."

Spend the night there with those beasts running around loose? No way. "We'd better get started," she said and headed for the ledge down into the ravine. She'd feel better having the gorge between her and the cats.

At the bottom, she threw her stick aside and bent beside the stream of water. "I may have got into some poison oak."

"Use sand to scrub your hands good. That'll take the oils off as well as soap would." Paul tossed his stick and stooped beside her.

They washed up like a couple of surgeons preparing for an operation. When their skin was pink and glowing, they shook off the water and started on their way. Dinah looked at her watch.

"Four hours, minimum," he said, apology in his tone.

When she glanced at him, he gave her a wry grin. She grinned back. "You know, as a child, I loved adventure stories. Looks like I'm finally going to get to live one." She pointed down the trail. "Lead on, MacDuff."

A funny expression crossed his face. "You're a good sport, Dinah," he said quietly, surprising her.

It made her feel warm all over.

Time ceased to have meaning. To Dinah, it seemed as if they had walked for days, with no end in sight. Twilight had come upon them. At the split in the trail where they'd turned west to check out the creek, Paul stopped.

"I saw a snow cabin through the trees when we were over that way," he said, more to himself than to her. He scanned the sky, his alert gaze taking in the approaching dark and the rapid drop in the temperature. He turned and studied her. "Let's head for the cabin."

She looked at the path they'd followed earlier. It was mostly downhill and would take them to the ranch. "I'd rather try for the ranch. When we get out of the woods, we'll be in the meadow—"

"We won't make the meadow before nightfall. There won't be a moon. It rises late tonight." He shook his head. "It's too dangerous to traipse along the ledge in the dark. We'll stay the night in the cabin."

He looked around, found three rocks and stacked them to make a duck pointing in the direction they'd take. Just to be sure no one missed the clue, he drew an arrow in the dirt with a stick.

"Come on." He headed off at a brisk pace.

Dinah huffed in irritation and with the effort to keep up. Paul was in a big hurry. Maybe he was worried about those cats and didn't want to tell her. Fear surged through her body.

They crossed the saddle and headed down a steep slope. He slowed a bit and waited for her as they descended a rocky incline. In the trees, she spied the cabin.

As they came to it, she noticed it was sturdily built of pine logs and even had windows. Through the gloom, she could see the insignia of the forest service cut into the door. There was also a big padlock on it.

Paul ignored the door and went to one of the windows. He studied it for a minute, then removed a knife from his pocket. Slipping the blade into the crack between the window and the frame, he carefully pried the lock open. He pushed on the window, and it moved easily, opening by sliding to the side. He grinned at her.

"Welcome," he said and indicated she should go first.

Feeling like a thief, she scrambled over the sill and into the dim interior. Paul did the same, then closed the window against the night chill. Dinah looked around.

An old-fashioned iron cooking stove held pride of place at one end of the room. Apparently it was used for heating the cabin, too. Six bunks, stacked three on three, lined one wall. A metal sink with a hand pump was opposite the bunks. Two barrels were stored on each side of the door.

Paul removed the lid from a barrel. "Blankets," he said. He pulled four out and tossed them to the bunks, which had solid wood bottoms and no mattresses. He checked the other barrel. More of the same. "No food. I guess that was hoping for too much."

"There's a pantry," she said.

She pulled out the metal rod that served to prevent animals from getting through the doors and peered at the shelves. Pots and pans. A metal canister set. Paul came over.

"Hey," he said when she opened the first canister. "Coffee."

They also found rice, salt and crackers, several cans of soup and a package of lemon drops. "Lemon drops?" he questioned.

"For fire fighters," she said. "It keeps the mouth moist."

Paul frowned. "Sounds like you've used them."

"Uh-huh. Would you like vegetable beef or chicken noodle soup for supper?"

"Vegetable beef. When were you in a fire?" He didn't like the idea of her being in danger. It seemed reckless on the part of the forest service to chance wasting a brilliant mind like hers in a fire.

"We've had lots of them in California the past couple of years. The drought, you know. I suspect this cabin was used recently for the same reason."

"Yeah, there were several fires in the area last year."

She selected two cans and a pan for heating them. "We need water and a fire for the soup."

He put aside thoughts of danger and turned to the job at hand. "I'll get some water from the creek."

"We have a pump," she pointed out.

"It'll need priming."

"Let's try it." She pumped vigorously for several minutes. Nothing happened.

"Like I said, I'll get water from the creek," he remarked. He grabbed a kettle and climbed out of the window.

While he hiked back up the steep slope and down the saddle to the creek, he considered his reactions to spending the night with Dinah in the deserted cabin. It couldn't be helped, of course, but it was damned uncomfortable.

The problem was his libido. His body seemed to think this was a romantic interlude. It wasn't. But he had to admit he wanted her with a deep, raging hunger that wouldn't let up.

He stooped and lowered the kettle into the cold water. As soon as it was full, he headed back. It was almost too dark to see the trail. A light suddenly gleamed in the window of the cabin to guide him to safety.

"Look, I found a lamp," Dinah exclaimed when he set the bucket through the window and into the sink. She turned down the wick.

The softly flickering light played over her face as she beamed at him across the room. The tension in his body increased.

"I'll find some firewood," he said and stalked off.

He hoped she hadn't noticed the strain in his voice. This was going to be a long night. An understatement. It was going to be a hell of a long night. He didn't think she even realized the problem.

His problem, not hers.

She was busily playing the role of a good sport with not a word of reprimand about his not having tied up the horses. Well, who would have thought a damned cougar would consider them as dinner on the hoof? Usually cats were intimidated by much bigger animals.

The scent of humans should have driven the big male off, too. The fact that it hadn't had prompted him to get Dinah out of the woods. It had also influenced his decision to risk a night at the cabin with her rather than heading for the ranch.

He realized again it was going to be a long night.

He grimaced and started picking up pinecones and as many branches as he could carry. He piled the wood beside the cabin. When he had enough for the night and morning, he handed it through the window to Dinah, who stacked it neatly in a corner.

When they were finished, he climbed inside and closed the window securely against the encroaching darkness. He tried not to notice the blankets on the bunks, already arranged into two neat beds for them. My, but she had been busy.

"I poured some of the water down the pump and got it going. The well water seems okay, not rusty or smelly," she said. "We also have matches, but I can't find a can opener."

"I have one on my knife." He got the fire going in the stove, then opened the cans.

Dinah dumped the soup into two pans and set them on the stove. She looked around. There was nothing to do but wait. She risked a glance at Paul. He was silent, lost in his own thoughts, which weren't pleasant, she decided. He looked grim.

While the meal warmed, she looked around again to make sure she hadn't missed anything. "There doesn't seem to be any dishes or cutlery. We'll have to drink directly from the pans."

He stirred from his introspection at her words. His gaze roamed down her body to her boots and back to her face. She thought he sighed before turning away.

"I'll see what I can do." He chose some dry pieces of wood and began carving them.

To her surprise, he made each of them a crude but serviceable spoon.

"It's ready," she announced after stirring the pans. She handed one pan to him and took the other for herself. After setting the tin of crackers out, she sat on the bunk nearest the stove while Paul sat on the floor.

She realized she was very hungry and tired. It had been a long day. And might prove an even longer night, she thought ruefully. How did she get herself into these situations?

"Finished?" he asked.

"Yes."

"I'll wash up."

He pumped water into the pans and washed them as best he could without benefit of soap. He left them in the sink to drain. Next, he added several large branches to the stove until the fire was burning in a lively manner. The room began to warm. He resumed his seat on the floor.

"The cabin is well chinked," she noted. She slid to the floor and propped her back against the leg of the bunk bed.

An uncomfortable silence spread between them. When she shifted and stretched her legs straight out in front of her, one crossed over the other, he gave her a sharp glance; then she saw his gaze go to the bed behind her. He went back to contemplating the stove.

A tremor danced through her. He was thinking of the night, of them, of being alone in the cabin with her. She had to open her mouth to take a breath. Slowly, slowly, she forced the air in and out of her lungs while her blood rioted in her veins.

All the old tumult caused by him rampaged through her. She hadn't let herself think on the hours ahead. Not that anything would happen. But it would be a very long night....

Dinah jumped when Paul suddenly moved. He got a log and, opening the front of the stove, poked the wood inside. He glanced at her when she stirred restlessly.

"Relax, Dinah," he ordered softly.

"I am," she asserted. She sounded breathless.

Outlined against the flickering fire, he looked like an ancient god who had left his throne and come to earth for some strange reason to mingle with the mortals.

Remembering the stories from Greek mythology, she recalled the reason Zeus had taken on other forms—a bull and a swan, for instance. He'd wanted to lull maidens into a false sense of security, gain their trust, then seduce them. He'd succeeded, of course. Foolish maidens.

Paul had said he would wait until asked. Was that a ploy to regain her trust . . . a part of his seduction technique?

Her heart chugged like a steam locomotive going uphill. The fact was, foolish or not, she did believe him.

She watched him while he added a hefty log to the fire. There was so much about him that beguiled the senses. She hated to think she was so shallow that looks alone would appeal to her.

In college, that might have been true, she reflected. Her pride had been involved. Carl had set all the female hearts a-flutter with his blond handsomeness, his clever repartee.

Paul wasn't like that. He liked to tease her—he could be the very devil with his laughter and quips—but he'd won her trust with other qualities . . . his gentleness, the quiet way he sometimes had, the intelligence in him. Like her father.

She realized that was why she trusted him. Her father was a gentle man and a man of his word. Paul was, too.

When Paul closed the stove and resumed his seat on the floor, Dinah couldn't help but be aware of the bed at her back. She huffed out a tired sigh as wild imaginings romped through her mind.

First man. First woman.

Being alone here in the rough country of the national forest, it was as if they were the only two people on earth. It could be dangerous to the heart to think like that. Next thing she knew, she'd begin to believe her own fantasies.

She had other things to think about. The ruined yew trees. The cougars. The long hike out tomorrow.

"There," Paul said. "That should keep us warm for a while. The embers will last until morning. Ready for bed?"

She nodded, her mouth going dry, and looked away. There was fire in those blue depths, and it wasn't merely a reflection of the flames leaping in the stove. He wanted her.

Paul gave an exasperated sigh. "Dinah, it's okay to look. Hell, I've been doing more than looking since we arrived here."

Her head jerked up. What was he saying?

His slow grin curved his mouth. "I've been thinking, too."

The heat started deep inside her, at that secret place no one had ever penetrated . . . except this man. "Thinking?" Her voice sounded more like a croak. She cleared her throat.

"About us."

"There is no us," she quickly informed him.

He snorted impatiently. "Not yet," he agreed. "Maybe never. But there is something. I feel it. You feel it—"

"No."

"Yes," he said softly, insistently. "But we're also rational human beings. We don't have to act on our impulses. We can consider the consequences."

She didn't feel very rational right then. She was being consumed from within and without—the fire inside and the one in his eyes. "Of course," she agreed, managing a cool edge. "I, uh, need to go outside, then I think I'll go to bed."

Getting to her feet, she pulled on her parka, climbed out the window, carefully felt her way into the dark and returned without mishap. After climbing back through the window, she laid the coat on the bunk, then washed her face and rinsed her mouth.

"Here." Paul pushed a piece of cloth into her hand.

"Thanks."

She wiped her face, then laid the bandanna over the rim of the sink to dry. It must have been in his pocket, she thought. The material had been warm. It had carried his scent—a tangy, masculine smell of soap and after-shave lotion.

Sitting on the bunk, she pulled off her boots, made a pillow from her parka and laid down, tucking the two blankets around her neck to hold in the heat. She had a feeling it was going to be a long night. A long, cold night.

Dinah discovered just how cold in the early hours of the morning. She woke, shivering, drawn up into a little ball. The air felt as if it came directly from the Arctic, sweeping through every crack and crevice of the cabin to poke her with icy fingers. Her feet were aching with cold.

"Dinah?"

"Yes?"

"Are you cold?"

She hesitated. Would he suggest they pool their body heat by sleeping together? "Yes."

She heard him moving around in the dark, but he didn't come to her. Instead, he added some pinecones to the fire, then blew on the embers to ignite them. When the cones were blazing, he added wood until the fire was going again.

He closed the door, and they watched the flames through the isinglass panels.

"That should help." He peered at her through the flickering firelight. "I'll fold your top blanket. That will give you another layer. You might have to put on your jacket and do without a pillow. Are your feet cold?"

"Freezing."

He folded the top blanket in half and covered her, tucking it around her neck. She tensed when he sat at the end of her bunk. He searched under the covers and found her numb feet. He removed one sock and began rubbing. A chuckle escaped him.

"If the saying, cold feet, warm heart is true, your heart must be very warm," he explained.

She smiled at his humor and closed her eyes. His hands felt wonderful. "I think it's frozen, too," she complained with a droll laugh. "You'd better get back in bed before you freeze."

"I have my coat on."

"Oh."

She opened her eyes. In the glow of the fire, his eyes seemed golden, as if lit by a magical sun inside him. A shimmer of emotion, strange and compelling, went through her.

Paul must have felt the tremor. He rubbed her ankles, his long, lean fingers so very gentle on her, then he massaged the calves of her legs through her jeans. Moving back to her foot, he warmed it, then replaced the sock and started on the other one.

The old longing spread slowly over her, leaving her feeling wretched and lonely in its wake. She stared at Paul's mouth as he bent over his task. The warmth from his hands worked its way up her legs. It lodged deep within, joining the other mysterious fire that sometimes burned there.

Her mouth tingled as she remembered the kisses she'd received from him. She pressed her lips together, desperately wishing she could forget the incidents. Maybe she should give in to the desire they both felt.

If she and Paul made love, she would finally know what she'd only dimly glimpsed—the special interconnectedness of life she'd observed at the ranch.

She must have gasped because he looked up suddenly. His eyes locked with hers. She couldn't breathe....

He pulled her sock on, then covered her feet with the greatest of care, tucking the covers all around and under them.

"Better?" he asked. His voice was husky, deeper.

"Yes. Thank you." She said hoarsely.

He stood, then stayed where he was. He took a step forward. She watched him, feeling as if she were in a dream, as he sat beside her. He reached out and smoothed the hair from her forehead. She felt a tremor in his fingers that hadn't been there before.

"Your eyes are asking. Do you mean them to?"

"I . . . I don't know."

A smile flicked over his lips and was gone. "Well," he said. He heaved a deep breath. "We could try a couple of things and see what you like." He waited.

She couldn't answer. She didn't know if she wanted him to touch her or not. Danger signals buzzed inside her. But it didn't feel dangerous . . . only exciting and scary and breathtaking . . .

"Let's try this," he suggested.

She tensed as he came nearer.

"This is just a friendly kiss. No strings attached." He bent to her. His lips were dry, warm, soft on hers.

Tingles shot down her throat from her mouth and caused her heart to speed up. She closed her eyes. The kiss ended.

He smiled at her when she looked at him. "That wasn't so bad, was it?"

She shook her head.

"That was the kiss of one friend to another, or maybe a close relative. This one will be the same, except the friend might *wish* there was more between you."

He kissed her again. This time his lips were moist when they met hers, but just as soft, just as gentle. Her eyes flickered closed. The heat inside leaped like flames over a fresh log. She pushed the blankets away, freeing her arms.

Her hand brushed his jacket. The kiss deepened ever so slightly. She sensed restraint in him, as if he longed to crush her in his arms but wouldn't permit himself that luxury. She caught the edge of his jacket and clenched her hand on it as sensation piled on sensation. The tingles went all the way to the middle of her abdomen where the fire burned brightly.

She stilled when he moved his hand. He touched her shoulder, then he lifted his mouth from hers. She sighed as she experienced the loss. He'd been so gentle, so sweet.

He stared down at her for a long minute. "What did you think?" he asked.

"It was . . . nice."

"Not too demanding?"

She shook her head. A smile forced its way to the surface. He'd remembered her previous comparison. In many ways, he was a generous man, concerned with her pleasure, not his own.

He leaned near. "This one will ask a bit more of you."

Before she could speak, he slipped his arms around her and pulled her close, not crushing, but she could feel his warmth on her breasts through her thermal top and undershirt.

His lips were exquisitely gentle on hers.

She tensed when they opened on hers, enclosing her lips in his moist warmth. She felt a slight kneading movement from his mouth, but it went no further. His hands repeated the motion on her back. A lethargy crept into her muscles.

This was nice . . . very nice.

Her heart beat heavily, but the rest of her relaxed. It was like melting, yet the excitement still fluttered inside. More than fluttered, she realized. It was building into a strange tension.

She moved as a faint restlessness seized her. Lifting one arm, she laid her hand on his shoulder, sliding her fingers under the fleecy collar of his shearling jacket. Her other hand still held the lapel tightly in her fist.

When he drew back, she instinctively followed, wanting that wonderful contact to continue.

"Dinah?" he whispered.

"Mmm," she said, frowning slightly.

Paul wondered if she realized what she was asking with her little crooning demand. Hunger raged through his blood. He was in control, but it wouldn't take a lot to lose it. He wanted to let go and bury himself in her warmth, to take them both to the highest peak of pleasure. He knew with a certainty he'd never before felt that it would be there for them—hot and hungry and mind-shattering.

Her lips touched his. Flames erupted. A heaviness grew in his lower body. He had to fight his own instincts that told him she was as ready for him as he was for her.

She was lost in passion, but something held him back. With any other woman, he would have taken her right then and there. But with this one, he wanted to go slowly, to win her completely. . . .

It was a crazy thought.

He tried to concentrate on breathing, pulling the air slowly and easily into his burning lungs. It wasn't working.

Her hand slipped to the back of his head. She pulled him closer, again giving the little kitten cry of demand in the back of her throat.

"I know, darling," he whispered. "I want it, too."

He gave her his mouth and felt the pressure of her response. His mind whirled into a red haze of desire, and all thinking was lost in the wonder of her, of touching her.

He pressed her against the bed, holding her as close as possible. Before he thought about what he was doing, he laid down, partially covering her long, exciting curves with his body, on fire for her.

"Dinah," he said, a growl of need too strong to be denied.

Dinah felt the urgency in Paul, the gentle strength of his body over hers. Emotion flamed in her like the hot, curling blaze of a sunspot. It flared into the cold, empty space of her heart.

But there was also a panicky drum of danger within her. She was setting herself up for heartbreak all over again.

It didn't matter. She wanted him, wanted this wildly sweet connection with life that he could give her.

This is but a moment, not a lifetime.

She shook her head, trying to ignore the voice of self-preservation that warned her against the passion, but the warning was relentless. Finally she twisted from him, breaking the contact of their lips. He reached for her again.

"No," she whispered, struggling against her terrible need. "Don't."

He drew back, puzzled. "What is it?"

"I'm sorry. I can't," she said. She scooted away from him, her back against the wall as they stared at each other in the dim light of the fire.

His expression changed as passion was replaced by anger. Then that, too, was gone, and his expression settled into his usual cynical half smile. "Is this a game we're playing, Dinah? If it is, I'd like a list of the rules so I can play my part correctly."

She shook her head helplessly. How could she tell him that she was afraid of herself and her own emotions? That she wanted to make love with him, that she wanted to experience all the bliss of being in his arms, but was frightened of making another mistake.

If she were foolish enough to let herself fall in love with him again, she was afraid she'd never get over it. And yet, there was this driving hunger to experience all of love, all of life . . . with him . . . only him.

He moved, and she shrunk back. He gave a soft snort of disgust, walked to the stove and added more wood to the fire.

"I didn't mean to . . . to lead you on," she finally said, taking the blame for the fiasco. "I know I must seem a tease of the worst kind. . . ."

He gave her a cool, studied perusal. "Not at all. If you'll just tell me what you want, I'll try to deliver."

She stared at him stupidly. "What?"

His laughter chilled the fire in her blood. "Oh, come on, Dinah. I'm not exactly a callow youth. I've been around the block, as one might say. Are you angling for a promotion and need me to put in a good word for you again?"

She was aghast that he would put such an interpretation on her actions. He thought she was trying to butter him up again for some devious reason of her own. Tears filled her eyes and softened the image of him and the dance of the firelight across the cabin to a blurred pastel of shadows, like an old painting. Like a scene from a time that was never meant to be.

"No," she said, fighting the sadness. "I realized that the price of a night of ecstasy might be too high to pay."

"Your virginity?" he suggested, mocking her despair. "You could be right."

Paul turned from her and admitted to an acute sense of disappointment. With Dinah, he'd thought... hell, he'd thought they might be friends as well as lovers. He should have known better.

She would probably laugh if he told her that. No woman he'd met had ever wanted to know the man inside—the one with dreams of finding a woman who'd stay by him, who'd work with him, love him, have his children....

Bitterness rose in him. He shouldn't have agreed to come up and help his cousins. Being at the ranch stirred up old emotions and longings better left undisturbed.

He swore silently. What had brought on that line of morbid thinking? A few kisses and a night in an isolated cabin didn't mean a damned thing.

"Go to sleep, Dinah," he said, his voice a little rougher than he'd intended. "Believe me, you're entirely safe."

After a minute, she slipped under the blankets and curled up with her back to him. A curious pang echoed through him, coming from deep inside.

He stoked the fire again, then plopped his blankets on the floor in front of the stove. As he'd suspected—it was proving to be a long night.

Chapter Seven

Dinah woke with a start. She looked around, alarmed, then remembered where she was when she saw Paul. He was busy at the stove. She remembered the night, and her lips became soft and warm all of a sudden.

The scent of chicken noodle soup filled the cabin, triggering a memory that made her smile, although sadly.

At that moment, Paul glanced around. His eyes seemed to darken when he caught her expression, but he didn't speak.

She tried to adopt a humorous tone. "The soup reminds me of my mother," she said. "When anyone in my family got sick, no matter what the illness, my mother made chicken noodle soup. That was her cure-all for the common cold, pneumonia, a stomach virus or being down in the dumps." Or having a bruised heart.

He made a brief sound, which could have been amusement. She doubted it, though. She wished he would smile at her. Even his sardonic quips were better than this. For a second, she thought of waking every morning and having someone to talk to and laugh with. For so long, her life had been lonely.

It was strange how clear that fact was to her now. Watching the ebb and flow of life at the ranch, she realized a whole segment had been missing from hers, things like companionship and a kindred spirit to share joy and sorrow as well as various interests and activities. Those were the things necessary for a full existence.

She risked a quick glance at Paul. He looked domesticated, standing there at the old-fashioned stove, but she had no false hopes that he wanted the same things his cousins had.

While he stirred the pans on the stove, something painful inside her contracted. He seemed to have firmly put aside the fiery passion of the night before.

If only it was as easy for her. She couldn't forget it, nor the fact that he thought she was using him. She wished she'd never asked for that letter of reference from him, especially since he obviously thought so little of her character.

"Soup's on."

His call to breakfast interrupted her useless ruminations. She shook off her depression and determinedly adopted a nonchalant manner. "It's barely dawn. Why are we up before the birds?"

"To hit the trail for home."

It didn't take a rocket scientist to figure out he wanted to leave as soon as possible. She scrambled out of bed, pulled on her boots and went to stand by the stove. She looked at the stack of wood. Most of it was gone.

"Did you keep the fire going all night?" she asked. She'd faked sleep at first, then had fallen into a deep but restless slumber after that. She still felt tired.

"What was left of it, yes," he said. "Eat up. I want to get an early start."

He probably wasn't used to women who froze up on him when he kissed them. Bet that was a new experience, she silently mocked both of them. But the idea didn't amuse her. The odd hurting attacked her again.

She looked away from his much-too-handsome form and quickly ate her soup. The sooner they were out of there, the better. She was as susceptible to him as Leda had been to the swan that had won her trust before changing back into Zeus and seducing her.

"I didn't make coffee," he said while she was washing her pan at the sink.

"That's okay." She stored the pan, then folded and put her blankets in the barrel. She noted he'd already put his away.

"You're remarkably domesticated for a rogue," she blurted out without thinking. The idea intrigued and puzzled her. Paul had so many interlocking facets, some hard and cynical, some endearing and gentle. Which was the real man? Which was the facade?

He put his pan away and closed the pantry, then secured the latch with the metal rod. He thrust his hands into his back pockets and faced her. "Why is that surprising?"

"Well..." She thought about it. "I don't know. I guess I thought someone like you would expect the woman to do it."

She was taken aback when fury blazed in his eyes, then it was gone. He smiled dryly. "Never let it be said that you don't speak your mind," he said. "Sounds like you've figured me out, so why don't you tell me what 'someone like me' is like?''

"Oh, you know." She gestured vaguely, feeling as if she were suddenly treading upon thin ice, although Paul stood perfectly still and expressionless, waiting for her answer.

"No, I don't," he said, his eyes narrowed like laser beams on her. "Tell me the way you see it."

She'd started this, she'd have to stick it out and tell the truth. "I think you're a cynic, a man who questions other people's motives with undeserved skepticism but never looks at his own. But when a woman holds back, not sure of *your* motives, you accuse her of having clandestine reasons for withdrawing. At times I see a gentleness in you, at others, a determined callousness that I don't understand."

Hands closed harshly on her shoulders, putting an end to her nervous, rambling impressions of Paul's character. She stared up into blue eyes that were definitely blazing with fury.

"You don't know a damn thing about it," he snarled at her.

The hair lifted on the back of her neck. Paul, in his anger, was much scarier than the mountain cats, she discovered.

"Who are you to pass judgment on me?" he demanded, giving her a little shake. "You tried your little ploy two years ago. When I saw through it, you put on your innocent act. Hell, you knew I'd send the letter."

He paused, but she said nothing. She'd defended herself against that charge two years ago. She wouldn't do it a second time.

He spoke again, his voice was soft but no less menacing. "I learned a long time ago that men don't hold a candle to women when it comes to being callous. What do you know of my life, my hopes, my dreams? Not a damned thing!"

He let go so suddenly she stumbled backward. She caught herself with a hand on the log wall, never taking her eyes off him.

Going to the stove, he removed one of the lids and stirred the embers with one of the carved spoons. He sprinkled water on the hot ashes until it was safe to leave them.

Dinah stayed out of his way. There was a controlled rage to his movements that warned her not to rile him further.

"Let's go," he said. He waited by the sink.

She crawled out the window and stood aside. He came out behind her and slid it closed. Using his knife, he pushed the lock into place. Without another word, he started off up the steep slope on the first leg of their journey.

Dinah fell into step behind him. His forbidding anger seemed to radiate around her. She was still stunned at his reaction. He'd always been a laughing, teasing devil of a man, too handsome for his own good—or the good of any woman he set his sights on—but she'd never seen this grim stranger who wouldn't speak to her.

She seemed to have strummed some chord in him that would have been better left untouched. What had happened to make him so cynical of women? Maybe she would ask him sometime. When she felt brave enough to risk getting her head snapped off.

She sighed and shook her head. She didn't understand him at all, but she wanted to. There was more to Paul McPherson than a handsome face and a charming manner. There was a man behind the facade. She wondered if she could find him.

An hour passed. The sun came up over the eastern peaks, its rays hitting them intermittently as clouds scudded across the horizon. She unzipped her parka. Another hour passed. They were on the long ledge leading out of the hills and down to the meadow.

A scream erupted from the woods.

Every cell in her body went on instant alert. Paul stopped and listened, his eyes scanning the trees intently. A faint sound reached them, not a snarl, but lower, softer, like a groan.

"They're together now," Paul told her. "They won't be interested in us."

She realized the lower tones were more a purr than a groan. Heat singed her face when she realized the cats must be mating. She felt like an intruder in their private Eden.

"Good," she said, proud of the level tone of her voice.

He looked at her for the first time since leaving the cabin. His eyes held a moody cast. He hadn't forgiven her for her off-hand assessment of his character, she realized.

An apology pushed its way forward. She tamped it back. *Handsome is as handsome does*. She'd seen no evidence that Paul was other than what he appeared—a man who took what pleasures life offered. Heaven knew there must have been plenty of offers from the women he'd known.

She wrinkled her nose at the thought, not liking it. Well, his personal life had nothing to do with her. He obviously wasn't interested in her; she was just a passing fancy.

Regret caused the earlier depression to return. Be practical, she warned herself. She had a job to do. Maybe it wasn't meant for her to have all the other stuff of life, too.

A gust of cold air hit her. She glanced up. The sky was rapidly becoming overcast. Oh, no. Rain. Just what they needed. She trudged on behind her silent companion.

"Here they are," someone shouted.

Dinah jerked out of her introspection as a cowboy rode into view. She thought she recognized him as one of the Sky Eagle men. He was leading two saddled mounts.

"Hank," Paul said. He smiled for the first time that day. "Glad to see you."

"I'll bet. Your horses got back last night. We figured you'd hole up someplace and start out early."

"Right. We found the service cabin."

Hank was the one who'd helped birth the filly, Dinah remembered. The cowboy who wrote songs. She watched him pull his rifle out and fire it twice, the shots spaced about five seconds apart. The horses threw up their heads, but didn't panic.

"That'll let the others at the homeplace know you've been found," he explained when he saw her watching him.

Paul caught the reins of one horse and gave them to Dinah. He took the other and swung into the saddle. She did the same. She realized she was tired. They'd walked for two hours, and there was still over an hour's ride across the meadow before they reached the homeplace, as they called it.

It seemed to take longer to cross the huge pasture on the return trip. She remembered the exuberant race on the journey out. This time was very different. A quiet despondency pervaded her spirits. She felt she'd missed something important, a clue to life that had dangled before her for a brief moment. She wondered if she'd feel this way if she and Paul had made love.

Ignoring the soreness in her bones, she let her mount keep pace with the lead horse. They finally arrived at the house.

Rachel waved from the deck. "Hello," she called.

Dinah waved back, glad to see a welcoming face. Paul and Hank had hardly spoken on the ride, much less smiled. Paul had taken the lead, she'd been put in the middle and Hank had brought up the rear. She'd felt like a prisoner being taken in.

Hank took their horses to the stable. She and Paul joined Rachel at the house.

She took one look at Dinah and clucked sympathetically. "You must be exhausted. Did you have to sleep in the woods?"

"We found the service cabin," Paul explained tersely. He didn't elaborate.

"Are you hungry? I can fix breakfast, or we can have an early lunch. I made a pot of chili."

"I'd like a shower, if you don't mind." Dinah could feel fatigue creeping over her.

"Of course," Rachel said graciously. "We'll eat when you're finished."

Dinah went to her room. She was aware that Paul stayed in the kitchen. She heard him speaking to Rachel in low tones when she left, telling of the cougars.

Thirty minutes later, bathed and in fresh clothing, she returned to the lower level of the attractive house. Paul was in the family room, looking at the local newspaper.

He looked up when she passed. "Finished?"

"Yes."

He stood and stretched, his body long and lean and powerful. Electricity ran through her, hot and frightening. The longing returned. She recognized it now. Like the cougars, she yearned for a mate. It was that simple.

Right. The way quantum theory was simple.

Dinah was mostly silent during lunch. Paul expounded on their adventure to his cousins. "We might have to move those cats. They're no problem where they are, but if they range lower, some of the ranchers might take a shot at them," he finished.

Rachel touched her husband on the arm. "Do you think it's the same one?" A slight smile played at the corners of her mouth.

Kerrigan chuckled. "Could be. Cats are territorial animals. They're better than dogs at finding their way home." He gave his wife a roguish look. "Of course, one should watch out for attack from unexpected places when tracking the big cats, I've found."

"I think I sense a story here," Paul deduced, glancing from his cousin's teasing grin to Rachel's pinkening cheeks.

"Should I tell it?" Kerrigan asked his wife.

"No. I made a terrible fool of myself. But don't mind me," she said airily. "I can see you're dying to disclose all."

"Well, maybe not all," he murmured.

The couple exchanged a tender glance.

While Kerrigan recounted a story about meeting Rachel in the woods while tracking a cougar, Dinah resisted the pangs of envy that plagued her at their obvious pleasure with each other.

There was more to marriage than raging hormones. Obviously. The McPherson couples were prime examples of partners who were friends as well as lovers. Again she felt the strong flow of life around her, of connections made and bonds forged for eternity. It was there for those who weren't afraid to reach out for it.

"Well, we have to get on the road," their host announced after he concluded his story and they finished the meal. "We'll be down at the Rogue Valley Ranch for the rest of the month before moving the cows and calves back up here for the summer."

"What?" Dinah said stupidly. Her gaze flew to Rachel.

Rachel smiled reassuringly at her. "We move part of our herd back and forth each year. Beth calls them snow cows because they go south for the winter." She gathered the dishes. "You and Paul are perfectly free to make yourselves at home here. Use whatever you need. Hank is the foreman. If you want help, he'll assign as many men as we can spare."

"You're leaving, too?"

"Yes, Kelly and I go. We help put on ear tags and count the spring calves."

"Paul, I have a couple of things I'd like to go over with you before we leave," Kerrigan said. The men left the kitchen.

"Is there some problem?" Rachel asked, her eyes concerned.

"Oh, no. I was just . . . surprised."

"I guess we forgot to mention it. There have been so many other things to discuss. I'm excited about your study. Finding a universal cure for cancer would be wonderful, wouldn't it?"

"Yes." Dinah helped with the dishes and waved the family off an hour later. The clouds were heavier and darker. The afternoon storm loomed over them like a sinister promise. "Well," she said, turning to face Paul.

"Alone at last," he murmured, a taunt in the phrase.

"Why didn't you tell me they were leaving?" Although she tried to keep her tone level, the accusation broke through.

He gave her a narrow-eyed scrutiny. "Maybe I vanted you to myself," he replied, mocking her with a Dracula accent.

"Very funny." A raindrop hit her on the nose. She wiped it away and marched into the house. Ten seconds later, the bottom dropped out of the clouds. The deluge began.

Dinah went to her bedroom, read a report until the words blurred, then laid down for a nap.

She heard Paul's steps in the hall, then his bedroom door opening and closing. It hit her that they were truly alone in the house. She shivered uncontrollably and pulled the afghan tightly around her as if shutting out demons. Finally, she slept.

She was awake and reading again when she heard the telephone ring. The rain still fell steadily, blotting out the hills in the distance. She watched it for a minute. A knock sounded on her door. She opened it. Paul stood in the hall.

"Wills called. Supper is ready at the bunkhouse. I can get us a couple of plates and bring them back here, or we can go over and eat with the men, whichever you prefer."

"The bunkhouse will be fine," she quickly decided. She was used to being around men at logging operations and such. There was safety in numbers.

"Let's go if you're ready," Paul said without further ado.

It seemed he had decided to be brisk and businesslike now. Fine with her. It was the practical way. It had been the same two years ago when she'd turned on him, hurt and angered that he could think her motives so selfish. He'd withdrawn to a faraway place. As if she'd hurt him...

Maybe she had been callous in her flippant judgment of his character at the cabin, but she'd never meant to cause him pain. She hadn't known she could, to tell the truth. She'd thought only of her own.

Pulling on her parka and putting up the hood, she followed him through the rain from the main house over to the bunkhouse. They shook off the excess water on the broad deck and went inside.

The old man, Wills, was at the stove while several cowboys—six, she counted—watched the news on TV in the lounge area. A seventh one set the long table. When he saw them, he added a couple more plates. The men stood when they spotted her.

"Hi," she said, more at ease than she'd been in two days. "Thanks for letting us join you. I wasn't sure about Paul's cooking skills."

"Hey, I'm great with bacon and eggs and peanut-butter sandwiches," Paul said, rallying to her attempt at lightness.

"Yeah, but who wants to have them for breakfast, dinner and supper?" one of the men quipped.

That broke the ice. The television was turned down, and they all trooped to the table.

"What's the general schedule for the ranch this month?" Paul asked the other men.

Wills spoke up. "You'll have to ask the foreman. He'll be along in a minute."

Hank came from the back of the bunkhouse. He had on new jeans and his good boots. The fresh scent of aftershave overlaid the aroma of roast and potatoes.

"O-o-o-oh," the cowboys chorused when he appeared.

"Don't he look nice?" Wills commented. "Going to town for supper again, Hank?"

The foreman's ears turned a furious red. "Uh, yeah."

"Looks like we might need to get started on another cabin," Wills said with a knowing look.

"Yeah," one of the men agreed. "One with room for Sita's two kids plus...how many you think you'll have, Hank...two or three?"

Hank ignored them, spoke to Paul and Dinah, then grabbed his hat and dashed out to his truck.

Dinah laughed along with the men. She felt at home with this type of rough humor. Glancing at Paul, she saw he wasn't amused. In fact, he was frowning.

A silence fell, with only the drumming of the rain on the tin roof to dispel the quiet. She was used to that, too. Hungry men didn't jaw a lot.

After the meal, two men cleaned up while Wills and Paul discussed the work schedule. A card game started over in one corner. Dinah listened to Paul's plans.

"I need to talk to Hank tomorrow about two men to help me reroute the runoff up at the saddle into the pond on the Triple R. That'll take most of a week, maybe longer if the rain doesn't let up soon."

Wills shifted in the chair. "It's set in for a spell," he advised. "Feel it in my bones."

Paul nodded.

Dinah saw he took Wills's forecast just as seriously as the old rodeo clown did himself. A warm feeling spread through her. Paul could be so kind. It was part of his technique, she knew, but it was still very appealing.

She became lost in her *first man-first woman* fantasy, in which she and her husband started their ranch from scratch and built their house with their own two hands, making a life together.

She thought of the cougar—the big, golden male, fierce and restless. He would leave the female to raise her young alone.

The sadness of it hit her. Dinah wanted a steady sort of man, one who would stay with her and raise their family and grow old with her. She didn't think a creature as beautiful as the cougar was meant to be tied down. He had to be free to roam.

Wills got up and ambled off toward the back of the bunkhouse. Paul stirred, resting his arms on the table and locking his fingers together under his chin. He was seated across from her. He stared at her, his thoughts obviously far away.

Despair settled over her. She felt very dissatisfied with her life. There was a natural sort of beauty in the male-female relationship. She wanted to share the discovery of that beauty with someone. Her gaze flicked to Paul, then away.

She knew better than to think of him as a mate—that was a lifetime relationship as far as she was concerned—but as a lover he would be knowledgeable, confident and considerate. That, too, was part of his charm. He could read a woman's response the way Wills could read the weather.

That ability came with experience. She needed to know about herself and passion before she could get on with life. Paul could teach her. She caught her breath, then let it out very slowly. Yes. Yes. She wanted him to be the one to show her....

"Ready?" Paul broke into her deep introspection.

She looked up, startled, then felt a blush heat her face. He observed her without a word.

Flustered, she rose. He held her parka for her. She slipped her arms inside and followed him out.

"Could we go see the new foals?" she requested. Anything to keep them out of that silent, vacant house.

He veered from a course to the house and headed for the stable. They went inside the warm, dark building. He flipped on the lights and dimmed them to a soft glow while she went to the stall and hooked her arms over the top railing.

The filly was nursing while her brother playfully nipped her ear. Dinah laughed softly, her emotions soothed by the quiet intimacy of the stable. The colt came over and stuck his head between the bars. He caught her parka and sucked at it. She pulled the red nylon away.

She tensed when Paul came over and laid one hand on the railing, his tall, powerful body close to hers. Her heart pounded as an urge to lean against him rose in her. If she did, would he wrap her in his arms and smile and tease her once again?

She missed that part of him, she realized. Her careless words at the cabin had caused a breach she didn't know how to mend. It was up to her to apologize this time.

"I'm sorry for what I said," she said before she lost courage. "At the cabin. I didn't mean to hurt you."

"You didn't."

He gave her a long assessing study. She stood still and let him see the regret in her eyes. What were his hopes and dreams? she wondered. Would he have shared them if they'd made love?

His eyes narrowed as if he'd divined the thought. He laid a hand on her throat. "Your pulse is suddenly pounding very fast," he commented. "Why is that?"

The question was the perfect opening. They were alone in a quiet, dark place. She could tell him of her longing.

"It's nothing," she said. "Just some silly thoughts."

"Such as?" He dropped his hand and rubbed the colt's ears.

"I'd like to have a ranch," she said, thinking of her earlier fantasy. "It's the American dream, isn't it? To have your own spread and feel you're the ruler of all you survey."

"I suppose."

"Your farm in Tennessee, is it large?"

"Nothing like this, but it's about six hundred acres near my parents' farm. They look after the place for me."

"I see. Does it have a house?"

"No. I had the original farmhouse torn down. It was in a bad state and poorly made in the first place. Someday I'll build a new one out of red-clay brick, the color of the soil along the banks of the river."

"There's a river?"

"Along one border of the property."

Visions of green fields and giant Belgian horses with their huge hooves and dainty steps came to her. She saw a sturdy but graceful house built from the elements of the earth itself. So, that was one of his dreams.

He'd probably get around to choosing a wife for that house someday, some sophisticated debutante who'd be at home in a brick mansion by a river. Only someone very beautiful would do.

When the filly finished her dinner and came over, Dinah petted it absently. A darkness fell over her spirits. She thought of the facets of Paul she'd discovered the past few days at the ranch.

He was good with children. There was respect and affection between him and his cousins and their wives. He was kind to others. And gentle. A man like him deserved a special woman. . . .

"Ready to go in?" he asked. "The storm seems to be settling in for the night."

Listening, she realized it had started raining furiously again. The weather matched her mood—unpredictable and dismal.

The storm continued unabated throughout the night. Not a ray of sun broke through the clouds the next day. Paul and his cousin Keegan consulted on the new waterway, using the aerial maps of the two ranches to plan the project.

Dinah read one book, then another, a repeat of the previous night when she and Paul had listened to the news on TV, then read the rest of the evening. At ten, she'd scuttled off to bed, still fighting the wild impulse to ask Paul to show her the wonder of making love.

In the cloudy light of day, she decided he'd probably laugh himself silly if she tried. But it was tempting.

That afternoon, she got a call from her supervisor. "What are you doing?" he asked.

"Reading," she said, disgruntled.

He chuckled. "You want a job?"

She perked up. That might get her out of the house. "Yes."

"One of the rangers reported pine borers up near Crater Lake. We could use your advice on how to stop them."

"Right." She felt better with an official duty to perform.

"I'll swing by and pick you up. Bring some clothes and plan to stay a few days while we check out the extent of the problem. We don't want another infestation that could kill thousands of trees like the one they had in Montana a few years ago."

"We might have to cut and burn," she warned.

"I know. I'll see you in about an hour."

They said goodbye. She looked up to find Paul and Keegan watching her. "I'll be leaving for a few days," she said.

Something flickered in Paul's eyes, then was gone.

"You're needed somewhere else?" his cousin asked.

"Yes." She explained the problem. "This rain will help. Sometimes the trees can drown the little devils. Well, I'd better get ready."

She escaped to the bedroom and packed several changes of clothes. She put in one good outfit. There was a nice lodge up at Crater Lake. Perhaps she'd eat there one night. She stayed in the bedroom until it was time for her ride to show up.

Paul was alone in the family room when she returned with her duffel and parka. He stood at a window with his hands in his back pockets and watched the rain sheet off the edge of the porch roof. He seemed moody. Maybe he was sorry to see her go.

"Uh, I'll call you as soon as I know when I'll be returning," she said, awkward with him and her wayward thoughts. "This will take a couple of weeks, maybe longer."

He turned toward her. His eyes ran over her... slowly... taking in every part of her jeans and sweater. There was no smile on his face, no sign of what he was thinking. Until he met her gaze.

Then she knew what had made him so quiet and tense all afternoon. He'd been thinking of her... of them... alone in the house, just as she had. It unnerved her to know they were on the same wavelength, so to speak.

"Keegan and I will be working on the creek while you're gone," he said, propping one hip on the window ledge. "As soon as you get back, you and I will map out all the yew trees in the area and plan your study, then we'll do the same for the wildlife project."

She nodded. Heat slowly spread through her while he talked. He had the most expressive mouth—mobile yet firm. She tried to look away, but couldn't.

He cursed softly, then stood and came to her. "Dammit," he muttered. "If you're not asking, say no...*now!*"

She didn't say a word. He reached for her.

She met him halfway, her lips already eager for the feel of his. He touched her carefully, controlling the kiss even as she broke into a wild response. She didn't understand her reaction, it frightened her, yet she couldn't resist.

His mouth stayed gentle on hers, touching her ten, twenty, a hundred times, making her ache with hunger.

If this was merely technique, she thought dizzily, it worked like a spell. By holding back, he made her want more.

When he moved closer, she didn't protest. His hands slipped from her shoulders to her back. He caressed up and down, leaving warmth wherever he touched.

An odd excitement rushed along her nerves. She trembled. He eased his touch until it was only a whisper, flowing over her like a gentle fire. It make her feel secure.

Raising her arms, she encircled his shoulders and let herself lean into him. A gasp was torn from her as her breasts touched him and absorbed his warmth. The kiss deepened subtly, in ways she couldn't describe. She only knew it was more intimate.

His lips opened over hers. She felt his tongue stroke her lips. He wanted in, was asking her permission. Her lips shook when she ceased holding them firmly together. She felt his tongue part them and move slowly, stroking her.

A roar filled her head. She was dazed by the magic he created. Tingles pulsed from her lips to all parts of her body. It was wild and exhilarating. Hesitantly, she touched his tongue and led him inside her mouth. Against her breasts, his chest rose in a sharply indrawn breath.

Suddenly his hand wasn't on her back. It was caressing her side, then moving upward, leaving fire wherever he touched.

Warnings echoed through her. She frowned, not wanting to heed them. Slowly, slowly, he moved, then his hand stopped just below her breast. She waited, suspended by elemental forces she couldn't deny. She wanted him to touch her there, she realized, somewhat shocked by the desire.

Then he did.

She gasped and jerked slightly.

He stared into her eyes, waiting, just waiting...

She remained motionless. Her heart beat so heavily, it seemed to fill her entire chest with its vibrant crashes.

Paul continued to cup her breast in his hand. He lowered his head slowly. While she watched, he closed his incredibly blue eyes and kissed her again. She let her lashes drift down, too. Passion was too powerful to watch. With a quiver of alarm, she let herself sink into it a bit more.

The blare of a horn jarred every nerve in her body.

They jerked apart, their breathing loud in the silent room.

"There's your ride," Paul said in a hoarse voice. His eyes were fathoms deep. She felt she could drown in them.

The horn sounded again. She frowned. The end of their kiss was anticlimactic. There was more territory to be explored.

He gave her an intense, probing stare, then picked up her luggage. "I'll help you with your stuff."

She left, her heart pounding wildly, not sure if she was running or not. One thing—passion was going to take some getting used to. She realized she'd made a decision regarding them.

Chapter Eight

Dinah paused in the lobby of the lodge. Standing by the plate-glass window, she watched a family of tourists go into the snow shelter. Another group of young men braved the snowbank and climbed on top of it to admire the view.

The snow wasn't as high as it had been when she'd first seen it. Tomorrow would make five weeks since she'd been sightseeing and picnicking on this very spot with Paul. Today was Saturday, the eleventh of May. Daffodils bloomed in a pot on the windowsill.

Turning toward the dining room, she admitted she wasn't sorry at the passing of time. It had rained or snowed or hailed on her nearly every day of the past month. She could live without it.

"Hey, Dinah, come join us."

She looked to her right. Two of the park rangers were seated at a table having coffee. She joined them reluctantly.

NO COST! NO OBLIGATION TO BUY! NO PURCHASE NECESSARY!

PLAY "LUCKY 7" AND GET AS MANY AS FIVE FREE GIFTS . . .

HOW TO PLAY:

1. With a coin, carefully scratch off the silver box at the right. This makes you eligible to receive two or more free books, and possibly another gift, depending on what is revealed beneath the scratch-off area.

2. Send back this card and you'll receive brand-new Silhouette Special Edition® novels. These books have a cover price of $3.50 each, but they are yours to keep absolutely free.

3. There's no catch. You're under no obligation to buy anything. We charge nothing—ZERO—for your first shipment. And you don't have to make any minimum number of purchases—not even one!

4. The fact is thousands of readers enjoy receiving books by mail from the Silhouette Reader Service™ months before they're available in stores. They like the convenience of home delivery and they love our discount prices!

5. We hope that after receiving your free books you'll want to remain a subscriber. But the choice is yours—to continue or cancel, anytime at all! So why not take us up on our invitation, with no risk of any kind. You'll be glad you did!

This lovely Victorian pewter-finish miniature is perfect for displaying a treasured photograph. And it's yours FREE as added thanks for giving our Reader Service a try!

PLAY "LUCKY 7"

**Just scratch off the silver box with a coin.
Then check below to see which gifts you get.**

YES! I have scratched off the silver box. Please send me all the gifts for which I qualify. I understand I am under no obligation to purchase any books, as explained on the back and on the opposite page.

235 CIS AK9Y
(U-SIL-SE-11/93)

NAME

ADDRESS _____ APT.

CITY _____ STATE _____ ZIP

 **WORTH FOUR FREE BOOKS PLUS A FREE VICTORIAN PICTURE FRAME**

WORTH THREE FREE BOOKS PLUS A FREE VICTORIAN PICTURE FRAME

 **WORTH THREE FREE BOOKS**

 **WORTH TWO FREE BOOKS**

THE SILHOUETTE READER SERVICE™: HERE'S HOW IT WORKS

Accepting free books places you under no obligation to buy anything. You may keep the books and gift and return the shipping statement marked "cancel." If you do not cancel, about a month later we will send you 6 additional novels, and bill you just $2.71 each plus 25¢ delivery and applicable sales tax, if any.* That's the complete price and—compared to cover prices of $3.50 each—quite a bargain! You may cancel at any time, but if you choose to continue, every month we'll send you 6 more books, which you may either purchase at the discount price...or return at our expense and cancel your subscription.

*Terms and prices subject to change without notice. Sales tax applicable in N.Y.

BUSINESS REPLY MAIL

FIRST CLASS MAIL   PERMIT NO. 717   BUFFALO, NY

POSTAGE WILL BE PAID BY ADDRESSEE

SILHOUETTE READER SERVICE
3010 WALDEN AVE
PO BOX 1867
BUFFALO NY 14240-9952

NO POSTAGE
NECESSARY
IF MAILED
IN THE
UNITED STATES

Actually, she was in a hurry. As soon as her ride arrived—it was five o'clock and he was already over an hour late—she would be on her way, back to the ranch and the yew trees. And Paul, some candid part of her insisted on adding.

Yes, and Paul, she admitted.

"I heard you were leaving," Rob said.

"Yes, it's back to the old-growth forest for me as soon as Chris arrives."

She and Chris, a local ranger, had been working together, assessing the pine borer infestation and deciding on a course of action. He was going to drop her by the cabin in the small town nearest the ranch for the night. She'd call someone from the ranch to come get her in the morning.

A pulse beat deep inside her. She knew Paul would come for her. She also knew they were going to become lovers. It was inevitable. When they were together, the awareness between them was impossible to ignore. He felt it as much as she did.

She realized the two rangers were looking at her. "I'm sorry. What did you say?"

"It was nice working with someone new. We'll miss you." His eyes conveyed his disappointment and frank interest.

She'd sized him up the first day on the job. He was bored in this remote location and looking for some fun. She'd kept out of his way, not giving him a chance to ask for a date so she wouldn't have to refuse. It made things easier, she'd found. Some men didn't take rejection with good grace.

"I'm anxious to get back," she said and launched into an enthusiastic description of her projects as if she hadn't another thought in her mind. During the time she waited, she managed to keep the conversation on forest service business.

When her ride came for her, she said goodbye, retrieved her duffel from her room and left with a friendly wave.

The trip from Crater Lake was uneventful and long. Night had descended when Chris dropped her at the cabin in the tiny town that served the ranches and the nearby lumberyard.

Inside, she made up the bunk bed, laid out her toothbrush, then decided to walk to the grocery and replenish her personal supplies in case it was a while before she returned to town.

As usual, it grew chilly after the sun went down. She hugged her parka around her and hurried down the side of the road. When she hit the one-block main section, the sidewalk started. She grinned and stepped up on it.

In the store, she shopped for toothpaste and shampoo, then lingered to look over the tourist items. A T-shirt with a picture of a spotted owl caught her attention. *Who-o-o are you?* was stenciled on the cotton.

Good question. She selected a pink T-shirt and added it to her basket. When she finished browsing, she paid for her items and left. For a minute, she stood on the sidewalk and looked around.

Lights were on at the little restaurant. She hadn't had supper yet. She could get some soup from the store. That reminded her of the soup she and Paul had shared at the other cabin. An odd restlessness invaded her. She didn't feel like being alone.

She'd eat in the—she peered at the name on the window—the Rogue River Diner and Saloon. The saloon part gave her pause, but she decided it would be okay. It was early yet.

The first person she saw was Hank, the foreman from the Sky Eagle spread. He stood when he saw her and smiled. When he pulled out a chair in silent invitation, she went over.

"Hello," she said, taking the seat and returning his greeting.

"You just getting into town?" he asked.

"Yes. I'm spending the night at the service cabin…." She had a thought. "Are you going back to the ranch tonight?"

"Well, uh, yes."

"I can ride with you," she decided. "That'll save Paul a trip into town and back tomorrow."

Hank looked embarrassed. "I hadn't planned on going back until late."

"Hi, you're Dinah, aren't you?" a feminine voice broke in. "I'm Sita. I met you at the birthday party."

Dinah remembered the woman. She'd asked Paul to dance. She remembered the men had teased Hank about going to town for supper. Oh, dear, she was probably horning in on his date.

"Hello. Yes, I'm Dinah." She flashed an apologetic smile at Hank. "I'm intruding—"

"No, no," Sita assured her. "I don't get off work until nine. That's another hour. Do you want to see a menu?"

"Yes, please."

After she ordered, she and Hank sat there in companionable silence, listening to the music from the jukebox in the next room.

"Did Paul know you were coming in tonight?" he asked.

"No. I didn't call him from the lodge since I wasn't sure what time I'd get back. I thought this would be simpler."

"Hmm," Hank said.

A man of few words. She mentally grinned. Through the open archway into the saloon part of the building, she could see a couple dancing on the tiny hardwood floor. By the time their meal arrived, a few other couples and several single men had gathered in the saloon. It was a popular Saturday-night spot, it seemed.

An uncomfortable sensation washed over her. She glanced up to see a man watching her from the next room. He leaned against the bar, a beer in his hand. He was tall, a big man with a belly that hung over his belt, probably good-looking at one time, but he'd gone to seed, as her mother would have said. He gave her a smile and raised the bottle in her direction like a toast before he took a drink.

Dinah focused on her plate. Each time she looked up after that, she encountered his slightly leering grin.

"Someone making you uneasy?" Hank asked.

She was surprised at his perception. "Not really. There's a man in the bar. He keeps looking this way." She shrugged, dismissing the local Lothario.

Hank twisted around. He stared hard at the man, then turned back to Dinah. "Name's Cawe," he informed her. "He's bad news."

"Somehow, I'm not surprised."

A shadow loomed over their table. She and Hank glanced up.

"This a new hand at the Sky Eagle, Hank?" the man inquired. He gave her a grin.

Hank hesitated, obviously not wanting to introduce her.

Dinah had found a direct approach worked best. She stood, but her height didn't match the newcomer's. He was taller than Paul.

"Dinah St. Cloud," she said pleasantly, but without welcome. "I'm with the forest service."

"Well, the rangers are getting prettier every day." Cawe gave her a once-over through narrowed eyes. "Maybe I ought to see if there's another opening and join up."

She felt her skin crawl at his assessing look. "Excuse me. I want to finish my meal and get back—" She stopped abruptly. She didn't want this man to know where she was staying.

"There'll be a band at nine, if you'd like to stay for the dancing," Cawe invited.

"No, thanks." She sat down, took up her fork and then stared at him in a way that had run off better men than he would ever be.

The smile disappeared from his face. He nodded and ambled back into the bar, taking a chair at a table so he could watch her. Which he did the entire time she ate.

"He's a mean one," Hank said. "Watch yourself around him."

Sita came over. "Was that Bobby Cawe over here?"

"Yeah. He has an eye for Dinah," Hank said.

"You at the forest service cabin?" Sita asked. When Dinah nodded, Sita turned to Hank. "Maybe you'd better drive her to the ranch tonight. Cawe can get mean. Besides, he has a grudge against the McPhersons . . . and anybody connected with them."

"That's true," the foreman agreed.

"I'm sure I'll be fine," Dinah said firmly. She wasn't going to ruin their date. "If you'll give me my check, I'll be going."

Hank waved her off. "I'll get it. Hold on and I'll walk you to the cabin. Sure you won't head in tonight?"

She shook her head. Since Sita was still on duty, Dinah let Hank escort her to the cabin and see that she was securely locked in. She even put one of the straight chairs under the doorknob.

At ten, she went to bed and fell asleep at once. She'd been up since dawn that morning and had hiked for hours through the woods, spot-checking the trees and daydreaming about being the first person to explore the area.

She woke with a sense of danger. She lay still and listened. A life spent attuned to nature had taught her not to disregard her instincts. They often picked up something the conscious mind could not. She scanned the windows.

A shadow there.

A man was trying to peer through the crack in the curtain into the dark interior of the cabin. A tall man. A big man. His form was dimly backlit by the streetlight on the corner where the sidewalk began. With something—a knife, she thought—her intruder started working on the window.

She eased out of bed and into the tiny kitchen alcove. She found a hefty iron skillet. Just right. Taking up a position by the window, she waited. If he got inside, he was in for a big surprise . . . and a bigger headache.

At that moment, lights came into view around a bend in the road. A vehicle, traveling at great speed, tore through town, not bothering to stop at the one Stop sign on Main Street.

The figure outside her window froze.

The truck skidded to a stop right outside the cabin. Leaving the lights on, the driver leaped out and stood surveying the front of the small building. Dinah heard her intruder curse.

The driver must have heard it, too, for he walked purposefully around the side of the cabin toward the window. The big man faded into the shadows. She heard footsteps. Running. The man from the truck ran, too.

Dinah took the skillet with her and looked out the front windows. She couldn't see or hear anyone.

After an interminable time, the driver returned. "Dinah? Open up." *Paul*.

She flipped on the light, laid her weapon on the table, then pulled on her jeans, moved the chair and opened the door. "A little late for visits, isn't it?"

He gave her an assessing once-over. "Get your things together. We're heading for the ranch."

She put her hands on her hips. "Would you mind telling me what the heck is going on?"

"Someone was trying to break in," he said. He started rolling up her sleeping bag.

"I saw him." She picked up the skillet. "I had a welcoming gift ready."

Paul raised his eyebrows at her grin. "You were going to fight him off with that?"

"There wasn't going to be a fight. I was going to clobber him as soon as he stuck his head through the window."

Paul looked heavenward, then glared at her. "Get the rest of your clothes on."

She held on to her temper with an effort while she selected underclothes and a shirt, then went into the bathroom. "How did you know to come?" she called through the closed door.

"Hank got worried and decided to call when he and Sita left the diner. He said Cawe had been making some suggestive remarks about you after you left. I decided to come in and get you."

She finished buttoning her shirt and opened the door. "Why?"

Paul closed her duffel and hefted it to his shoulder. "A gut feeling," he said. "Cawe has been a problem for the McPhersons for years." His anger returned. "Why the hell didn't you let us know when you were returning? Don't they have telephones up at the lake?" he asked sarcastically.

She sat in the chair and put her shoes on, not sure if his ire with her was due to the danger from Cawe or to the inconvenience of his having to rescue her. She stood. "Ready."

They went outside. She locked up and stored the key in its usual place. They began the long drive to the ranch.

"Are Rachel and her family back yet?" she asked.

"No," he snapped.

That effectively ended the conversation.

Dinah woke to bright sunlight. She checked the time. Almost nine. It had been a while since she'd slept this late. She lay in bed, not wanting to get up. Not wanting to face Paul.

She wasn't sure of herself around him. Last night, with the intruder at the cabin, there hadn't been time to think of her reaction to him. On the long drive to the ranch, he'd been withdrawn, with no sign of the passion they'd shared. She'd found that pretty daunting.

Doubts returned to assail her over the wisdom of getting involved with a handsome, cosmopolitan charmer like him. Perhaps she wouldn't get a chance to. From his attitude last night, she surmised he'd decided he didn't want to waste his time with someone as inexperienced as she obviously was.

Sighing, she went into the bathroom. She inhaled deeply as she stepped into the shower. Paul's scent lingered on the air. His shaving cream can and toothbrush were on the counter. Sharing a bathroom was almost as intimate as sharing a bath.

At once, visions stirred in her mind. What if he was still in bed...what if he heard the shower and joined her...what if he touched her breast the way he had just before her ride blew the horn to pick her up...and then he caressed her all over...and took her to his bed....

The warm water pelted her breasts as she rinsed herself. It reminded her of his touch. He had been so exquisitely gentle when he'd cupped her and held her in his large hand. Suddenly, she couldn't get enough air. She leaned against the wall and forced herself to breathe deeply, calmly.

Don't think about what almost happened, she admonished her imagination. But she couldn't help it.

She turned off the shower and dried her awakened body harshly, as if to punish it for her runaway thoughts. A few minutes later, she emerged from the bedroom, dressed in her usual jeans and cotton turtleneck. Her damp hair was caught in a banana clip. She wore no makeup. About as far from a *femme fatale* as a woman could get.

No one was in the house. She ate cereal for breakfast, then took her coffee cup and drifted out to the stable. Hank was there, treating a sick cow.

"Paul went to Medford to pick up the latest batch of aerial photos. He said to tell you he had business to take care of and will be back tonight sometime." Hank paused. "Uh, you're to make yourself at home. You can eat at the bunkhouse if you want, or you can find something at the main house."

"Thank you. I'll go see if Wills needs any help."

Was Paul avoiding her? She suddenly found the prospect of a silent house more than she could face. She spent the rest of the day helping Wills or tagging calves with Hank and another cowboy. It was during the evening meal at the bunkhouse that Paul returned.

Her heart started beating like mad when she heard a vehicle on the gravel driveway. She forced herself to continue eating. In a minute, Paul came in the door. He tossed his hat on a hook, washed up at the sink and pulled up a chair.

After one quick meeting of the eyes, Dinah kept her attention on her plate. She felt singed by that glance.

He looked incredibly handsome. His jeans fit without a wrinkle. The cowboy shirt matched the summer blue of his eyes perfectly. His dark hair was attractively tousled.

"Chicken and dumplings," he said on a note of satisfaction. "I didn't get a chance to eat today. I'm starved."

Paul loaded up his plate and dug in. Food wasn't the only thing he was starved for, he acknowledged. The taste and feel of the woman who sat so silently across from him had filled his dreams for weeks.

That she wasn't on fire for him was evident by the fact that she'd been gone almost a month and hadn't called once, not even to let him know she was ready to return. That ought to tell him something. He just wasn't sure what.

When she'd left, after letting him touch her breast—the start of intimacy between them—he had thought things would be different.

Hell, it didn't matter what he'd thought. Paul's past convinced him that women had their own schemes, and the poor dumb chump of a male never knew exactly where he fit in them. He'd learned that lesson well.

But there were things he wanted to share with Dinah, he admitted. All the sweet magic of making love with her swept over him. He would go slowly, showing her one pleasure at a time until they both reached the final ecstasy....

A groan forced its way to the back of his throat. He swallowed it with a gulp of hot coffee and nearly burned the hide off his tongue. He muttered a curse and grabbed his water glass.

"Ol' Wills boils that coffee twice to make sure it's hot," one of the men advised.

"It is," Paul confirmed when he could speak.

Nothing like making a fool of yourself mooning over a woman. She was smiling at his mishap, but there was sympathy in those black velvet eyes . . . and more than a bit of sensual interest. His libido perked up.

But maybe he was reading her all wrong. With another woman, he'd have known exactly what was on her mind. With Dinah, it was hard to tell. She was unpredictable.

One thing for sure—if he kept thinking of her and all the things he wanted to show her, he'd have to dump the ice water into his lap before he'd be able to stand. Hell, he'd never had this much trouble with a woman before. It was like being an adolescent all over again and trying to figure girls out, showing off for them and thinking of great deeds to perform.

He wanted to do the same with Dinah. That didn't include burning his tongue on the damned coffee, he silently mocked.

Would she be impressed if he did something wonderful?

Hardly. One sharp glance from those obsidian eyes cut a man right down to size. A niggle of admiration touched him. She wasn't a woman who'd fall for a face or a charming manner. Not Dinah. She'd require a lot from her man— gentleness, patience and a strength of character to match her own.

If a man won her love, he'd find a loyal companion— she'd grabbed a stick and marched right along with him to fight the cougar, a good sport—she'd never said a cross word about roughing it in the cabin—and a passionate woman. She'd be able to take his desire and give it back tenfold.

In her innocence, she just didn't know about that part yet. The thought nearly made him go up in smoke. He'd never fantasized so much about a woman in his life. That was one reason he'd stayed away from her last night. He'd been too tempted, too near the edge of control, after almost a month apart. That plus the fact that she hadn't contacted him had forced him to hold himself at bay. After all, she might have changed her mind.

If she'd said no last night, it would have been hard as hell to stop, especially with his adrenaline running over the worry about Cawe. He'd give her some space, wait and see how things developed between them, before he made a move. That was as fair as a man could be.

He finished his meal and settled back in the chair, aware of the restlessness in him but bound by a sense of honor to his decision. "The sun will dry the ground out today and tomorrow. Are you ready to start our study?"

Dinah nodded. She cleared her throat, aware that eight men listened with varying degrees of interest to their conversation. "The sooner, the better. Have you decided on a section?"

"Yeah. We'll look over the maps I picked up in Medford. The old-growth forest is marked on it. Logging operations and dates are inked in. What do you want to start with?"

She'd thought this out. "Cross-over in wildlife. We want to see if the spotted owl and other animals that inhabit only old-growth areas will cross logged spaces."

"Okay. We'll head out tomorrow after lunch. With a packhorse, we should be able to stay two weeks. Ready to look at the maps?" He stood and took his plate to the sink.

She did the same, then went with him to the house to pore over the maps and areas sectioned off on it. She forced her mind to stay on the business at hand. It took a lot of willpower.

They decided to start at the northern boundary of the ranch, where it met the national forest land. She knew the superintendent was holding up logging requests, pending her report on the impact of felling trees on the wildlife and natural resources.

A thrill of excitement charged through her. She loved the woods. She enjoyed studying and analyzing nature. Her gaze slid to Paul. She could see them doing this for a lifetime, sharing their mutual interests, making love...making a life together.

"I . . . what did you say?" She looked at him blankly.

"Do you know how to pitch a tent?"

A strange question. "Of course."

"Of course," he repeated with a smile. "Dinah, the girl wonder. Competent at everything."

Except making love. He didn't say the words, but she heard them in her mind. He had probably been amused at her nervous reaction when he'd touched her breast.

No, Paul wasn't that way. He might tease, but he wouldn't laugh at or humiliate another person. There was an innate kindness in him that she'd only recently realized he possessed.

"My parents sent me to camp each summer," she explained.

"Good. We'll be sleeping in tents the first few days. I thought we'd move to the service cabin later."

It came to her that if they were lovers, they could share a tent. She took a careful breath, vulnerable all at once.

He watched her as if gauging her reaction to this plan. She'd known the way things would be, but that didn't stop her lungs and heart from going erratic at the thought of being isolated with him for days on end.

"Fine," she said.

For another minute, he studied her, then he shrugged. "That's it then. I'll get our supplies together. We can check them in the morning, then leave right after lunch. That'll give us time to get in and set up camp before dark."

"All right."

"No questions?" he asked softly.

"No." She met his gaze levelly.

He nodded and left abruptly. She saw him stop and talk to Hank, then both men headed for the stable. A tremor ran over her.

Two weeks. Alone. In the woods.

Dinah pulled her hat down lower and made a face at the back of Paul's head. He rode ahead, keeping a sharp lookout for danger and hardly speaking to her at all. Except to be very polite. He'd made sure the supplies met with her approval. He'd given her a choice among several horses. A perfect host.

The previous night, after they'd studied the maps, he'd played cards at the bunkhouse until long after she went to bed. She didn't understand him. Was he waiting for her to ask him to be her lover?

If he would look at her again with those searing flames in the depths of his eyes, as if he'd consume her in a glance, he'd know how she felt. She couldn't just blurt it out, not to this cool stranger who hardly looked at her at all.

"It isn't far now," he called back to her. "There's a pretty spot with a bit of grass up ahead. I thought we'd set up camp there for a couple of days, then move to the logged area."

"That sounds fine."

The woods gave way to a lovely meadow, filled with the first spring flowers—pussytoes and wild buckwheat. A tiny creek ran beside a row of alders and willows already green with new leaves.

"An enchanted place," Dinah murmured.

Paul swung off his mount. He got to work unloading the packhorse without a word. She climbed down, unsaddled the gelding and left him cropping grass.

"There's a good tent site. Here's another," Paul announced. "Which one do you want?"

The one with you. "Uh, that one." She pointed to the spot beneath a giant hemlock that was thick with fallen needles. She went over and smoothed it, removing stones and lumps. "I'll do my tent," she said when Paul started to unfold it.

He grunted and left her to it. She smiled in relief when she saw it was a tent she was familiar with. She put it up as fast as she could, wanting to beat him. No such luck, but she did finish at the same time. A tie, she scored them.

When he gathered firewood, she did the same. They each came back with an armload at the same time. Another tie.

She decided to start the fire and prepare their supper. After making a fire ring, she placed a wadded paper towel in the center, added a pyramid of pinecones, then a tent of sticks. She lit the paper. It flamed up, then fizzled out.

Paul came over. He dumped some charcoal starter on the wood and dropped a match on it. It flamed instantly with a sizzling sound, then settled to a steady burn. He added larger logs until they had sufficient coals to cook on.

"The wood is still damp from the rain," he said. He retrieved supplies from the pack, then put water on to boil for coffee and a skillet to heat the ham-and-potato hash he removed from a can.

Dinah did a slow burn. His attitude was insufferable. He was as remote as Jackass Mountain . . . with a stubborn streak to match.

"What have I done to tweak you off?" she demanded after ten minutes of stark silence.

"Not a damned thing," he said. *Snarled* was perhaps the correct term.

"No, tell me. I can take it. If you have a bone to pick with me, let's hear it. Two weeks of the silent treatment is more than I can contemplate. Without resorting to murder," she added.

He paused in stirring the hash and returned her steady gaze. A reluctant smile picked up the corners of his mouth. "It isn't you," he said finally. "It's me."

Something must have gone wrong. "Oh?"

He gave a snort of laughter.

"Something terrible happen to you?" She was openly curious.

"Yeah. Call it poetic justice." There was a flash of emotion in his eyes. Wry humor. Resignation. Maybe even pain.

Fascinated, she probed further. "Can you talk about it?"

He dished up their supper. "No."

She was disappointed. She'd hoped a sharing of confidences would lead, in some sort of natural way she hadn't figured out, to a greater closeness. Sighing, she ate without noticing the food.

It was just as well to forget any idea of intimacy between them. Paul must have realized just how foolish it was to get mixed up with someone he worked with. She agreed. It would really be stupid to get involved with a heartbreaker like Paul.

But she couldn't stop thinking about it. Nor keep from studying him covertly. What would he say if she said...

"Oh, hell," he said. He threw down the fork on the plate and the plate to the ground. He stood and stalked off, leaving her sitting there with her mouth open.

Honestly, he really was a moody person, not at all the teasing devil she'd always thought him, ready with a smile and a wink.

He put his bedroll in his tent, hobbled the horses and yanked their supply bag into the air to dangle from a rope tossed over a tall limb. She cleaned the dishes and put them away, then brushed her teeth and washed up. Night was falling.

When she returned to the fire, Paul was there. He had added a log and brought the saddles over for backrests for them. The fire flickered over his features, turning them golden. Her heart contracted painfully. He was so beautiful.

He met her gaze. It was a moment before she realized he was watching her stare at him.

"Do you have any idea how arousing it is to watch a woman look you over?" he asked. His smile was mocking.

She felt heat rush up her neck. She shook her head.

"It is. If you keep looking at me, I'm going to take it as an invitation. Do you understand?" His tone was harsh.

She cleared her throat. "Yes," she said, her breath leaving her in a rush. "It is. It is an invitation."

His eyes narrowed to golden slits in the firelight. The woods around them seemed to quiet. The silence grew. "Why?" he asked.

She stared at him, speechless.

"Why?" he demanded.

"I want to . . . *know*."

"Know?"

"What life is all about. I want you to teach me about making love . . . and everything," she finished lamely. Her heart seemed to have moved to her throat.

"Why me?" He was relentless in his probing.

"Because you're an expert." At his darkening face, she quickly added, "I mean, with your looks, you must have . . . that is, with women throwing themselves at you and all . . ."

He watched her without speaking for a full minute. Then he cursed savagely, got up and left her sitting by the fire while night enclosed the tiny meadow.

After a minute, she drew a shaky breath, her thoughts in turmoil. She wasn't sure how, but she'd said it all wrong. Paul was furious with her.

Chapter Nine

Paul stomped through the woods at a reckless pace. The anger churned in him like water in a boiling cauldron. The leash on his control chafed, and he wanted to break free of it.

Coming to an opening in the woods at a rock outcropping over a ravine, he picked up a tree limb that was lying on the ground and hit the tree with a resounding blow. That helped . . . a little.

He cursed and dropped the stick. Sitting on a boulder, he watched the moon rise above the peak of the mountain. The air was cold now. He zipped his jacket and jammed his hands into the pockets, his thoughts on the woman he'd left at their camp.

The irony of the situation struck him, but he didn't find it amusing. Most men would jump at the chance to make love to a woman like Dinah. In fact, he'd been on fire for her for ages.

So what was the problem? the cynical half of his libido inquired. Go for it.

He couldn't. Not with Dinah.

Well, hell, at least it wasn't his pretty face that impressed her. She'd made that clear from their first meeting. Instead, she assumed he'd be a great lover due to vast experience. That was what she wanted from him—his expertise.

Usually he didn't mind when women used him for their own purposes. Like Sita at the birthday party, wanting to make a guy notice her. He could laugh about it most of the time, but not this time. Not with this woman.

He should be used to it. Women, he'd learned, always wanted something from a man. When things changed, when life got tough, when the man no longer met their expectations, they left. Yeah, he'd learned that lesson. His ex-fiancée had taught him well.

Once he'd thought Dinah was different, but her wanting him was only a variation—an interesting one, he admitted—on the same theme. She'd leave when it suited her, as she had when she'd gotten the job she wanted.

He had to give her credit, though. She was unique in some ways. Standoffish. Aloof. A challenge. Yet there was a core of fire in her. He wanted to reach inside her and claim it.

So why didn't he?

She'd given him the perfect opening. He could seduce her...at her request. No strings attached. No lies. No promises.

A shaft of desire hit him, making him gasp with the force of it. Maybe he'd take her up on the offer. Although, with her, he wasn't sure what kind of lover he'd be. He'd wanted her too long, too fiercely. He'd probably scare her to death if he revealed a tenth of his passion for her.

He realized he'd made up his mind.

A scream jarred him out of his musing. He bolted upright, then realized it was one of the mountain cats. He had better head back to camp before Dinah came dashing to his rescue.

The thought smoothed the last of his temper. For just a second, he wondered how it would feel to be married to a woman who would stand beside her man no matter what the odds. A strange sensation lodged in his chest, sort of like an ache. He wanted a life, he thought. A whole life.

Turning from the moonlight, he hurried back to camp.

The scream of a cougar froze every cell in Dinah's body for a second. Her first thought was of Paul, alone in the dark. Then reason returned. He could take care of himself.

She sat in front of the fire while the logs fell to softly glowing embers. At last, with a sigh, she covered the coals with ashes and prepared for bed.

Sitting inside the tent with her feet outside, she removed her shoes and socks. She decided a candid, humorous note was called for when she saw Paul again. If she ever did.

A rustle in the woods stilled her hands for a moment. She stared into the darkness between the trees.

"It's me," Paul called out, his tone gruff.

He walked toward his tent without looking at her. The moonlight cast silver beams over his handsome face. There was a stillness about him.

"I'm glad," she said with wry relief. "I was concerned that the thought of being attacked by a man-crazed woman might scare you off for good."

He stopped abruptly. In the dead silence, she could hear him draw a sharp breath, then let it out in an exasperated sigh. "You don't cut a man much slack."

"I didn't know you needed any," she retorted.

"With you, I don't know what I need."

His statement surprised her so much, she couldn't think of a retort. She simply observed while he added a log to the embers and sat on a blanket, resting against his saddle.

"You want a cup of hot cocoa?" he asked.

"Yes."

While he prepared the drink, she pulled on her socks and shoes, then returned to the fire. He handed her a cup. She held it between her palms, feeling the warmth seep into her.

Her wayward memory supplied images of Paul's warmth—in the stable, at the snow shelter, during the times he'd kissed her. His lips had been so warm on hers. She silently groaned as the much too familiar tingle invaded her lips. She took a sip of cocoa.

"We'd better talk," he said in a quiet tone.

She studied him with quick, covert glances. It was impossible to ferret out his mood.

The firelight enhanced his features. Shadows, mysterious and alluring, danced in his eyes. He was a temptation sent by the gods to lure her into danger. And she was tempted. Very, very tempted.

"I didn't mean to make you angry," she apologized.

His snort of laughter was brief. "It was a rather odd reaction," he admitted. "After all, it isn't every day that a woman like you offers herself to a man, his for the taking."

"A woman like me?"

"Yeah. One I've wanted for years. I've fantasized about you for so long, I'm still not sure I didn't dream what you said."

Every part of her body went haywire when she realized what he'd said. Her heart skipped, clenched, then beat like mad. She felt the same. "You didn't," she assured him.

"I admit I'm surprised." He sounded cynical.

She swallowed the cocoa nervously, unable to fathom his thoughts. She sensed an odd disappointment in him. Maybe he didn't want her . . . no, one look into his eyes told her he did.

"Remember the kiss under the mistletoe?" he asked, confusing her with the change in subject. "It nearly did me in. If I could have taken you home and made love to you at that moment, I would have. I waited for a signal from you all the next month."

His confession should have made the conversation easier. It only made her more uncertain in light of his earlier anger with her. However, she hadn't changed her mind about her earlier request. "So what's wrong with now?" she asked bravely. Her voice quavered only a little.

He flicked her an odd glance. "Your timing is off." He stood. "Finished?"

Totally perplexed, she nodded. He took her cup and washed it along with his. She rinsed her mouth, said good-night and went to her tent.

Inside, she removed her clothing and snuggled into her sleeping bag. She wondered why his initial reaction to making love to her had filled him with rage.

There was also the question of timing. If *now* was wrong, how would she know when the right moment came along?

Dinah climbed out of her tent in a grumpy mood. The sun backlit the eastern peaks with rosy dawn. The fire crackled merrily. The scent of fresh-brewed coffee wafted on the air. Paul was sitting in front of the fire with the maps spread around him.

"Good morning," she called.

His answer was a grunt of acknowledgment. She hurried through her morning ritual and joined him in front of the fire. She ate her cereal, then poured a cup of coffee. He continued his study of the maps. He apparently intended to ignore her.

She told him her plans. "I'm going to check the area and see what signs of wildlife I can spot. If I find a likely place, I'll set up a blind and use it to study the local animal population."

He looked up. His blue eyes made her weak with longing. She wrapped her arms across her chest as if the action could shut out the feeling. It was hard to face him, she found.

"What's wrong?" he demanded, seeing right through her pose of self-control.

She decided on the truth. "It's embarrassing to be rejected," she said. "Is this how a man feels when a woman turns him down?"

That got his attention. His gaze skimmed along her figure, which was mostly hidden under her bulky coat. "I haven't turned you down," he said grimly.

"I thought you had. That's the way I took it." Her mind filled with fragments of their previous conversation. "Then, what did you mean?"

"Just what I said—you're timing was off."

"When will it be on?" she demanded with a boldness that surprised her.

"I'll let you know." He folded the maps and packed them away. "I found a watering hole last night. It looks like a gathering place for animals. I'll help you with your blind, if you like."

Dinah followed him to a rocky ledge along a ravine. Over the ravine was a volcano tube that allowed an easy crossing of the creek below. There was also an open pool of flowing water where animals could drink.

She and Paul made a blind for her to hide in with tree limbs and fir branches. For the rest of the day, she observed the wildlife that came to the watering hole.

The isolation gave her a lot of time to think about her timing.

The fifteenth of May, a Wednesday, was one of those incredibly beautiful days that restored the soul. The warm breath of spring wafted across the tiny meadow. The dawn cast a rosy halo around the skyline.

"We'll move to the service cabin after lunch," Paul told her over breakfast. "If you're ready."

"Yes, I am. I want to study the patterns of the spotted owls in the area."

Paul nodded.

She took up her position at the blind once more and took note of the several deer, one bear and the rabbits who made use of the pool. A brown-spotted owl stopped briefly, then late in the morning several blackbirds came to bathe. They were a noisy bunch.

A sound like the distant bark of a rifle sent the raucous group off into the trees. The smile left Dinah's face. She listened intently for several minutes. A premonition of danger had her crawling out of the blind and heading for camp.

No one was there.

The hair lifted on the back of her neck as another shot echoed off the rocky peaks around her. Instinctively, she raced for the path through the woods that led to the forest service cabin.

Watching the path for roots and other hazards, she almost careened right into Paul's broad chest as he came down the trail toward her. He caught her with hands on her shoulders.

"Where are you off to?" he asked with his usual sardonic amusement at her expense.

She was so glad to see him, she didn't care if he was laughing at her mad dash. "I heard gunshots."

"So did I." He scrutinized her rapidly rising and falling chest. He brought his gaze back to her face. "Were you off to rescue me?"

"Of course not." She moved out of his grip, disgusted with herself. Naturally, her first thought had been concern for him, but he wasn't going to know that. "I wondered what was going on."

"Someone is taking potshots ... at an inanimate target, I hope." He motioned for her to lead the way. "Let's get packed up. I think we'll be safer away from here. There's an old logging road over the next ridge. It gives hunters easy access to the area."

He herded her along the trail like a collie with one sheep. She pondered his protective manner and what it might mean.

They broke camp in silence. Paul loaded their gear onto the horses. They mounted and headed out at noon exactly, she noted with a glance at her watch.

Shortly before three, they reached the service cabin. This time, Paul had a key for the padlock. They could use the door rather than climbing in and out of the window.

"It was more fun sneaking in," she said, giving him a smile as she carried her sleeping bag and supplies inside. "More of an adventure. Walking in the front door is too staid."

He gave her a thoughtful perusal before tossing his stuff to one of the hard bunk beds. After unpacking and bringing everything inside the cabin, including the saddles, he took the horses to the creek. Dinah went along with a bucket for water to prime the pump, which had dried out in the month since they'd been there.

"Oh," she said in surprise when they reached the place where the stagnant pool used to be.

"We got the creek turned," he said.

"A very nice job," she commented, noting the opening that had been blasted through the rocks to let the pool drain toward the west. She followed the newly dug trench that had been lined with rocks. It led into the creek channel on the down side of the saddle where the Triple R Ranch started.

"This will give the ranch a year-round water supply in the upper pastures," Paul explained.

They stood there for a minute in the warm spring sunshine. From this vantage point, they could see for miles across the wide, rolling hills. The upper slopes were covered with evergreen trees. Farther down, the land opened up into meadows with meandering lines of alders and willows indicating the creeks.

Dinah gazed over it as if enchanted. She became caught up in her *first man-first woman* fantasy.

"Don't you wonder what it was like?" she murmured.

"Before the white man came?"

"Before anyone."

Paul's shoulder brushed hers when he stepped up beside her and looked out over the far hills. "A land of plenty. Deer. Elk. Bear. Beaver. Miles of fields suitable for grazing. The first settlers must have thought they'd found paradise."

"Yes." Her voice trembled.

Unable to stop, she turned to him, knowing her eyes reflected the deep need she felt to be held by him.

He looked from the horizon to her. A flash of hunger flamed in the depths of his eyes, then his face became closed. "We have work to do."

She swallowed the disappointment and followed him back to the cabin. He strung a tether line for the horses so they could graze at will in the clearing. Dinah went inside and prepared sandwiches from canned meat for lunch.

On an impulse, she took the food outside and set up a picnic, complete with cool glasses of lemonade from a mix.

After the meal, Paul went into the cabin. He emerged in a few minutes with a fanny pack around his waist, his coat tied on it. She knew he was leaving.

"Where are you going?" she demanded, jumping to her feet.

"I want to scout out the area."

"You're going to see if you can find whoever fired those shots," she interrupted, instinctively knowing she was right.

His slow grin spread over his mouth. "You're sharp."

A shudder of fear raced through her. "What will you do if you find them?"

"Don't worry. I can take care of myself."

"They have a gun . . . or guns."

"So do I." He gave her a level stare.

"I'll go with you."

"No."

She picked her parka off the ground and tied the sleeves around her waist. "Do you have another gun?"

He heaved an exasperated sigh. "No. You're to stay here, Dinah. I mean it." He gave her a threatening glare.

She glared right back. "I'm going. Either with you or behind you. I mean it."

The expletive that greeted this statement didn't faze her. She simply resettled her hat on her head and waited for him to accept the inevitable.

"All right," he conceded. "But you do exactly what I tell you, when I tell you, got that?"

"Yes."

"Get a couple of granola bars from the supplies. We might miss supper."

She scurried inside to do his bidding. He was gone when she returned. "Paul, you sneak," she yelled.

Only the chuckle of the wind answered. She headed for the trail. She wasn't an expert, but she knew something about tracking through the wilderness. She found the imprint of his boot, studied it, then began to follow it back the way they'd come.

The woods were silent as a grave, she thought at one point. She reached the damaged yew trees. An idea came to her. Paul must be heading for the old logging road. That was the logical place for hunters to leave their truck. She hiked over the ridge.

Paul was kneeling by the side of the logging road when she arrived an hour later. He glanced up, not surprised to see her.

"Three men were here," he said. "Something happened."

She knelt beside him. He pointed to the telltale signs in the dust. She leaned closer. There were spots in the dust. She touched one with a finger, then studied the stain.

Blood.

"Someone was hurt," she whispered, worried that a madman with a gun was going to rush from the woods and shoot them.

"The three men left," Paul told her. He began tracking the trail of blood.

Dinah followed behind. Since Paul was so engrossed in his task, she kept a sharp eye out for any suspicious sounds or movements around them. She heard nothing, not even a birdcall in the distance.

That in itself was alarming. Birds were silent when danger was near. She paused and listened intently. Only the sound of her heartbeat, surprisingly strong and even, echoed in her ears.

She realized she wasn't afraid, not with Paul. Her life, since coming to Oregon, had been full of adventures ... of varying sorts. She loved it. She felt truly alive, as if she were finally living ... connecting with life, was the way she thought of it.

However, she didn't have time to dwell on these thoughts. Paul was about to leave her behind. She hurried to catch up, running on tiptoe so as not to break his concentration.

They lost the trail at a gully flowing with the runoff of the April showers. Paul muttered a curse under his breath.

"I'll try to pick up the track farther downstream," he said. "The path to the cabin is on the other side of that ridge. Why don't you go back—"

"No."

He gave her a glare of pure irritation.

She returned it with a steady gaze.

"You'd drive a saint to sin," he said.

"What are we tracking?" she asked. "You said the men left, but someone obviously got hurt. Maybe they accidentally shot one of their party and carried him out of the woods."

"It wasn't a person," Paul broke in.

"What, then?"

"One of the cougars." He crossed the temporary creek and searched along the other side.

Dinah remembered the cry of the big cat the previous night. Had it stalked and attacked one of the hunters at the same time the man had been stalking a deer?

A case of poetic justice, except apparently the cat had been injured rather than the illegal hunter.

She joined Paul in his search for another sign of the mountain lion, but to no avail. The sun was very low before he gave up.

"Let's call it quits for the night," he said on a sober note. "We'll start here in the morning." He led the way back to the trail. It was dusk when they reached the cabin.

Dinah felt a frisson run down her arms as she entered the empty cabin. While Paul checked on the horses and strung the tether line between two different trees, she started their evening meal. She couldn't keep her gaze from straying out the window to where Paul worked.

There was a grim anger in him, she thought. He was angry at the hunters, or whoever, for hurting the cougar. She instinctively knew he would never leave an animal to die a long, painful death.

"Supper's ready," she called out.

When he came in, he closed the door behind him, shutting in the heat that radiated from the stove. The temperature was dropping rapidly with the approach of night.

Another shiver chased down her spine as Dinah saw Paul glance at the bunk beds, then away. He frowned heavily, then pumped a pan of water and washed up. He waited until she was seated before taking his place on the floor beside her.

They ate and watched the flames flicker behind the isinglass panels of the stove. For the life of her, Dinah couldn't think of one thing to say. Her mind whirled with half thoughts and bits and pieces of past conversations with Paul.

"Let it go," he suddenly said.

"I beg your pardon?"

He collected the dishes and washed them at the sink. "The time will come when neither of us will be able to resist the other," he announced without a trace of humor. "Then . . . whatever happens, will happen."

"As simple as that?" she asked. Heat erupted inside her at the thought of his lovemaking. The moment seemed wrought with complexities as obscure as the hieroglyphics on an ancient temple.

"I don't think it will be simple at all," he said.

He left the dishes in the sink to drain and returned to his place on the floor. He looked at her, a probing perusal that reached right down inside her and added fuel to the fire there. An insight came to her.

"But you don't want it," she said slowly. The shock of the realization lodged in her chest.

"No, I don't want it."

She felt stricken to the soul. "I don't understand."

His laugh was brief and bitter. "Maybe I don't feel like being your tutor in the sexual games between men and women. This may be hard to believe, but not all men are ready to leap into bed on the slightest pretext."

The message finally got through to her. She'd insulted him!

Worse, what he said was true. She had expected him to sweep her off her feet and into bed, so to speak, without a thought.

But, some part of her protested, he did want her. She wasn't so lacking in feminine instinct not to know that.

This wasn't the time to think about it. She had fences to mend. "I'm sorry," she said. She laid a hand on his arm.

He looked at it, then back at her. "For what?"

"For being callous. I've never thought you were promiscuous, but I must have given that impression." She let him go, regretting the lose of contact with his warmth.

"You're something," he said slowly, shaking his head as if perplexed. "I can never figure you out."

She decided the evening should end on a light note. "Who would want to?" Her smile invited him to share her amusement at her own expense.

He didn't smile. "Me. I would."

She felt her lips tremble when his gaze lingered on her mouth as if he thought of the kisses they'd shared. She was totally at a loss to understand him, either. One experience with the campus heartthrob hadn't prepared her to deal with a man of Paul's depth.

"Ask me anything," she said.

Her voice was husky instead of humorous. She wasn't sure if she really meant it. At the moment, she wasn't sure of anything except the hard beat of her heart that rattled her whole body.

Abruptly he stood and paced the small room. "After we make love, what then?"

She gestured helplessly. "I . . . I don't know."

They seemed to be in the middle of a quarrel, only she didn't know what the bone of contention was. And he thought *she* was hard to figure out!

"Are we talking about a one-night stand? A week? A full-blown affair for the time we're up here in the woods?"

"I hadn't thought that far ahead," she admitted truthfully.

Obviously an affair would be much more complicated than she'd thought. Paul, of course, knew from experience how things like this worked. He should be the one to tell her. . . .

"You've had a bad experience," she realized all at once. Of course! Why hadn't she seen that before?

"Haven't we all?" he retorted, with a cynical smile.

"Tell me about it," she requested. When he didn't reply, she reminded him, "I've told you what I want. It's only fair that I should know where you're coming from."

When he spoke, his voice was cold and emotionless. "I was engaged once...."

Paul? Engaged?

"When my face got smashed in an accident, she walked out. I was a pretty gruesome sight. The thought of being tied to someone who might be a candidate for a freak in a sideshow was more than she could contemplate."

"She was shallow," Dinah declared. "You were lucky to be rid of her."

An ache settled in Dinah's chest. The idea of Paul's being hurt sent a surge of adrenaline into her blood. She was ready to fight for him, she realized. She studied his handsome face.

"But you look wonderful," she said.

His eyes roamed her face restlessly. There was emotion in those azure depths, but she couldn't read its meaning.

"Seven operations," he said laconically, "and a year out of my life."

She heard the pain behind the carelessly spoken words. Months of pain, of uncertainty, of being alone when the woman he'd loved had walked out on him. Dinah felt his loss as a sharp ache in the vicinity of her heart. His hurt had been much greater than hers, she realized. He'd given his love and trust, had asked the woman to marry him and she had betrayed him.

Without thinking, Dinah stood and reached out to him, wanting to offer the comfort of her arms.

He caught her hands and held her off. "Are you feeling sorry for me, Dinah?"

"Yes."

He dropped her hands and stepped back. "Forget it. I don't need it."

"Yes, you do." She moved nearer. "I asked you to teach me about life and…and making love. Perhaps we can learn from each other." She searched for the words to express a gut-deep feeling she had. "Perhaps we were meant to help each other."

His smile was cynical. "By sleeping together?"

"Maybe." She pushed closer still, until there was only six inches between them. She couldn't explain it, but she felt it was terribly important that they make contact. "Maybe it's time we both let go of the past and move on from here."

With one step, she closed the distance between them. Never had she laid herself so open to another person before, but she felt a kinship with this man. It was something she'd never experienced with another.

They'd both fallen for the wrong people. They'd both suffered, Paul much more than she had, but still, it was something they shared.

They could share passion, too. The conviction that it was right for them to do so made her determined. A luminous joy washed over her as she put aside doubts and simply followed her instincts.

"The time is right," she murmured, sure of it.

"Maybe," he said coolly. "Or maybe you're confusing lust with some star-crossed, romantic nonsense. That's one thing I never do."

She stepped back from him. Their eyes met in a gaze she was powerless to break. There was turbulence in him and a return of his earlier anger. She knew he wanted her, but there were other emotions involved. That was what he was fighting.

Turning away, she went to the sink to brush her teeth and prepare for bed. "We'll wait," she said and was pleased at the confidence she displayed.

"Don't hold your breath," he told her.

She laughed. "Really, Paul, that's such a cliché."

When he muttered something about checking on the horses and slammed out of the cabin, she realized the wait wouldn't be terribly long. The hunger between them was too great.

Chapter Ten

Paul was up before dawn. Dinah heard him prowling the cabin like a restless predator. She knew he'd be off as soon as possible to search for the cougar. She wanted to go, too. She heard him put coffee on, then go check on the horses.

She rose and dressed as quickly as she could. When he returned, she had oatmeal prepared. He nodded to her, then ate without wasting time talking. As soon as it was light enough to see the trail through the woods, they were off.

Birds sang and squirrels chirped in the woods as the world woke to the new day. She felt refreshed and ready to tackle whatever the morning brought. At the creek, Paul set her to searching for signs of the big cat on one side and he took the other. She kept her eyes on the ground, searching for a paw print to indicate the cougar had come that way.

The sky had brightened to dawn before Paul called to her. "Over here," he said.

She leaped across the tiny creek and joined him. He was bent over the ground, walking slowly while he followed the trail. Dinah saw a bloodstain on the earth where the cat had rested briefly, then a bloody paw print on a granite ledge a short distance away.

Sticking close to Paul, she helped him find the trail. A half hour later, they caught up with the animal.

The big cat was under a tree, lying in a niche between two boulders, which formed a partial shelter. Blood stained the tawny fur and the pine needles around the animal. It had tried to lick the wound clean, but the task had proven too much.

Dinah wondered if the cat was dead when it didn't stir at their approach.

Paul tossed a stone. The cougar didn't move.

"It's unconscious," he said in a low tone. "Stay here while I muzzle her."

He picked up a stick, removed a rope from his jacket pocket and eased toward the cat. When he yelled at the animal, Dinah jumped, but the cat remained still. He prodded it with the stick. The cat didn't open an eye.

The hair stood on end on Dinah's neck.

Paul moved in quickly, lifted the tawny head and tied the crude but effective muzzle on. He proceeded to lash the big front paws together. "Okay," he called.

Dinah joined him. "Oh," she breathed, seeing the animal more closely. "A female."

"A pregnant female," he elaborated. He checked the wound. "It missed her lungs. At least the bullet went all the way through. I was afraid it might be lodged against her spine."

"Can we save her?" Dinah asked. She ran her hand over the soft pelt and felt the telltale protrusion of the cat's belly. "How far along do you think she is?"

"It was early April when the male cougar was here. She's probably halfway to term."

"Domestic cats take sixty to sixty-three days. Is it the same for wild cats?"

"No. She'll take about three months."

Dinah figured the time. "So she has six weeks to go. Do you think she'll lose the babies?" She petted the big cat's head while her heart ached as if the loss were her own.

Paul laid a hand on her shoulder. "I don't know," he answered truthfully, his voice dropping to a low, husky note. "We'll do what we can. Let's get her to the cabin."

Dinah looked up in surprise.

Paul bit back a groan as she gazed at him as if posing for a statue of Hope Reborn. Her black eyes gleamed in soft approval of his actions. It was all he could do not to take her right there and to hell with the consequences.

"How can we move her?"

The question brought him back to reality. He mulled it over. "We'll make a travois from our coats."

He searched the area for two branches or saplings of a good size and finally found two young lodgepole pines. He cut them down and returned to Dinah and the cat. While she watched, her eyes filled with admiration, he attached their coats to the pines to make a sling.

"I'll need your help," he murmured, slipping his hands under the animal's head and shoulders. Dinah joined him and slid her arms under the hips and abdomen. Together they heaved the one hundred and thirty-or-forty pounds of limp weight onto the makeshift stretcher.

It took most of the morning to return to the cabin. Paul kept an eye on the cat. The lioness opened her eyes once and gazed at him, then closed them again as if resigned to her fate.

He also watched Dinah and stopped often to let her rest. She never complained once on the long trip. Of course, he'd learned to expect that stiff-upper-lip stoicism from her.

When they reached the cabin, she started a fire in the stove and put on a pot of water to boil while he secured their patient's paws to the saplings so it couldn't take a swipe at them.

Carefully, aware of Dinah's worried gaze, he washed and cleaned the wound as best he could. After shaving off the fur next to the punctures, he tore open an iodine packet from their first-aid supplies and sprinkled the antiseptic powder over the entrance and exit holes. After he'd secured bandages over both places, he set back on his heels.

"That's the best we can do," he decided. "We'll have to let nature take its course."

"Yes," Dinah agreed. She reached out with a bandanna and solemnly wiped the sweat off his forehead.

He hadn't realized it was there. He heaved out a deep breath, letting go of the tension of the past couple of hours, then turned to his companion. It was almost his undoing.

She gazed at him with a sweet, disarming smile of approval on her face. Her eyes were filled with more than lambent regard. He wondered if she knew of the desire he saw reflected in those dark, volcanic depths. She gave off an aura of sensuality, hot and smoldering, ready to burst into flame at a touch.

When she laid a hand on his upper arm, he almost came apart. It wouldn't be long before he gave in to what she was unconsciously asking for. He didn't even know why the hell he was fighting it.

"We'll need a better muzzle," he murmured and moved away.

Dinah blinked in disappointment. For a second, she'd thought he was going to kiss her. Her lips burned for it. She turned so he couldn't see her face and read the desire she felt.

She wanted him. It had become an echoing theme in her. She didn't understand it. After months of suppression, she was suddenly bursting with needs she couldn't control.

Staring out the window over the sink at the willow shrubs along a low point in the tiny meadow, she felt like a new bud opening to the warmth of the sun. That sun was Paul.

Why did she respond to only him? she wondered, confused by the intensity of it all. A hand touched her chin and turned her face. She whipped her head around, startled by the touch.

"Let it go," he advised softly. "You'll only drive yourself crazy worrying about it."

"About what?" She was pleased at how calm she sounded.

"Us," he said with his cool, know-it-all grin.

Her shoulders slumped. "I've never felt like this before," she explained, not bothering to hide her puzzlement. "I don't know how to handle it...or what to do..."

"Gets you tied into knots, doesn't it?"

"What?" she asked, her heart beating hard as she waited for his answer, even if it was likely to be one of his cynical, man-of-the-world remarks.

"This." He leaned down and kissed her parted lips.

She went up in smoke. She lifted her hands and clung to his shirtfront shamelessly as her legs trembled and weakened. When he raised his head, she protested with a breathless murmur and tried to follow his lips.

"More?"

He was taunting her, she vaguely realized. She slipped her hands behind his head. He let her touch his mouth with hers.

"It hurts," she whispered. "Inside. I'm all hot and aching. Why does it hurt?"

She felt the sizzling electricity increase between them. He tensed under her caressing fingers. Then he groaned and caught her to him, all traces of the cynic evaporating in the heat of passion.

Dinah experienced a jolt of triumph. He was no longer toying with her or fighting the need.

When he shifted, she was instantly aware of him all along her body. Her breasts, stomach and thighs meshed with his, each part fitting perfectly. He was right. They were made for each other.

A whimpering sound forced them to reluctantly draw apart. They looked at the cat. She watched them with a golden, unblinking stare. She tried to snarl, but the bandanna and twine held her mouth nearly closed. After a brief moment, she gave up and dropped her head back to Dinah's parka.

"She needs water," Paul said. He went to the sink and pumped a pan half full. Kneeling by the cat, he dribbled a few drops on her lips from a cautious distance.

Dinah held her breath. The beautiful female opened her mouth the fraction of an inch the muzzle allowed and licked at the water. Dinah smiled in relief.

For a quarter of an hour, Paul patiently let the cat drink as much as she would take. When she ignored the last dribble, Paul didn't urge her to take more. Instead, he sat beside the animal, who lay on their two coats, and stroked her head and scratched her ears while speaking in a low, crooning voice.

It would be wonderful, Dinah knew, to be touched like that by him. He would be gentle. He would be passionate. He would give as much to his partner as he took for himself. She licked her lips and looked away.

Seeing the sun on the meadow, she realized the morning was gone. It was time for lunch. She prepared sandwiches and chips with slices of apples and oranges from their supplies. She kept visualizing Paul's long, lean fingers, stroking and caressing through her dark hair rather than the tawny fur.

"Lunch," she said softly when it was ready. She placed his plate on the floor beside him along with instant lemonade. She chose a place nearby.

They ate in silence. When she risked a glance at him, he was watching her, but his thoughts seemed faraway, focused on some inner place that only he knew. She wondered what it would be like to be there with him. Tears stung her eyes, surprising her.

What was it she longed for? It was more than passion or some vague connection with life. Her gaze returned to Paul. He was the key. It was true, but she didn't know why.

She sighed with fatalistic humor. Maybe she was one of those women whose fate was to reform handsome rakes . . . or break their hearts trying. That was more likely the case.

For the rest of the day, they stayed close to the cougar. Paul gave the cat water often as the animal stayed alert longer. That evening after supper, he motioned Dinah close and handed her a piece of wood.

"I'm going to try something," he said.

"What?" she asked, worry starting up.

He trailed a fingertip along the frown line between her eyes. "Nothing too dangerous. I'm going to take the muzzle off."

She batted his hand away. "That's not dangerous?"

He laughed. "Not as dangerous as some things I could name."

"Such as?" she challenged, annoyed with him. Didn't he have any sense of self-preservation? The cat could take his hand off with one bite.

"Getting involved with curious virgins," he replied.

"I'm not—" She broke off abruptly. Well, she was a virgin. And she was curious. Plus a few other things she couldn't decipher. The situation was maddening.

He gave her a challenging smile, then reached slowly down to the cougar. The golden eyes opened to slits. He spoke softly and rubbed her. She closed her eyes. Paul untied the twine behind her head. Now there was only the relatively loose circle of bandanna around her nose. It would easily slip off if she moved.

Paul continued to speak in a crooning tone. He scratched behind the alert ears and along the cat's muzzle. Each stroke slipped the bandanna farther down. Then it was off.

Dinah moved closer with the stick of firewood, prepared to jam it into the cat's mouth if she tried to bite. Suddenly, the cat raised her head two inches off the pallet.

"Easy," Paul said.

Dinah wasn't sure if he meant the cat or her.

The cougar yawned with a delicate roll of her pink tongue and laid her head down again, eyes closed. As Paul stroked the cat's head and neck, a deep rumble came out of the tawny chest.

The cougar was purring!

"Hand the water over," he said.

Dinah gave it to him. He placed the pan near the cat's head. Her nose twitched; then she raised her head and lapped the water until the pan was dry. She laid her big head down wearily and gave a sigh.

"Good girl," Paul said.

Dinah found herself jealous of a wild animal. Paul had never spoken to her in that soft, caressing tone of voice, as if she'd done some brave and wonderful thing. She wished he would.

"She seems to have accepted us...you," she said, knowing the cat's trust was due to Paul. "Is there no female on earth immune to your charm?"

Her laugh was slightly shaky, a bit envious and not at all secure. Heavens, but she was coming unglued.

"One," he told her. "You."

She shook her head. "I'm going down for the third time."

He smiled at her half-desperate attempt to hold the aching need at bay. It was useless. If he wanted her, she was his for the taking. She sighed in despair.

"Maybe it won't be so bad," he suggested.

She looked at him, wide-eyed.

"Making love," he clarified.

Every nerve in her went to red alert. "So, this is it then?"

"I think so." He stood and pulled her to her feet. "Let's bed the cat down, then we'll see about us."

She gulped and set about doing as he suggested. He filled the pan with water again while she broke bread into another one and soaked it in powdered milk and water. She put the concoction by the water pan.

When she looked at Paul, she knew her eyes revealed her every thought, but she no longer cared. She was helpless against the deep, aching need for him. It was more powerful than anything she'd ever felt. He was the key to her passion. She moved toward him, wanting to unlock the door.

His arms opened for her.

"Now?" he whispered against her hair.

She nodded. A tremor shook her, from her or him, she couldn't say. He drew back to gaze at her. She was set ablaze by the fire in his eyes. He wanted her. Oh, yes, he wanted her!

He moved and his mouth trailed along her temple, her cheek. He kissed her eyes closed, then continued to her mouth. Her lips trembled. She couldn't control the reaction.

"I won't hurt you," he said huskily.

"I...I know." Wouldn't he? She was suddenly afraid of all this hectic passion. She wasn't sure what it was leading to. Or if she'd like it once she got there.

"I'm as scared as you are."

"You are?" Her voice quavered, and she was embarrassed by her nervousness even as she longed for more from him.

"Ah, Dinah, Dinah," he said, almost laughing; then he crushed her mouth under his as if he was tired of games and was down to serious business.

His hands went to her hips, bringing her into full contact with him, making her aware of his desire in a more factual way.

She felt odd. Light-headed. Her heart was jumpy. So was his. His chest heaved against hers in quick, deep breaths.

He moved, and his hand slid along her side to her waist and above. He took the weight of her breast into his palm.

"I want you," he said when he bent to kiss her throat. "I want you wild and hungry in my arms, so far gone that you'll accept everything I do to you, no questions asked."

Flames erupted like a volcano exploding in her. She was consumed by them, by his passion. She turned her head, wanting his mouth...wanting him!

Their lips met.

Yes, yes, yes! some wild part of her cried, breaking free under the passion of his kiss. For once in her life, she welcomed the loss of control.

She arched against him, loving the feel of his body against hers. His hands swept over her again and again, pressing her closer as he explored every dip and curve of her torso and hips.

When he at last turned and, in a slow waltz, danced her to the bed, she followed willingly, her thighs enmeshed with his as they glided—one, two, three, one, two, three—to the soundless music of their desire.

He stopped beside the bunk bed. "Wait," he said. Reaching over, he grabbed his sleeping bag and tossed it over hers, then smoothed the fabric. "That'll give us a bit more padding."

His hands went to her shirt buttons. He smiled as he leaned his head toward hers. She lifted her mouth for his kiss.

With delicate strokes of his tongue, he asked permission to come inside. She let him. Slowly, he tasted and sipped at her lips. He coaxed her tongue into erotic play with his.

It all seemed so natural. His hands moved down her shirtfront, so slowly that she never felt a second's alarm about being undressed, so confidently that she never once thought of pulling back or protesting.

His open mouth glided over hers, fitting perfectly to her. He established a rhythm that set off a pulsing sensation deep within. The rhythm built and built and built until the whole world was filled with the sound of it. It thrummed in her ears and in her blood. Her heart changed, matching its beat to the erratic impulse of their passion.

A cool wind wafted over her. She realized he'd pushed her shirt down her arms. It dropped to the floor.

"Do me," he requested, encircling her shoulders.

She slipped her arms from around his neck, not realizing until then that she'd been clinging shamelessly to him.

She laughed breathlessly as she raised shaky fingers to his shirt and started on the first button.

"What?" he asked, nuzzling her ear.

"Everything seems...new," was the best she could come up with to explain how she felt.

"Yes. New and exciting, as if we're the first to know this." He chuckled. "Adam and Eve. In our own rustic Eden."

She looked up at him, surprised at his understanding and at his comparison of them to the first couple on earth. A pang went through her as she realized he felt the same way she did. Kindred souls, she thought hazily.

"Hurry," he said. He kissed her nose.

She got back to work on his buttons. He sucked in his stomach and let her pull the material from his jeans. She finished and pushed it off his shoulders.

At the moment his shirt fell to the floor, she felt another tickle of air across her chest. Paul slipped her bra down her arms. It joined the shirts. His hands cupped her breasts.

"Dinah," she heard him say.

The pulsing beat increased to a steady roar as if she held seashells to each ear. It was wonderful and scary.

He flicked his thumbs over her taut breasts until the nipples stood out in blatant invitation. Electric shocks spiraled through her, arousing a need as strong as pain.

"Paul," she breathed. "Your touch...it makes me ache. I never knew it would be like this. So achy..."

Paul felt her body arch into his. Her thighs brushed his. He knew about the aches of passion. He was hurting, his need for her was so great.

With swift movements, he unfastened both their jeans and stripped them away. The last of their clothing followed. As she trembled and weakened in his arms, he felt the hard strength of desire flow into every part of him.

He lifted her and laid her on the bed. She clung to his shoulders and urged him down with her. He stretched out beside her and ran his hands over her silky flesh.

"Please," she said, her eyes closed tightly, a slight frown etched across her forehead. She clamped her teeth into her bottom lip, but she couldn't recall the plea. He was glad.

"Do you want me that much?" he asked, fascinated by her passion. No woman had ever wanted him like this, as if he held the key to life for her. A hot shaft of hunger and an emotion he couldn't name speared right through him.

"Yes. It hurts," she whispered, "to need like this. I don't understand..."

"Shh," he murmured. Another shaft of emotion hit him. This time he could identify it. Tenderness.

She knew the torment of passion; he wanted to show her the sweet, wild pleasure of their joining. But not yet. She wasn't ready. He'd have to let the torment build a bit longer.

He lifted a hand to her rib cage and slowly slid it over her breast. She bucked against him and lifted into his hand. Her body quivered like an aspen leaf in the wind.

When she cried out, he was stunned by the sound of her need. He wanted to crush her to him and give and give and give until every drop of his passion had sated every hunger in her. It was a new feeling, one that left him vulnerable and shaken... and somehow humble.

This was a first for her. It was for him, too.

"Dinah," he said, a husky ache in his voice. "Relax, love. I'll take care of you. I promise. Can you feel my hand stroking you? Can you feel how much I want you?"

After a minute, she nodded. He felt the passionate need slow down in her, not much, but some. She sighed, her breath ragged against his chest. The tenderness rose in him.

He caressed her trembling body, feeling her silky heat radiate over his palm, feeling her heart race. He pressed his hips against her, letting her feel his heat and the hard shaft of his desire.

She opened her legs and caught him between her thighs, taking him by surprise. Fire leaped in him, and he nearly lost it right then. He thought of ice floes, of northern seas and icy rivers, until he regained control.

With the back of one hand, he wiped the sweat off his forehead. He saw her eyes were open, her pupils so wide they looked like black velvet under pure crystalline pools of some magic substance as she watched him.

"Better?" he asked.

"Yes. The . . . ache is easier."

She smiled, a tiny smile, but he was glad to see it. The need was still there, but the trust was growing. It wouldn't be so frightening for her to lose herself to passion's madness when he began building the hunger again.

He returned her smile. "Sex can be scary. It can be rough, too," he told her.

A flicker of worry appeared in her eyes.

"But it can be as gentle as a baby's kiss."

He showed her.

"It can be as tender as a mother's touch."

He feathered a caress along her cheek.

"When you're more experienced, we'll try some different things. And maybe we won't be so gentle, but nothing will hurt, either." He paused, then gave her a knowing smile. "At least, not in *painful* ways, only passionate ones. I know how to take care of those. Soon you will, too," he promised.

He looked into her eyes for a long minute, aware of her and nothing else. He knew it was the same for her.

With exquisite gentleness, he stroked her breast. She caught her breath and pressed upward against his hand. He smiled again, knowing there would be no stopping for either of them.

Dinah felt Paul move back from her, removing the intimate contact between her thighs.

"That gets me too excited," he explained.

His confession pleased her. When he bent to her, she opened her mouth to his. His tongue invaded her, and a sound like the rush of wind filled her head.

She relaxed as his hand moved over her shoulder, her breasts, down her side, down... down... until he stroked her thighs, first one, then the other. He pushed on her leg, asking for more.

Closing her eyes, she kissed his face, all over. He remained still, letting her regain her courage. She again felt the pressure of his fingertips on her. She moved one leg to the side.

He cupped her with his hand, which felt incredibly warm to her. For long minutes, he simply stroked the tight black curls there, running his fingers through them.

When the tension oozed out of her, he began to kiss her once more, taking it deeper, harder and hungrier than before. He demanded more from her. She kissed him back just as hard, just as hungry. A wild clamoring rose in her.

"More," she murmured when he freed her mouth and ran his tongue down her neck, tasting and nibbling at her.

"More?" he asked.

"Yes." She was desperate now.

He eased over her, caressing her breasts by rubbing his chest back and forth against her. She liked the tactile sensation this produced as the dark, wiry hair teased her sensitive nipples.

With a gasp of pleasure, she pressed upward and felt an even more intense pleasure farther down her body. She writhed against him as the quickening tingle grew and grew. His fingers were magic, stroking and urging her to greater heights.

She whimpered suddenly, hearing the sound from a long way off. The terrible need had taken control now. She couldn't fight it nor stop it. She didn't want to.

"It's all right," he whispered against her throbbing mouth. "I've got you. Let it happen. Let it take you. I'll be here."

Her body was trembling. She couldn't stop it. Wrapping her arms around him, she clung to him mindlessly and gave him back kiss for kiss until she was only aware of the points where they touched.

He established a rhythm with her. When, in her eager desperation, she lost it, he patiently brought it back. The roar inside her grew louder... louder... She clutched him, afraid of what was happening.

"I've got you," he assured her. "It's all right. Trust me."

And suddenly a wave of pure delight, of pure sensation, burst over her and she was carried up, up, up until there was nothing but the ecstasy where he touched her. She cried out, once, then again, then went very still.

He quit stroking in that shockingly intimate fashion and was motionless, holding her while she came back down.

All she could hear was the sound of her own breath. Then she heard his breath rasping gently in her ear as he nuzzled her there. She pressed her head against his shoulder, unable to look at him.

"Dinah," he said. There was a smile in his voice.

She kept her face buried against him, unable to believe she'd behaved as she had. She'd been so... abandoned.

"Don't be shy," he said. "I loved making you feel like that. Don't you know what it does to a man's ego to have a woman respond to him like that?"

She shook her head.

His chest moved against hers as he laughed softly. "It makes him feel like a king, a hero of the highest order."

"But you haven't..."

"Not yet. I wanted to show you the best part first. The next is a little harder. Can you stand more?"

With him, she had no doubts. "Yes."

"I've seen you take a pill each morning," he mentioned. "You are protected?"

"Yes." It was easier to work in the wilds if she had control over the phases of the moon in regard to her body.

He began to kiss her face, moving over it in a circle. His hand, she noted, was idly rubbing circles around her breasts. To her surprise, a shimmer of sensation curled through her. She realized she wanted him again.

"I'm safe, but I have protection with me if you'll feel better that way," he said. "I haven't been without it in years."

"Since your fiancée?" She couldn't believe she'd asked that.

A bleakness passed through his eyes, just for a second, then it was gone. He smiled at her. "Not since then."

Her heart skipped when he began to move against her, his whole body caressing hers. When he placed his knee against her thighs, she moved them apart. He shifted over her. Again, he touched her intimately with his long, slender fingers.

She felt her breath catch as he again explored the moist warmth. When he stroked her, she moaned and closed her eyes. The hunger came upon her, even stronger than before. She said his name, a sob of need and encouragement. She moved restlessly beneath him, wanting more from him.

He poised himself above her. "Watch," he murmured hoarsely.

Her eyes flew open. He looked at her, then down. She let her gaze follow his. His body was powerful, intent on its purpose as he pressed forward. She felt the contact, then the strange sensation of having him become part of her.

Doubt assailed her. He was so...masculine. Her body couldn't possibly accommodate him.

His warmth burned into her. She laid her hands on his arms and felt him tremble. His muscles clenched under her fingers, his control etched in bands of steel, as he lowered himself into her.

He closed his eyes and held on, breathing deeply, not moving for several seconds. Suddenly her confidence returned.

This man would never hurt her deliberately. These few seconds might prove uncomfortable, but he would help her past them as gently as he could. Taking a breath, she rose to meet him.

She heard him gasp as they melted together in one fluid thrust that made their union complete.

"Be still," he ordered and clenched his teeth as he fought visibly for control.

A smile curled over her mouth. She felt so foolishly proud, as if she'd accomplished some great feat.

"Witch," he said and looked into her eyes. "Damned pleased with yourself, aren't you?"

She laughed. This was life as it should be, she thought. This was right.

Unable to stop, she reached for him, running her hands all over his smooth, supple flesh. He groaned and swooped downward, taking her mouth in a thundering kiss. Soon her blood was racing again as pleasure caught her in its thousand delights.

I love him, was her last thought.

Chapter Eleven

Dinah woke abruptly. She stared into golden eyes.

The cougar stood beside the bunk, her nose no more than six inches from Dinah's. The cat yawned, huffing her breath over Dinah's face. Dinah's mouth went dry. She lay perfectly still.

Show no fear.

She tried not to, but it was hard when she thought she was being looked upon as a breakfast pastry.

The cat yawned again, then turned and headed for the door. She lifted one big paw and scratched at it. On the second try, she caught the latch. The door opened.

The magnificent lioness walked outside into the sun like a golden queen surveying her realm.

Dinah went limp. That was certainly a jolting way to wake. She stretched and felt the fabric of the sleeping bag caress her skin. She'd never slept in the buff before.

A shot echoed through the woods.

She leaped out of bed, heart pounding. Had the cat attacked Paul? How could she help him? She grabbed a length of firewood and headed for the door. She stopped right outside.

Paul appeared at the edge of the woods. He carried a carcass, which he laid in the meadow grass. The cat came to him, obviously in pain as she walked, and sniffed at the offering.

The cool morning breeze blew over Dinah, causing her breasts to contract into hard points. Paul glanced toward the cabin and froze. She realized she must look ridiculous, standing there stark naked with a piece of wood in her hand for a weapon.

She bolted inside, tossed the stick on the woodpile and grabbed at her clothing. She didn't make it.

Paul leaped into the cabin and dashed across the room. He swooped and caught her in his arms. With a laugh, he hugged her to him, then tucked her under the covers on the bed.

He bent over her. She turned her face away, self-conscious in the full light of day.

When he left her, she whipped around. He poured a cup of coffee and brought it to her. She tucked the sleeping bag under her arms and took the cup. While she sipped, he studied her.

"How are you?" he asked in a solemn tone.

She swallowed before answering. "Fine. A little stiff." Now that her adrenaline had quit flowing, she felt foolish.

He studied her intently for a moment. "I've never had a woman come to my rescue. My experience has been the opposite..." His voice trailed off while he thought about that.

"I thought...I heard the shot and thought the men who wounded the cougar might have come back."

Paul smiled. "Did you think we were having a shoot-out?"

Before she could answer, he removed the cup from her hand, set it on the floor and lifted her into his arms. She had only a second to think before his mouth covered hers. Then she was lost to everything but them.

The morning proved the night had been no fluke. He took her to those marvelous heights again, until she could only cling to him and whisper raggedly of needs long unmet. He answered them all.

She drowsed, clasped against his lean, hard body. A snuffling sound brought her to full alert.

The cougar stopped in the middle of the room. She watched them with an unblinking stare for several seconds, then she went to her pallet and lay down, weariness in every move.

"Did you let her loose?" Dinah asked.

"No. She chewed through the bindings on her legs during the night. Fortunately, she seems to consider us friends rather than snacks. However, I thought I'd better find her something more substantial to eat than our food in case she changed her mind."

He rose and stretched, his body rippling in shades of bronze, except for the lighter strip around his hips.

Her throat filled with emotions too large and mingled to sort through. She remembered the troubling thought of the previous night. She had fallen in love with him all over again.

For a moment, she worried over the future, then realized it was futile. What would be, would be. A warm glow spread through her. She would always have this memory, no matter what happened.

She watched him stoke up the fire and put a pan of water on to heat. He selected fresh clothing and headed out.

"You use the warm water. I'll wash at the creek," he said and left her alone.

She quickly bathed and dressed. After combing the tangles out of her hair and clipping it into a ponytail, she started breakfast.

When Paul returned, he helped her. They ate in silence, which neither of them wanted to break. She wasn't sure what to say. The love she felt filled her chest and pressed against her throat.

After eating, Paul checked the wound on their patient. The cougar lifted her head and glanced at him. With a loud sigh, she closed her eyes and lay back down. A purr filled the quiet of the cabin.

Dinah went over and stroked the tawny fur. "Last night... and this morning... I don't know what to say."

"Yeah," he agreed. There was no laughter in the word.

"I think... I think I'm in love with you."

His head whipped around. The tightening of his mouth didn't bode well for her confession. "It's gratitude you're feeling," he told her. The sardonic tone was back.

She wasn't experienced enough to argue with him. It seemed ironic to her that she had wanted that very thing from him—experience—so she would understand more about the male-female attraction, but now that she knew passion, she felt more confused.

"Is it?" She stared at him, troubled by feelings she couldn't put into words. "I'm not so sure."

He rose to his feet. "You're confused right now, but with a bit more experience, you'll calm down."

She disliked his implication that all she felt was sexual excitement. He walked out before she thought of another question.

"How long does it take to understand the relationship between members of the human species?" she asked the cat.

The cougar sniffed her empty water pan.

Sighing, Dinah pumped water and kept an eye on their patient the rest of the day. Paul stayed out until night.

"There's beef stew," she said when he came in.

"Thanks."

The cougar opened the latch and went outside while Paul ate. He raised his eyebrows at the feat.

"She's smart." Dinah closed the door against the night chill.

"You could take some lessons there," he suggested. He washed his dishes and added wood to the fire. "I found a couple of logs."

With this cryptic statement, he went outside. In a moment, he returned with a section sawed from a tree trunk. He went out and came back with a second one. Moving the barrels to form backrests, he fashioned crude chairs for them.

Dinah took a seat and propped her elbows on her knees, her chin on her clasped hands. She'd have to take a page from his book, she decided, and treat the situation with a light touch.

A scratch at the door had Paul on his feet. He let the cat in. She took her place on their coats and cleaned the fur between her toes, then kneaded her paws against the pallet. Dinah wondered if she'd get her old red parka back in one piece.

"We'd better talk," Paul said.

It was the last thing he felt like doing. He wanted to lift that ebony-haired Venus into his arms and take her to bed. There, all their differences were resolved . . . for the moment.

Unfortunately, sex, as mind-consuming as it was, occupied only an hour or so out of the day. That left twenty-three hours to live through. His experience with women indicated they had no staying power when the going got rough during those other hours. His first love sure hadn't hung around.

His gaze went to Dinah. She had fortitude, he had to admit. And courage he'd rarely seen in a human being.

Right now, she was having fantasies about them. Hell, he was having them himself. He kept envisioning them together, working on various projects, then returning home to the farm in Tennessee where they'd raise a family.

He cursed silently. He'd been around his cousins too much of late. All that domestic bliss did things to a man's judgment. To finally make love to the woman of your dreams was the crowning blow. It threw a man off balance. He needed to think through this passionate interlude in a logical way.

Naturally, he and Dinah were having wild illusions. Their lovemaking had been incredible. The best either of them had ever had. The *only* intimacy she'd ever had. He summoned the sardonic amusement he maintained toward life. It wouldn't come.

Damn.

Next thing, *he'd* be thinking they were in love.

"What happens next?" she asked.

He heaved a deep breath. "I don't know."

"Well, I suppose we can have an affair. I mean, we've already started it, haven't we?" She batted her lashes at him.

The realization that she had turned the tables and was taunting him didn't set well. "Don't get cute," he said.

At the look of hurt in her eyes, he immediately regretted his snappish words. He tried to soften his tone.

"Look," he began patiently, "things happen between people when they share what we did last night."

Dinah noted he didn't refer to their lovemaking simply as "sex." Neither did he deny something had happened between them. A spark flared inside her.

"You're right," she said.

He gave her a sharp glance, but his voice was gentle when he spoke. "Last night, I showed you the natural woman you'd buried inside yourself. It would have happened sooner or later. That much passion couldn't be suppressed forever. I just happened to be the man—"

"Don't you dare say it!" She sat up straight and glared at him. "I've never felt like that. Not with anyone. Not ever."

"Only with me?" he jeered, not mockingly but lightly, as if to tease her out of this frame of mind.

"Yes."

A tense silence stretched between them. He reached out all of a sudden, clasped her arm and pulled her to him. Before she knew what was happening, he had her on his lap.

"Hormones," he told her quite gently.

He kissed her until desire flowed like molten gold in her, until she couldn't argue or protest or breathe. His lips and hands did wonderful things to her. She did the same to him.

It was primitive. It was wild. It was even a little rough.

When the tempest quieted, he kissed her eyes, her nose and then her mouth. "See?" he murmured.

She frowned at the knowing look in his eyes. "You've got to get over this cynical attitude of yours," she advised him.

The cougar stayed with them from Friday until the following Saturday. Late in the afternoon of the eighth day, she went outside. By dark, she hadn't returned.

"Do you think she'll be all right?" Dinah asked. She took their coats outside and brushed the cat hair off.

"She has things to do," Paul said. "She has to decide on a den for the birth. Later, she'll probably move to another."

Dinah watched him clean the fish he'd caught for their dinner, his hands sure and deft at the task—the way they were when he made love to her each night.

A shimmer of desire attacked her, and she wrapped her arms across her chest and gazed into the distance, trying to regain control of her senses. She wondered if people ever got over the rapture of making love.

Did it finally become like so many other things in life— just an appetite to be satisfied with no more thought than it took to grab a snack and be off again?

A finger lightly touched the frown line between her eyes. "Don't you know it's bad for you to think such dark thoughts? It can color your whole outlook on life."

She smiled up into Paul's eyes and caught his hand. She kissed the palm, then held it to her cheek, loving the feel of him.

"Have you ever had fish cooked the Indian way, skewered on a stick and slow-roasted over an open fire?" he asked.

She released his hand. "No."

"Let's try it." He hooked his hand behind her neck and pulled her against him. Together they collected firewood, and she watched while Paul made a small fire in the clearing. He made her hold her own two trout over the fire.

They sat there in the deepening twilight before the flickering fire. Another first, she thought. Their days here in the mountains had been full of first-time adventures.

First man-first woman.

"Watch it," he warned when she let the stick dip close to the cinders. "No daydreaming on the job."

She laughed and concentrated on the task.

"How's the bark study going?" he asked later.

She laid the fish bones on her plate and licked her fingers. "Fine. I've found three stands of yew near here."

They discussed their projects during the meal. When they went inside, Paul checked the pantry. "We need to go in and pick up supplies. How about tomorrow?"

She realized she was reluctant to face civilization again. The fantasy of being here in the woods with him had taken hold in her heart. If they left, it might disappear.

"Fine," she said without much enthusiasm.

He caught her chin and turned her face to his. After a careful scrutiny, he murmured, "Don't think this is real."

She managed a nonchalant shrug. "I don't. You've warned me it isn't nearly every day."

A frown appeared on his handsome face. He looked worried. For her, she realized. He didn't love her—he'd made that plain—but he wasn't a callous person. He was concerned that she would be hurt when the summer, or their affair, was over... whichever came first. She felt her smile wobble a bit.

"Good." He spread an aerial map on the floor and studied the contours of the land in that sector and the contrast between old and new growth in the forests that covered it.

She saw the map was a section of the Sky Eagle Ranch east of the cabin, too far to commute back and forth each day.

The ranch was in an uproar when they returned the next day.

"You're just in time," Rachel called to them when they rode in around noon on Sunday. "Hank and Sita are getting married this afternoon."

Paul raised an eyebrow in that devilishly handsome way he had. "A bit sudden, isn't it?"

Rachel rolled her eyes. "They announced they were getting married just after you left...what was that?...two weeks ago?"

Paul nodded.

"They were going to drive down to Lake Tahoe, get married in one of those quickie wedding chapels, spend the night and come back the next day. Beth and I thought it was unfair to deprive the ranch hands of an occasion. Have you noticed that cowboys love a party?" she demanded of Dinah with a delightful giggle.

Dinah smiled and nodded.

"So," Rachel concluded, "we're having the wedding here at three this afternoon, and the happy couple will honeymoon in Tahoe for a week, courtesy of the McPherson brothers."

"Sounds like we'd better make ourselves presentable," Paul suggested to Dinah.

He dismounted. After Dinah swung down, he led both horses toward the stables. Dinah followed her hostess into the house. Beth, the other McPherson wife, was there. She brushed her dark hair off her forehead and greeted Dinah with a weary grin.

"I think we should have let them elope," she said. "I'd forgotten how much work weddings are."

"Not really," Rachel protested. "This is fun."

"Right," Beth agreed drolly.

"Dinah, your room is ready for you," Rachel advised. "Why don't you take a leisurely bath and have a nap? You must have been on the trail at the crack of dawn."

"That sounds wonderful. Thanks."

In the quiet of the peaceful bedroom, Dinah shed her clothing and went into the bathroom. A warm shower after days of bathing in a pan of tepid water was pure luxury. After blow-drying her hair, she slipped into her red football nightshirt and lay down with an afghan spread over her.

She awakened to the pressure of a warm mouth on hers. Her eyes snapped open.

"Hello, Sleeping Beauty." Paul sat beside her on the bed. He had a towel wrapped around his waist. "Time to get dressed."

"Already?" She looked at the clock. She had thirty minutes. She ran her fingers through the damp, wiry hair on his chest. "I didn't hear the shower."

"You were sound asleep." He smoothed the hair back from her forehead. "You should have told me you were tired. We could have rested on the way."

"I'm fine." She sat up. "We'd better get dressed."

"Yes," he murmured, his eyes going dark as his gaze strayed over her. He heaved a sigh, kissed her again, then left.

She was pleased at his reluctance to go, and yet—she paused after putting on her underclothes and considered the situation—and yet, she sensed a growing distance between them.

An echo of sadness yet to come strummed through her.

Shaking off the mood, she dressed in a ruby-red blouse and a skirt printed with roses on a black background. That was as festive as she could get with her limited wardrobe. She put on makeup and added a gold chain and earrings. There.

When she went into the hall, she found Paul outside his door, his hands thrust in his pockets while he leaned on the wall and waited for her. He fell into step when she drew even with him.

He wore dark pants and a white shirt with a subtly striped tie in blue and red. His eyes looked as blue as the sky outside.

The kitchen was a busy place. All the women from town and the neighboring ranches had brought covered dishes for the event. Sita was pacing back and forth. She wore a dress of creamy lace with pink silk roses around the neckline. The real roses clutched in her hands trembled.

"Why am I so nervous?" she asked, then paced some more.

"Wedding nerves," an older woman suggested.

"I've been married before," Sita told her.

"Sometimes it's scarier the second time," someone else said. "You worry more because you know how easily things can go wrong."

"I'll see you outside," Paul said and escaped the roomful of women offering helpful advice to the bride.

The ceremony was held in the side yard. Spring flowers were in bloom and roses had been trucked in by a florist from Medford who was busily arranging a double row of candles to form an altar. A white mat had been spread over the grass. Chairs lined the newly mown lawn. A portable organ had been set up to one side.

"It's time," Rachel said.

Dinah went outside with the rest of the women. Paul stood and indicated a seat beside him. She slipped into it. Hank, dressed splendidly in a light blue summer suit, took his place after the minister stepped in front of the bower of candles and roses. Kerrigan was his best man. Keegan, she noticed, played usher and escorted Sita's mother and father to the front row.

"I wonder how Hank decided on who was to be best man?" she whispered to Paul.

"He didn't. He asked them to choose. The twins flipped a coin," Paul said with a grin.

"And the loser had to stand up with the groom," she concluded.

"No," he corrected. "The loser had to be usher."

Did she imagine the hard edge in Paul's voice when he'd corrected her conclusion? She glanced at him and found him watching her through narrowed eyes. She looked away.

The organist played the wedding march. The audience stood while Sita came down the aisle with her children on each side of her. When the minister asked, "Who giveth this woman?" the son and daughter answered, "We do." The children sat down.

The scene was so tender, Dinah got all misty-eyed.

By the time the vows were spoken and Hank had, with shaky fingers, lifted the chin-length veil and kissed his equally shaky bride, several women in the crowd had to dry their eyes.

At last it was over. The grinning couple faced the guests and raised clasped hands. Everyone clapped and cheered.

"Here."

A white handkerchief was thrust into Dinah's hands. She stared at it for a second. Paul gave an impatient snort, took it back and patted the moisture that clung to her lower lashes.

"You'll do," he said, surveying his handiwork. "No smears or anything."

She grimaced at him. "Thanks."

"Why do weddings make women cry?" He resumed the sardonic tone she associated with him. "It should be the men who weep. They're shackled for life."

Anger rose in her. "No more than women," she began, then shrugged. It wasn't worth an argument.

Leaving him, she went into the kitchen and helped place the food on the linen-covered tables lining the deck. It was a perfect day—bright and warm, but not hot. A sycamore tree shaded the deck and part of the lawn. The ranch hands, dressed in suits and their best boots, arranged the chairs into groups and set up more tables.

I want this, Dinah thought. She paused after setting down a platter of thin-sliced smoked turkey and gazed at the crowd.

Keegan stood with his arm around his wife while he and his twin suggested various outrageous activities to the bridal pair to fill the time while on their honeymoon. Children raced across the lawn in a game of tag. Parents chatted and kept an eye on their kids, calling reprimands or warnings every once in a while.

Beth McPherson leaned against her husband's arm with a contented smile. Her dress was gathered under her breasts and comfortably loose over her waist, but to the discerning eye, a slight roundness was visible in her figure.

Dinah's throat squeezed shut. She wanted that, too—the sense of purpose and fulfillment the McPherson couples had. Now that she knew the ecstasy of making love and the joy of waking in her lover's arms every morning, she wanted more.

She wanted it to go on and on forever. With Paul.

A sigh pushed its way past her aching throat. He was trying to distance himself from their involvement. She sensed it in some deep, intuitive part of her. She'd expected it, but that didn't stop the knowledge from hurting.

She'd been right from the first. Working with Paul again had been a mistake. She felt a hand on her arm and looked up into eyes as blue as a summer sky. . . and as remote as a mountain peak.

"Ready to eat?" he asked. "We seem to have missed lunch."

"Yes, we did," she said in surprise. She handed him a plate and took one for herself. "I'm starved."

They sat at an empty table. Soon Beth and Keegan joined them. They discussed the study Paul was doing for them on managing their land efficiently and preserving the sections of old-growth forest, then Dinah reported on her experiments with bark regrowth.

Later, after the bride and groom and the guests were gone, she and Paul helped straighten up. That night, she and Paul and the McPherson couples stayed up late. Their talk covered a variety of topics with a good dollop of teasing and humor thrown in.

It was after midnight when they went to bed. Paul walked with her down the hall. He'd become remote since the wedding. Was he afraid she'd try to trap him into marriage?

The fatigue of the long day caught up with her, leaving her vaguely depressed.

He stopped at his door. "You'd better get a good night's sleep. We need to go to town for supplies tomorrow, then head out early Tuesday morning." He went into his room.

Dinah did the same. She brushed her teeth and washed her face quickly in the bathroom, then undressed in the dark and put on her nightshirt in her room.

A cloud had covered the moon, and heat lightning played along the mountain peaks, she noticed. She climbed in bed and watched nature's fireworks through the windows.

When she lay down and closed her eyes, restlessness invaded her. She couldn't seem to drift off, although she was tired. She did finally go to sleep but woke when thunder crashed overhead.

She realized she'd crept all the way across the mattress, looking for the hard, masculine body that had cuddled her close for the past two weeks. She scooted back to the side she usually slept on and frowned into the darkness.

Lightning lit the room. The storm was moving in. The rain began with an abrupt downpour. She would have liked the sound of it on the roof... if she'd been in Paul's arms.

If he'd wanted her, he would have come to her, wouldn't he?

She recalled the way he'd looked at her earlier. The passion had been there, but something else intruded.

Not sure of the protocol of lovers, she decided bravado was called for. She got up, boldly went through the double doors of the bathroom and entered his room.

He was sitting up in bed, watching the storm. The sheet was pooled around his hips, and she could see the gleam of his bare chest in the faint glow of the quadrangle lights shining through the windows.

She dashed across the carpet. He had the cover lifted by the time she dived into the bed. He pulled her shivering body into his arms. His heat surrounded her.

"The temperature has dropped with the storm," he murmured, his face buried in her hair. "Did you get cold?"

"Yes." She leaned back against his arm. "I missed you." There was a tense pause, and she thought he wouldn't answer.

"I missed you, too," he said in a low, husky tone. "I couldn't sleep."

"Me, either."

She snuggled against him and laid her thigh between his. They watched the storm and felt the electricity arc between them. When he moved his hand so he could cup her breast, she turned her face to his chest and kissed him everywhere she could reach.

Moving up his throat, she tasted and nibbled and enticed until she reached his chin. He dipped his head, and her mouth met his.

She felt a shudder go through him. Then he gathered her closer, pulling her up until she lay over him. She opened her legs and clasped his hard arousal between her thighs. He thrust his hips against her. With his hands, he showed her how to move.

The kiss deepened as excitement grew, until she could no longer tell the storm without from the one within. Heat collected deep inside her body, and a rhythm was established.

"Let's ride the storm," he whispered. "Take me in."

Trembling, she rose and let herself down over him, taking him into her, welcoming the fullness of his body as they merged.

Their coupling was wild and ecstatic, as restless as the storm that shook the earth outside the windows. His hands raced over her, touching her everywhere and bringing her greater and greater pleasure. He kissed her breasts. She kissed his. Their lips were never still, but roamed at will, seeking always to give more and yet more to each other.

When the last crescendo of lightning flashed through them, she was unable to withhold the cry that rose in her. "I love you."

He held her hips and thrust against her, causing aftershocks of pleasure to jolt through her.

"I love you," she said mindlessly.

She stilled as the pleasure became unbearable. He tensed in her arms. She felt his powerful release pulse through her, giving her more sensation when she was sure she could take no more.

"I love you," she whispered raggedly and collapsed against him, letting his strength take her weight. She was unable to move.

They stayed that way for a long time. At last he turned and laid her on her side. He went to the bathroom and returned with a washcloth. As if she were totally helpless, he sponged the heat from her. When he left her again, she felt the loneliness.

She heard the shower come on, then go off before she drifted into a half sleep. Outside, the rain fell with a monotony of sound, and the thunder rolled into the distance.

Paul returned. She curled up against his side when he lay down beside her. "Dinah," he said.

She squinched her eyes tightly closed. She didn't want to hear any lectures. Perhaps if she pretended to be asleep...

"I never promised you a future," he continued.

"I know." She raised herself to where he was propped against the headboard and leaned against him. He linked his hands around her. "But I still love you."

"For now, maybe, but what about later?"

"What do you mean?"

"It's easy to love someone when life is good, when we have *this.*" He stroked her body. "But what happens when things get rough, when the passion dies down and the everyday pitfalls have to be endured?"

"That depends on us." She sat up and wrapped her arms around her knees. "If you stayed the same person I fell in love with, then I'd still love you. But if you became bitter and angry with life and took it out on me, I'd grow to hate you. You'd do the same with me." She thought for a second. "I think that's the way life is. What we make of it is up to us."

"You certainly lay it on the line."

"I see no reason to skirt the issue." She listened to the rain fill the silence between them.

He didn't say anything, but seemed to be thinking about what she'd said. Dinah stayed quiet. She had no further arguments. This was something he had to work through in his own mind.

"Your story sounds good," he finally said. "I just don't happen to believe it."

Before she could react, he swung out of bed. While she watched, he pulled on his clothes and left.

She returned to her room, defeated by the past, *his* rather than hers. She'd been right to think Paul meant trouble as far as her heart was concerned. Unless she could get him to trust again, hers was going to be broken all over again.

Chapter Twelve

Dinah woke at first light. She sighed wearily. The night had not been refreshing. She wondered what the day would bring.

After a shower, she dressed, then washed and packed all her camping clothes for the return trip to the woods. Looking around the comfortable room, she acknowledged that some people were never lucky enough to find the things in life that they wanted.

She thought she was one of those.

Going into the kitchen, she found coffee in the pot and poured herself a cup. She made toast and ate it at the round table where she'd watched the McPherson family, with envy eating at her soul.

Paul came in, letting in a blast of chilly air. As usual, the storm had brought a jet of cold temperatures with it.

''Good morning,'' she said equably, forcing herself not to stare at him, with all her love shining in her eyes.

He nodded silently and filled a cup with coffee. Turning, he leaned against the counter and studied her for a long minute while he moodily sipped the hot liquid.

Dinah waited. She noted idly that her fingers shook slightly when she picked up her own cup. When she was a hundred years old, Paul could walk into the room and still have an effect on her.

"I've decided to head out this morning," he said abruptly.

"To where?" she said. The salty taste of tears filled her throat. She'd been expecting the news, but that didn't make it any easier to take.

"I need to check out the areas east of the cabin. It'll be too far to come back each night. I'll pitch a tent."

"Okay."

There was a salient pause.

"Okay?" he repeated. "Just like that?"

"What do you want—for me to throw myself on the floor and beg you to stay with me? You have a job to do. I understand that."

He ran his fingers through his hair, looking dumbfounded by her statement. "It's more than that," he said. "I think we need some space from each other...some time to think...."

She raised her head to look him in the eye. "I'm not going to interfere in your life, if that's what you're thinking. No matter how I might feel, I know I have no claim on you, so you don't have to worry—"

"I'm not," he snapped. "Look, you've never known sexual fulfillment before. It's a powerful thing, easy to mistake for other feelings." He gave her a smile, half mocking, half serious. "As strong as it is between us, it's no wonder you're confused."

He'd once been in love, she recalled. He wouldn't confuse lust with love. That's what he was telling her.

"You think I need some time to get my bearings and get over my infatuation for you," she concluded. "After the sensual wonder cools a bit."

"Something like that," he muttered. "Although I wouldn't have stated it quite so cold-bloodedly."

She sensed his displeasure, but didn't understand it. She was trying to be mature about the situation. She'd gone into his arms with her eyes open. She'd asked him to be her lover. The rules had been clear to her from the start.

"I'm trying to be a good sport," she told him with a calm she didn't feel. "Isn't that what you want—a woman who doesn't become hysterical or demanding?"

Paul cursed when she gazed at him with that cool reserve she possessed. There was no subterfuge with this woman. She was all candor and honesty. It disarmed him, threw him off balance...and made him want to hold her...forever.

No. A man was a fool to get caught up in those fantasies. He'd been down that road once, but never again.

Dinah got up and came to him. He watched her warily. She lifted both hands to his face and stroked it gently. He gazed into her dark eyes. Deep inside them, he saw the hot embers of her passion, softly glowing, wanting only his touch to flame into life.

Would she have stood by him? If he'd met her first, would she have stayed with him through that year of pain and uncertainty, no matter what? Would her love have been strong enough to take it?

He'd gotten to the point where he'd hated going under the anesthesia, unconscious and dependent on the skill of the surgeon and the operating team to pull him back to reality, aware that there was nothing to come back to.

Hell, he'd made it. On his own. No one holding his hand. He hadn't needed anyone then. He didn't need anyone now.

"You're grateful for my expertise," he said, keeping his tone light, mocking the despair that suddenly descended on him. He caught her hands and pushed them down to her sides.

"Yes," she agreed. She sighed, then smiled.

It was almost his undoing. For a moment, he entertained the notion that he could be wrong about her. After all, two years ago she'd been highly insulted that he'd thought she was buttering him up for her own benefit. Of course she had been. Women just didn't like to get caught in their little games.

"We'll give it a couple of weeks," he stated, making the decision. "After that, we'll see."

"All right."

He frowned in annoyance. Did she have to be so damned agreeable? "Fine." He stormed out of the house.

Two hours later, he loaded up on supplies from the ranch kitchen, intending to head for the Rogue River, east of the ranch.

Rachel returned from town before he left and charged him with several tasks regarding the eagles she was studying. "The eagles had three eggs when we were up there. They should be hatching soon. Last year, the adults raised two babies, an unusual event." Her golden-brown eyes beamed with pride.

"Why is it so rare?" Dinah asked, forcing her mind to the conversation at hand and away from her thoughts.

"Well," Rachel began, then hesitated. "It depends on the food supply to a certain extent."

"Sometimes the first hatchling pushes the later ones out of the nest," Paul explained. "If food is scarce, one eaglet has a better chance of making it to adulthood than two or three.''

"Survival of the fittest,'' Dinah murmured. She watched Paul check the cinch on the saddle and wondered if mere survival was enough. Life didn't seem like much without love and hope.

Paul gave her a cool smile, his expression unreadable. "Yeah, it's a lesson we should all remember.''

"Every man for himself?'' she questioned, her voice sharper than she'd intended. "That can be a pretty lonely existence.''

He shrugged. "It's peaceful. All that wrestling with the soul can be wearisome.'' He swung up on the gelding.

"By the way, I saw the sheriff in town,'' Rachel told them. "He said they'd intercepted a load of yew bark stored in the old livery stable in town. Can you believe it?''

"Damn, that's pretty bold,'' Paul commented. "Did they find any clues that would lead them to the thieves?''

"No, not a thing.''

He cast a harsh glance at Dinah. "Stay close to the cabin,'' he ordered as if she were a Girl Scout on her first outing. "Don't show yourself if you see any strangers.''

"Right, Oh Great Leader,'' she said.

He gave her a look that would have dropped a charging bull at thirty yards. She returned it without flinching. With a click, he prodded his mount and started off, leading the pack animal.

Rachel watched him for a minute, then smiled sympathetically at Dinah. "I won't ask what that was all about. However, I must warn you—all the McPherson men have a stubborn streak a mile wide. It can be very frustrating to deal with.''

"I've noticed,'' Dinah admitted ruefully.

She and Rachel walked toward the ranch house.

"There's a loneliness in Paul," Rachel mused aloud. "I sense it sometimes when he holds Kelly. He's good with children. He'd make a wonderful father."

Dinah remembered seeing that strange trace of vulnerability in Paul while at the ranch. What do you know of my life, my hopes, my dreams? he'd demanded of her.

"The McPherson men can be maddening, but they're totally loyal to those they love," Rachel continued.

"Paul was hurt once." Dinah stopped on the deck and looked across the pasture at the horse and rider fading into the distance.

"I suspected as much. Did he tell you about it?"

"Yes. She left him when his face got smashed in a car wreck."

"That could warp a person's viewpoint," Rachel concluded sympathetically. "You love him, don't you?"

"I . . . I think so."

"Think?" Rachel sounded disappointed.

"I do," Dinah said.

"Good." Rachel laid a hand on Dinah's arm. "It's hard to get close to a McPherson. Paul needs you. Make him trust again."

Dinah hesitated. "I'll try," she said. She was probably setting herself up for a sharp letdown. Was it worth the pain? She'd find out . . . the hard way.

She smiled ruefully. The hard way was her usual mode of operation in life, it seemed.

She borrowed a truck and went into town for food and personal supplies. She bought a couple of aluminum plates and several cans of soup to replace those she and Paul had used.

"Well, howdy, ma'am," a masculine voice broke into her musing.

She looked up into a vaguely familiar face. A name came to her—an enemy of the McPhersons. "Oh, Mr. Cawe, isn't it?"

He was obviously pleased that she'd remembered him. She kept her smile deliberately cool, wondering if this man had been the one at the cabin that night.

She pondered what would have happened if Paul hadn't shown up—Sir Galahad to the rescue—in the nick of time. It only needed the villain to set fire to the cabin with her trapped inside to be a genuine, old-time melodrama of the Pearl Pureheart variety.

"Would you like a bite of lunch?" he invited.

She shook her head. At the narrowing of his eyes, she quickly explained. "I've got to get back. I'll be leaving to-day—" She stopped abruptly.

"Going back into the woods?" he asked.

A frisson of unease passed through her. What did this man know of her activities?

At her hesitation, he added, "Friend of mine in the forest service said you were studying the old-growth in these parts, also the yew trees. Is it true there's something in the bark that the drug companies are testing on cancer?"

Dinah studied his face, but could find nothing there other than polite interest. She nodded. It was hardly a secret.

"Who'd have thought it?" he marveled. "The loggers thought they were trash trees, the wood never good for anything but trinket boxes. Now they're a cure for cancer. Who'd have thought it?"

"Hardly a cure," she pointed out, not liking his awed manner. It didn't ring true. "Taxol is an experimental drug. It may come to nothing in the end or have very limited use."

He nodded his head several times as if gravely thinking the possibilities over.

"Well, I need to go." She pushed her basket past him and hurried toward the checkout counter, relieved to be rid of him.

On the way to the ranch, she thought about her reaction. She wondered if she disliked Cawe because he disliked the McPhersons.

Any enemy of my friends is an enemy of mine? she questioned. That wasn't necessarily true. Besides, Paul didn't think of her as a friend. He thought she was either lost in passion or playing games, luring him with the attraction between them for her own self-serving purposes.

Once, she realized, she'd been as wary as he was. It was knowing him that had opened her eyes. She'd learned to trust him, then to love him. He'd have to do the same.

Dinah returned to the cabin in the woods. She mapped the locations of the yew trees she was studying. Using the methods learned from working with cork oaks, she studied the stripped sections caused by thieves over the past three years. Trees with fifty percent or less of their bark removed were recovering, she discovered, providing their growth layer wasn't girdled.

She also went about her tasks with the old-growth study. In the early morning and evening, she listened and followed the trail of a pair of spotted owls. She found their nest at the end of the week, nestled in an old tree ten feet above the ground.

They were raising two fuzzy babies that were comical to look at. Watching the female poke food down the open beaks, she smiled.

Everywhere she roamed in the forest, she saw parents tending their young. It was the season. The longing inside her swelled like a tender new bud, ready to bloom but needing the nourishing rains of Paul's love to open.

She thought of Paul's cousins and their families, of Sita and Hank starting a life together. She thought of the farm in Tennessee, of her and Paul working together.

Mating. Raising children. Life begetting life.

It was the natural order of things.

Paul would make a wonderful husband and father. He wasn't a shallow person strictly out for his own pleasure. If she'd learned nothing else from knowing Paul, she knew she'd never again pass a quick judgment on a person because of superficial qualities.

He'd taught her more than that, much more. He'd taught her to trust again. She wanted to do the same for him.

She put the binoculars Rachel had loaned her into her knapsack, slung it on her back and returned to the cabin. Two horses grazed in the clearing beside her mount.

Happiness erupted in her. She broke into a run. Before she reached the door, two cowboys came around the side of the building. They stopped when they saw her. She stopped, too. Paul wasn't one of them.

"We were wondering where you were," Hank said with a friendly smile. He and the other man tipped their hats to her.

"Hello," she said, hiding the crushing disappointment. She wasn't going to mourn Paul. "You're just in time for supper. I left a beef stew out this morning."

She gestured toward the pan of stew. It had cooked in a solar oven in the sun all day. Hank grabbed the cooker and carried it inside for her. When she opened it, the mouth-watering aroma of stew filled the cabin. It appeared to be done.

After setting out the aluminum plates and a bowl, she dished up the meal and added a box of crackers. She sat on her parka and insisted they take the two chairs Paul had made from stumps and the barrels.

"What are you doing up here?" she asked.

"Checking the amount of water in the new creek, for one thing," Hank said. "Looking the cattle over for pink eye and such, for another. Seeing about you, for the third."

A chill crept up her neck. She sensed danger the way a wild creature did, like a faint scent on the air. "I'm fine," she told him. "You're welcome to stay here as long as you're in the area." She nodded toward the bunk beds.

"We got a camp just over the saddle." Hank tilted his head toward the double-crested hill where the creek had been diverted. "Paul rode by yesterday. He said there's been more tree rustling over the main ridge east of here."

She got out her maps. "Which sections did they strip?" she asked, unfolding the topography drawings.

The men pointed out the areas. "Paul had to go in for supplies," Hank told her. "He's going to talk to the sheriff and the forest service people about deputizing some of us."

The men grinned. They liked the idea of being included on the hunt for the thieves. Paul wouldn't hesitate to leap into a fray with the rustlers, either. The thought worried her.

Shortly after that, the ranch hands rode off to their camp. They had a small herd of cows to be treated for various ailments.

She was lonely when they left. While she listened to the hoofbeats die away, a chill danced over her skin. Paul was working alone in the woods. Rustlers were out there. Men with guns. She wished he were at the cabin. It seemed safer...for him, not for her. She sighed. It was too late for her. She was hopelessly in love with him. The past week had proven that beyond a doubt.

The following Friday, Hank came over again. After the first leap of her heart, she saw who it was and greeted him with a smile. He had a note from her supervisor.

She was to go to the ranch and wait for Chris to pick her up. They needed help at Crater Lake with the pine borers again. The heavy April rains hadn't been enough to stop the pests. The infestation was worse.

"Slash-and-burn time," she said.

Hank nodded. "Just what we need, a forest fire."

She closed the cabin, saddled her horse and headed for the ranch the next morning. She arrived at one. Her ride was already there, having coffee and pie while he and Rachel chatted.

Rachel wrinkled her nose in disappointment at the departure, then gave Dinah a hug when it was time to go. "Come back soon. I know a rogue who needs taming in the worst way."

"Worst for him or me?" Dinah quipped, returning the farewell.

"Good question." A worried frown settled on Rachel's face. "Paul has kept himself closed off for a long time. Perhaps his heart can't be reached."

Dinah shrugged as if accepting her fate. She ignored the fear in her heart. "It'll work out." She sounded surer than she felt. She turned to Chris. "Ready?"

They fought the borers at Crater Lake with a combination of logging and burning. June ended. She watched a fireworks display over the lake on the Fourth of July. A few days after that, tired but filled with anticipation, she returned to the ranch.

"Thanks," she said to Chris when he stopped the truck. She grabbed her duffel and walked toward the house. It seemed both familiar and strange after the weeks away. Although there was a light in the window, she knew no one was home. Rachel and her family had gone to visit her brother for a week.

Paul was in the room when she opened the door and went inside. "Hello, Dinah," he said in his husky, attractive baritone.

She was suddenly furious with him. He'd ridden off and left her alone for days. He'd caused her hours of worry about his safety with the rustlers over in his area. Now he greeted her as casually as an acquaintance on the street.

It hurt, but she kept her smile intact. As far as affairs went, theirs must have been one of the shortest on record. "Hi," she said, just as coolly in control.

She didn't fool him. "What's wrong? Aren't you glad to see me?" He tilted his head slightly and gave her a challenging stare. They were back to square one as if the moments at the cabin had never occurred.

"Not particularly."

He ambled over to her and laid a finger on the pulse in her neck. "Liar," he said softly.

She brushed his hand aside and walked toward the hall. She wanted a hot shower, fresh clothes and food that hadn't been dried, powdered and reconstituted. She *didn't* want the confrontation he seemed to be angling for.

Her lips tingled. She wanted his kiss, she realized. She wanted him to sweep her off her feet and make mad love to her until they couldn't stand up. She wanted him to never let her go.

She wasn't going to get that wish.

"Me and the boys are going to mosey into town for dinner and a little fun. Care to join us?"

The invitation was a dare. Pride came to her rescue. She'd known what to expect, she told herself. She'd known, so she had no right to complain about his attitude. She tried to think of practical matters.

If everyone was going to town, she'd have to cook a meal and eat alone. The prospect didn't appeal to her. If she went into town today rather than tomorrow, she could stock up, eat, then come back and turn in early. "What time?"

"Around five."

"Fine. I'll rest till then." She went to her room and lay down, her eyes burning with anger and frustration.

A knock on her door woke her sometime later. She glanced at the clock. Four-thirty. "Yes?"

"We'll be leaving soon," Paul called through.

"Okay."

She rose and looked over the spare outfits she'd left in the closet. The wool suit was too warm, the floral skirt seemed dressier than she wanted. She settled on clean jeans and a rib-knit turtleneck with a fitted vest over it.

A bandanna around her neck added a saucy touch. Good enough. Grabbing her wool jacket in case the temperature dropped after sundown, she left.

Paul was waiting for her when she went into the kitchen. "I'll drive," he said.

"Is there a vehicle I can use? I want to pick up some things at the grocery, eat, then call it a night."

"I'll bring you back. It's no trouble," he added.

She allowed the protest to fade into a frown. He followed her out of the house. Once in the truck, she stole a glance at him and found him watching her, his gaze fathoms deep and unreadable.

He put the truck in gear and drove off without a word.

She heaved a deep breath after they left and realized she was on emotionally shaky ground. She was still tired from a hard month of tough decisions, too little sleep and too much worry.

"What's the matter?" he asked after a few miles of silence. "Don't you love me anymore?"

Her heart, which she'd managed to keep under control, broke free. It rattled like loose rails under a heavy train. "I don't know," she said slowly. "I guess that's up to you."

Looking straight at him, she didn't miss the start of surprise on his handsome face at her calm retort... nor the sudden vulnerable pain that tightened his mouth for a second before he smiled.

"Don't you feel it's your duty to save me from myself?" he inquired.

"No." He was in one of his moods, she decided ... the one that signaled danger loud and clear.

"What kind of love is that? Sounds like the fair-weather variety to me." He lifted one eyebrow in that devilishly attractive way he had, a definite challenge in the act.

"Maybe," she responded softly, refusing to be drawn into an argument. He glanced away first.

For the rest of the journey, he mulled over his own thoughts without sharing them. When they arrived in town, she hopped out and went to the store. He followed and helped carry her packages to the truck when she finished. For a second, after putting the bags in the back, they looked at each other.

A shimmer of emotion skipped along her sensitive nerves. He seemed to be looking for something. She didn't know what.

"Come on," he said. His voice was deeper, the way it became when they made love.

Warnings flashed along her nerves. The two of them would be alone in the ranch house. Maybe they could sort it all out then, this storm that was brewing between them.

They went to the restaurant. Hank was there, waiting for Sita to finish up. He stood and motioned for them to join him.

Dinah saw the quiet happiness in his eyes. She looked away, an ache tearing through her.

"Well, the married man," Paul said. "Guess you won't be writing any more of those caterwauling love songs you used to sing in the bunkhouse, huh?"

"Paul," Dinah said in annoyance as Hank's ears turned pink.

"Did I say something wrong?" he declaimed, pressing a hand to his heart as if stricken.

"No," Hank said. "You're right. I don't have any more sad songs in me. Now I'm writing about how the love of a good woman fills a man's life." He grinned. "You ought to try it sometime."

Darkness flickered in Paul's eyes. For a long minute, he looked at Dinah without speaking. "Maybe you're right," he said to Hank, but watching her. "What do you think?"

She shrugged, feeling heat creep into her face. She'd known she was asking for trouble, getting involved with Paul. It might be worse than she'd ever dreamed.

Perhaps she'd awakened a beast in him that was better left sleeping, she decided. Perhaps in telling him she loved him, she had reminded him of his past and opened a scar that was too deep to heal. He might never give his trust a second time.

She wished she'd been his first love. She'd never have failed him. She'd have stood by him when he needed her. He'd do the same for the woman he loved.

That woman wasn't her though. If he was going to fall in love with her, she thought it would have happened by now. He wouldn't have been able to prevent it. Love didn't always beget love.

Hank excused himself, went to the counter and spoke to his wife. They talked for a few minutes. Dinah thought they looked very happy and very in love. She looked away.

Paul laid a hand on her arm. "Sorry," he said. "For mouthing off earlier."

She looked at him in surprise. "It's okay."

"Dinah, the kindhearted," he mocked, but gently.

"You're in a strange mood," she observed.

"Yeah," he said. "I am." He stared deeply into her eyes. "Was the past month as lonely for you as it was for me?"

Her heart skipped painfully. "Yes."

"I didn't think you'd admit it," he murmured. "But you've never been one to mince words."

"No, I don't. Leave off the hard-edged lover act tonight, Paul. I don't feel like sparring with you."

He tilted his head slightly and studied her. "You're tired," he concluded. "A hard month?"

She nodded, near tears for no good reason. Loving a man was hard on the nerves as well as the heart.

Hank returned, and they ordered their meal. When they finished, the music started in the saloon part of the building. The cowboys from the ranch trooped over. Dinah found herself going along with them. A man at the bar grinned at her.

She nodded without smiling.

"Friend of yours?" Paul asked.

"No. I don't like him. He gives me the creeps when he looks at me, like he's . . . undressing me."

Paul put an arm around her waist and pulled her into his arms for the first dance. "Shall I punch him out?"

"No!"

"I would. For you." He nuzzled his nose in her hair. "You always smell good. Like a forest or a meadow." He touched her ear. "I want you."

Her carefully constructed poise drained right away. "Paul." She meant it as a protest or a reprimand. It came out breathless.

"I can't stop thinking about you...about us." He gave an annoyed chuckle, then sighed. "Is that love, Dinah?"

Her heart stopped, literally stopped. "I think only you can decide that."

His gaze probed hers in the dim light of the saloon. The music weaved around them, casting its spell. A love song, she realized, and knew she would always think of it as *theirs*.

When the song ended, he held on to her hand. "Are you ready to leave?"

She nodded.

The drive to the ranch was made in near silence and filled with tension. It reminded her of the one in April, when they had attended the birthday party. April. Three months ago. A blink in the span of a life. A lifetime for the heart.

Chapter Thirteen

After a pleasant Sunday with all the McPhersons, who were at the ranch when she and Paul arrived there on Saturday night, Dinah headed back for the cabin in the woods bright and early on Monday.

Paul hadn't come to her either night. He'd withdrawn again, but she'd felt his gaze on her several times. He seemed to be thinking deep, dark thoughts, but he didn't share them with her.

So be it.

Hank hailed her when she turned at the fork of the trail toward the cabin. He rode down a ridge and joined her. At the cabin, he helped her unload her supplies, ate lunch, then left with her mount and packhorse trailing behind. He'd take them to graze with the other horses and bring them back in two weeks.

"But I'll see you every other day or so," he assured her.

"Fine." She realized he had been told to keep an eye on her and didn't protest. After she waved him off, she gathered her notebook, a topography map and the binoculars, then went to work.

One day passed, then another and another. She worked quietly and efficiently, as was her bent. In the solitude of the woods, she found a measure of peace.

While she performed her duties, she also had a sense of waiting. Premonitions filled each day. She greeted each dawn with a shimmer of expectancy, strong and certain.

On Thursday, she hiked to the creek in the warmest part of the day and took a dip, then washed her hair. Shivering, she dried and dressed and hurried back toward the cabin. A noise, sort of like a groan, stopped her before she emerged from the trees.

The thieves?

Dinah stepped behind a tree and waited, every sense acutely alert for danger. After several minutes, she ducked and peered from under a concealing branch. The wind stroked across her face, making her shiver. A movement caught her eye.

A long, powerful form glided through the trees and onto a rocky promontory above her, well upwind of her position. Her mouth dropped open in surprise. Then she smiled.

It was the cougar. In her mouth, she carried a tawny cub not more than three weeks old. She crouched, then disappeared into the rocks.

Dinah realized the mother cat must be moving her brood from the original den, a precaution from predators who might catch the scent of the young if they stayed in one place too long.

The big cat reappeared. The cub came out behind her. She carried it out of sight once more. When she returned, the cub stayed behind. The cougar tested the air, then trotted off into the woods above Dinah's hiding spot.

After another few minutes, Dinah quietly left the area and followed the edge of the woods to the cabin rather than cutting across the clearing.

After stoking up the fire, she put on a can of soup to heat. Keeping an eye on her supper, she dried her hair before the open door of the stove, then ate the soup and crackers.

She listened to the sounds of the night wind after that and wondered what Paul was doing. Seeing the cougar with her cub reminded Dinah that she might never have a child of her own. A dark-headed little boy with mischief in his blue eyes and love in his heart, she fantasized.

She looked at the dark window. The wind moaned around the eaves of the cabin. Most families were snug in their houses by now in the towns and on the farms. She sat on the stump of a chair and sipped a cup of instant cocoa. She'd never felt so alone.

At ten, she brushed her teeth, banked the fire and went to bed. Just before she went to sleep, she heard the snarl of the big cat out in the clearing. Her eyes snapped open.

There was no further noise. She wondered what had disturbed the mother cat. The big male? A bear? A person? It was a long time before she went to sleep.

Just before dawn, Dinah woke to the wake-up call of a raucous jaybird. She stoked the fire, dressed and opened the door. The cool air chilled her as she started to the latrine she'd made downslope of the cabin. Just as she stepped down, she saw the lioness dash across the edge of the little meadow and leap into the trees as if eager for a good run.

When Dinah returned, she quickly ate and headed out to observe the spotted owls. Later, she slipped into a blind near the pool that wound around the side of the saddle and counted the birds and small animals that came to drink. It was almost noon when she returned to the cabin.

After sharing a sandwich with the jaybird, which now thought he was party to the daily picnic, she sat in the shade and read a novel. Finally, she went to sleep.

A drop of rain slid warmly across her cheek.

She brushed it away.

Another hit the other cheek.

She opened her eyes. Four golden eyes stared back at her. When she sat up, the cubs dashed back a few paces in that joyful clumsiness of the very young, then sat down and watched her. When she didn't move, they stalked her, then leaped into her lap, tumbling over each other in a tawny heap.

Dinah sat very still. She quickly glanced around, but saw no signs of the mother cat, charging out to protect her little ones. The kittens kneaded her thighs, then began to purr.

Slowly, Dinah reached out and stroked the cubs' heads. They stopped their play and butted their heads against her hands. A tiny purr erupted from each of them.

"Oh, you lovely babies," she whispered and caressed them with longing eating at her heart.

A family, she thought. She'd like that. She'd like that very much. And there was only one man she wanted to share it with.

Paul would make a wonderful father.

Dinah decided to take Saturday off. She bathed in the creek at noon and ate a picnic lunch on a rock in the clearing by the cabin while her hair dried in the sun. Later she brushed the waves smooth and flipped the ends under.

The kittens, as she termed them to herself, joined her. When the mother cat was out hunting, they ventured freely into the clearing and came to her if she was there.

The mother cat had never caught them at it, or else she'd never made her presence known if she'd returned while the three of them played in the grass. The day before Dinah had seen the big cat nursing the little ones outside the new den. She'd carefully stayed away from the area.

With their tiny claws, the babies pulled themselves up on her lap, then made little growly noises as they tried to climb her shirt. She laughed and petted them, grimacing when their claws kneaded through the material into her skin.

That was where she was when Paul rode out of the trees into the sun. She heard the hoofbeats, then he came into sight over the saddle. He stopped the brown gelding at the edge of the woods and sat there, watching her and the cougar cubs.

The bright sun rays touched him with gold. He removed his hat and wiped the sweat from his forehead with a shirt-sleeve. After replacing the Stetson, he swung down, removed the saddle and bridle, then hobbled the horse and left it grazing.

He came over. "I'd like to have you painted like this," he said in a voice she'd never heard from him, utterly surprising her. "With the sun on your hair and the cubs in your lap. With the look of dreams in your eyes."

She couldn't speak.

Sometimes moments happen—those rare, perfect ones that catch a person unaware and, for that brief instant, gladden the human heart—this was one of those. She'd remember it always.

"How long have you had company?" he asked, gesturing toward the cubs who chewed on her blouse, then groomed their fur.

"I saw the mother bring them to a new den up in the rocks above the meadow on Thursday." She pointed up the hill near where the horse grazed. "I still can't get over it."

"Cats usually move their young after a couple of weeks," he mused. "She remembers being safe here."

"When you took care of her," Dinah murmured. The night they'd made love for the first time. She saw his eyes darken and knew he remembered, too.

Paul gestured behind him. "I've been tracking the bark rustlers again. They've been working their way over the ridge to this side. I wonder if it disturbed the mother to have them in the woods near the old den."

"Do you think she knows the ones who shot her?"

Paul turned from surveying the land east of them. "Yeah, she knows. She'll remember their scent for a long, long time."

"Did the thieves get more bark?"

"No, I think I scared them off. They took off for their truck when they stumbled upon my camp."

Alarmed, she asked, "Did you see them? Did they see you?"

"No to both questions. I was off taking a bath." He looked at her, his gaze so intense it caused a frisson to tremble over her. "I thought I'd ride over and warn you about keeping a sharp eye out for the men. It appears there are three of them. If they saw you…" He frowned. "They shot a deputy over near Elmer's ranch two days ago."

Her heart went to her throat. "Fatally?"

"A flesh wound. They're armed and dangerous. I'll be working over this way for a while."

"I see." Her mind scrambled through endless possibilities and came up with none. She hesitated. "Will you be staying for supper?" She sounded like a society hostess.

"If you have enough."

She laughed. "Hank and the boys keep me well supplied. I think a cowboy's favorite foods are cheese, chips and cookies."

Paul groaned. "That's what they've been bringing me. I'd hoped you have something different."

"Beef stew," she assured him. "Started on the stove and finished in the solar oven. It works fine. Have you used one?"

She realized she was chattering. When she rose, the cubs tugged at her shoelaces, then stopped, listened intently and dashed off up the slope and disappeared into the rocks that tumbled from the ledge below the saddle.

"That's too close to the trail," he said with a frown. "They should be over farther in the national forest land."

"Maybe she'll move them again," Dinah suggested. She wondered what he meant when he said he'd be working over this way.

When he turned back to her, there was a question in his eyes. She wasn't sure what he was asking. "You're invited to supper," she said, feeling awkward, like an untried youth.

"And?"

She waited.

"I need a place for the night." His expression was closed, but she thought she saw desire in his eyes.

She tilted her head. "Is our affair back on?"

He spread his hands, his eyes wary. "It's up to you. You'll have to say no if you don't want me."

The tension between them zoomed to the boiling point. Dinah knew she wasn't going to refuse, but it was hard to say yes right out loud, too.

She rubbed her arm where one of the kittens had licked her. Her skin felt very sensitive there. The cub's tongue had reminded her of Paul's stubble and the way it had felt at dawn against her fingertips and her lips.

"Dinah?"

For an instant, she observed uncertainty flicker over his face. Sometimes, it seemed, men as handsome as Greek gods could also be very human.

"I want you to stay," she responded quietly.

She heard him exhale suddenly, as if relieved. A warm feeling invaded her. Sometimes handsome men could even be vulnerable, she thought with a tender smile. She started for the cabin.

He caught her hand and held it tightly in his. "If you speak to me like that again, we'll never get to supper," he warned.

She smiled up at him, awash in happiness.

The sun was up when Dinah woke. Paul lay beside her on the narrow bunk bed, his arm across her waist, his leg nestled between her thighs. She sighed dreamily, remembering the night.

Ah, his touch...gentle, caressing...his hands gliding over her, tracing her eyebrows, her nose, her mouth and chin ... finding her breasts ... so gentle, so caressing ... bringing her fire and ecstasy, all mixed up ... oh, yes, his wonderful touch ...

His hand slid over her rib cage and cupped her breast. She was startled.

"Easy," he murmured.

Ah, his voice... soothing, encouraging... he'd told her how beautiful she was, how much she pleased him with her response...

He climbed out of bed, careful to disturb the covers as little as possible, and added kindling to the embers in the stove. He put on coffee and brought each of them a bowl of cereal. They ate in bed, curled side by side under the covers like two children.

After taking care of the morning ritual of washing and dressing, they ended up back in bed.

"Ready to get up?" he asked an hour or so later.

No. She wanted the idyll to continue forever. "I suppose."

They dressed again. It took a long time. Paul had to kiss each part of her before it was covered with cotton and denim. They sat in the sun while the heat warmed the meadow. By noon, the day would be hot, but now was perfect, she thought.

The cubs came and played in the grass. The big cat was gone longer and longer on her hunts, it appeared.

"I'm worried about the cubs," she told Paul, dragging a straw over the ground while the babies stalked it.

"About them getting too used to people?"

She was no longer surprised at his insight. "Yes." She mused on the problem. "Doesn't the mother cat smell my scent on them?"

"Yes, but she knows you're safe." He broke off a dry stem of grass and brushed it across her forearm. "I've been thinking about the cubs, too. There's a natural cave not too far from here. What if we move them there?"

"Will the mother let us?"

"I think so. She won't attack you, else she would have already. She's been watching us for more than an hour from the ridge."

Dinah looked up, startled. Sure enough, the tawny lioness was lying on a flat boulder, her gaze on the humans below.

"When the cubs come again, we'll carry them to the cave and see if the mother cat will follow without getting upset."

"If she gets upset, what will she do?"

Paul laughed, not with his old cynical humor, but with a merry chuckle. "Skin us alive, I suspect."

"Then there's no reason to hesitate, is there?" Dinah asked with a droll grimace. Then she, too, laughed. With Paul, life would always be an adventure.

That afternoon, they got the chance to try their strategy. She and Paul headed for a rocky ridge through the woods to the east of them. They each carried a cub tucked against their sides. The cubs looked around with interest. The mother cat didn't appear and leap upon them, but once, Dinah thought she heard a low growl in the trees behind them. The hair rose on her neck.

A tumbled layer of limestone thrust upward near the bluff where the ridge dropped to the next valley. Paul showed Dinah a small opening that had formed during the upheaval. He placed one cub inside, then the other.

"Come on," he whispered.

They backed away while the cubs sniffed the place out. Going back up the ridge, they hid among the pine trees. After ten minutes, the cougar walked slowly out of a group of trees and onto the rocks, her tail twitching, her ears flattened. The kittens yelped in greeting. After another long minute, the lioness bounded across the rocks and went into the cave.

"Come on," Paul said. "She's nervous about something."

They hurried back to the cabin a quarter mile away.

"I'll miss them," Dinah said, glancing back over her shoulder, but unable to see the little family. Her eyes burned with tears. She hurried on before Paul could notice.

He was quiet when they reached the cabin. He stayed outside when she went in to prepare a snack. When she brought cookies and filtered spring water to him and placed it between them on the grass, he studied her without speaking. She sat opposite him in the shade.

She sensed turmoil in him. He was probably afraid of getting too deeply involved. Maybe he thought she was waiting for a weak moment to ask him some great favor. A sigh escaped her.

"What is it?" he asked.

"Me," she said honestly. "You. Us."

He looked grim. "I know." He was silent for another long minute.

"The kittens," she murmured. She shouldn't have been surprised, but she was when he knew exactly what she meant.

"Are you thinking of a family, Dinah?"

Taking a deep breath, she admitted it. "Yes."

His face hardened. "Do you see me in this scenario?"

"I've watched you with Rachel's little boy," she hedged. "I've seen your eyes when we're with your cousins. I think you want a family, too."

He muttered a curse.

She continued softly, trying to make him see himself as she did. "You think women walk out when life isn't all laughter and sunshine, but you could be wrong. Maybe a woman exists who loves you enough to stick through anything."

"Such as yourself?" He watched her without blinking.

"Yes," she said, knowing there was a truth she had to face. "But it doesn't seem to be in the cards."

Once, she'd thought if you loved a person, it meant they loved you, too. That was the assumption of a child. She'd learned differently. Things didn't always work out. Life wasn't always fair, or even kind. And Paul didn't love her.

"We share a great passion, that's all," she ended and hoped he didn't hear the sadness singing through her like a mournful wind through the pines.

It came to her that she'd loved him since they'd first met. Paul, with his summer-warm blue eyes that warmed her clear through. Paul, with his teasing, devil-may-care ways that confused and infuriated her. Paul, with his heart locked carefully out of harm's way.

"And you're willing to settle for that?" he asked on a curious note. His voice had gone deeper, quieter. She thought she heard sorrow in it, perhaps other emotions, too.

"For now." She met his gaze levelly. If it was all she'd ever have of him, she'd take it.

There followed a tense silence. "For now," he repeated. His face hardened. "When this job is over, you'll have no trouble finding someone else."

She was shocked to her soul. Could he really contemplate someone else in her arms? If he could, then there really was no hope for them. She chose her answer carefully. "Perhaps someday. I have you to thank for teaching me how wonderful it can be between a woman and a man. It's...more than I'd ever dreamed."

As if she'd ever want anyone but him. Paul was her one true love. There would be no other.

"So," he concluded grimly, "having gotten what you want from me, you'll be ready to move on."

She didn't understand what he wanted from her. "Well..." she began, but was unable to speak past the pain in her heart.

His face looked as if it were carved from stone. He stood. "School is over. You graduated with honors. *Summa cum laude,* in fact—highest honors. You should be proud."

While she sat there, stunned, he saddled up and rode off. She stared at his back as he disappeared, then looked at their half-eaten snack. She would never, ever understand him, not in a million years. But she'd love him forever.

Dinah watched the mountain lion and her cubs from a discreet distance. They seemed content in their new den, having had all week to settle in. It was Friday. Tomorrow she would be going to the ranch, then to the forest service office in Butte Falls to turn in her reports on the various projects in the area.

She'd discovered that spotted owls did cross logged areas to hunt in other sections of the forest, but there was a limit to how far they'd go, and no animals seemed to want to live in the open areas. She'd marked the zones on a map.

The richness of life in the old sections was indisputably greater than in the clear-cut zones, but things improved after a few years of regrowth in the cut-over areas. She would explain all that in detail. By the end of the month, her study would be finished. She would return to California . . . older and far wiser.

Quietly withdrawing into the trees, she hiked through the thick pine needles, down the ridge and into an old-growth section where the yew trees grew. These trees, needed for cancer research, had to be protected. They died without the covering branches of taller trees to shelter them. That was a fact.

When she reached the small grove, she found all her careful work destroyed. The bark strippers had been at it again, girdling the trees, ripping off bark without a care to her color-coded marks and posted notices on the research. Much of the bark still lay on the ground. Pretty lousy thieves, she concluded.

While she checked to see if any of her handiwork had survived, she heard a sound behind her. She turned, expecting to find Paul.

Instead, she saw a smile she'd rather forget.

"Well, look who we have here," Cawe said, stepping from behind a large pine. Two men were with him. They carried burlap bags. Cawe had a handgun pushed into his waistband.

She looked from the bark to the bags. They were back for a second load, she realized. She'd stumbled right into the middle of their operation. Lucky her.

Could she bluff her way out of this one?

"Stripping bark is illegal," she said calmly, as if they might not know. "You men could be in serious trouble."

"Is that a fact?" one of the men said. He had a thin face with weasel eyes set close together.

The other man with Cawe and the weasely one had a crooked nose, probably broken in more than one fight during his misspent youth. He wasn't more than twenty-one or two, she guessed.

"Yes," she said gravely. "I'd advise you to leave before my partner arrives. He's an enforcement officer."

She saw by Cawe's face he knew an enforcement officer carried a gun and was trained to use it. He gave her a skeptical look. He wasn't impressed by her story. His expression changed while he assessed her. A cruel smile settled on his mouth.

"We saw the McPherson cousin's horse up at your cabin late yesterday. Seems he stayed all night."

Dinah remembered the man hated the McPhersons. Furthermore, he saw her as a means of revenge. Her courage wavered a bit.

She gave him a haughty stare. "Some of the Sky Eagle and Triple R hands have stayed at the cabin. The McPhersons have been very cooperative with the National Forest Service in helping with our studies here." She emphasized national to remind the crooks that they were dealing with the U.S. Government.

"Come on," the weasely one said. "Let's get the rest of the stuff and get out of here. I got a buyer waiting."

A buyer! It would be a boon to find the renegade outfit who was buying the bark. Maybe she could track them and find out...

"What're we going to do with her?" the young man with the broken nose asked. His hands twisted nervously on the burlap.

Cawe looked her over again. She didn't like his expression. "We'll take her with us," he said.

"What the hell for?" the weasel snapped. He spat into a pile of dried pine needles.

"In case the enforcement officer shows up and tries to cause us some grief. We'll have a bargaining chip."

The weasel shrugged as if he didn't care. The younger man looked worried. He might not want to hurt her, but he was too weak to stand up to Cawe. The weasel was indifferent to her fate.

She'd have to talk her way out of this with Cawe, and he already hated her for her association with the McPhersons. While he watched her, the other two men loaded up their bags with yew bark.

"This way," Cawe said, pointing toward the old logging road about a mile from where they were.

When Dinah hesitated, he grinned. A shiver went down her. *Show no fear.* Cawe had a sadistic personality. He would love to hear her beg. She stood her ground.

"Bark-stripping is a minor crime. Kidnapping is a fel-, ony. A criminal record hangs over you forever," she warned, hoping the others would insist on leaving her in the interest of self-preservation if nothing else.

The younger man shifted from foot to foot. "Look," he said, "maybe we'd better leave her."

"Who asked you?" Cawe snapped. His glance challenged the younger man, who subsided at once. He fixed a feral gaze on her. His leer made her skin crawl.

With a quick move, Cawe grabbed her arm and twisted it behind her, forcing her hand toward her neck so she had to bend forward to ease the pain of stretched muscles and tendons.

He bent over her. "Better be nice to me, and maybe I'll be nice to you later," he advised in a low, guttural growl near her ear. He moved back and let her straighten, his grin once more in place. "Maybe," he repeated.

Dinah didn't need a picture to know what he meant. The ultimate revenge of one male on another—to take his enemy's woman. Armies had been doing it for thousands of years.

"How far civilization has come since the time of the caveman," she said aloud, facing Cawe with a grim bravado.

He grinned and gave her a push toward the trees. "Jeb, you lead. The lady and I will follow. You keep on eye on the rear," he told the boy, making it clear who was boss.

Dinah had no choice. She walked as slowly as she dared while her thoughts flew in all directions. No brilliant plan of escape came to her. Unless . . .

Instead of heading straight for the trail to the old logging road, the weasely faced one, Jeb, took another route through the woods, one she wasn't familiar with. She worried about becoming lost if she did manage to escape.

They rested at intervals. The bark sacks were heavy. At one point, Dinah realized they were below the bluff where she and Paul had relocated the cougar den. She hoped the female didn't show up. Cawe would shoot the big cat if he got a chance.

"Let's go. It's getting late," she said as if afraid of the dark. She hiked off, not looking back. The thieves hurried to catch up with her. Jeb took the lead and headed over the crest and down toward the logging road.

Maybe after dark, she could slip away into the woods . . . no, Cawe was staying too close.

"I gotta rest," the weasel called out.

They stopped. The man sat on a fallen tree and removed his shoe and shook it out. She settled on a rock and breathed deeply of the pine-scented air.

"Keep an eye on her," Cawe said to the younger man. He and the weasel drew off to one side. They held a whispered conference. At one point, she heard the weasel say, " . . . get rid of the girl. We can't afford witnesses."

She realized they meant to kill her.

Paul stood in the open doorway of the cabin. Dinah wasn't in. She'd been gone earlier when he'd stopped by. He felt uneasy about her. The gelding was in the clearing, hobbled and munching on the sparse grass in the shade.

Dinah planned on starting for the ranch in the morning, the cowhands had told him when they met up on the southern trail earlier. They'd been returning to their camp after having had breakfast with her and delivering her mount for the trip out.

He left his horse munching grass and walked up the trail. Near the bluff, he veered to the left and checked on the den. The cubs were there, but the big cat was away. Through the trees, he caught a flash of color in the dip between the hills.

That must be Dinah, going over to check the yew trees. Since he'd come this far, he may as well catch up with her and tag along, he decided, ignoring the heavy beat of desire that coursed through him at the thought of seeing her.

He frowned. It was getting harder and harder to stay away from her. When she left for good . . . He dropped the thought.

A sigh escaped him. His life loomed before him—bleak and . . . okay, he admitted it . . . lonely. So what? He'd been lonely before. He turned to the problem at hand—how to get off the bluff.

The ridge along the cliff face divided into two narrow ledges, one going up, the other down. The down side was navigable, provided he was careful. He'd cut Dinah off on the trail.

After one near-fatal slip on a loose stone, he made it to the bottom and cut through the woods. If he kept going straight, he'd reach the yew study area first. He speeded up, anxious to see her now that she was near.

She wasn't at the site when he arrived. A quick glance at the trees told him the bark thieves had been there. Fear uncoiled in his belly. He bent and examined the ground. He found four pairs of footprints. One set was Dinah's.

The others were those of the three people from the logging road . . . the ones he'd been tracking for two days.

Scouting the area, he picked up the trail. The men had taken Dinah with them. Fear for her coiled into a knot inside him.

He followed the prints, then realized they were using an old logging cutthrough that came out on the main trail farther along.

It seemed logical that the men, carrying the stripped bark, would head for their truck over on the logging road. He headed that way in a quiet jog.

Hearing voices ahead of him on the trail, he slowed and crept as close as possible, keeping a stand of thick pines between him and the others. When he sneaked a quick look, he saw two men. One of them he recognized—Cawe, the enemy of his cousins.

"The damn woman belongs to the forest service," the smaller of the two men said. "You'll have to get rid of her for good."

"Yeah," Cawe agreed. "We'll have a bit of fun with her first." He laughed in wicked delight. "We'll eat when we get to the truck, then have *dessert.*"

Paul moved back down the trail. At a safe distance, he broke into a run parallel to the trail. He wanted to prepare a welcome for that bunch of rats when they arrived.

As he'd thought, the truck was at the end of the logging road. He checked it over and removed a shotgun and a case of shells. It was simple to dispose of those under a pile of needles and pinecones in the woods. He checked his own automatic. Ready.

He picked up the microphone on the truck radio, saw that the thieves had been listening to the local law channel and called the dispatcher. The sheriff came on and promised to send all the available officers to the area at once.

"Fine," Paul said and signed off. He checked the site and chose a tree to hide behind where he could see the trail but not be noticed by anyone approaching. He'd have to let Dinah and her escort pass him before he drew down on the men.

When the four silently marched past into the small clearing at the road, Paul joined them and waited until they fanned out so all were in his sights. "Stop where you are, gentlemen," he suggested in a calm tone. "Dinah, move aside if you will."

The three men spun around, two of them dropping burlap bags. Bark spilled out. Paul pointed the automatic directly at the men. They raised their hands. Dinah, careful to stay out of the firing line, moved off to one side. She gave him a warm glance.

"Good girl," Paul said. "The sheriff and some friends will be along shortly. We'll just wait here for them. You three sit down and put your hands on top of your heads."

"Cawe had a gun earlier. It was stuck in his belt, but I don't see it now," Dinah warned.

Paul saw the fury blaze into the man's eyes. Ah, Mr. Cawe had been working on a little surprise of his own. "Check his back," Paul told Dinah, "and see if he put it in his belt."

She walked cautiously behind the men. "Yes, it's there," she said, relief coming over her face.

"Get it." Paul swept the business end of his gun over the three and settled it back on Cawe. He'd welcome the chance to shoot the bastard for frightening Dinah.

Dinah bent down and tugged. She couldn't slip the gun out of the belt. She realized Cawe had expanded his torso so that the gun wouldn't pull free. Um, you kicked a horse in the ribs when it held its breath on the cinch.

Keeping hold of the gun, she straightened her legs, shifted her weight and aimed a toe at Cawe's back . . . not too hard, she didn't want to injure him. Suddenly, her leg was caught.

The next thing she knew, she was lifted off her feet like a sack of feed and heaved through the air. She hit in the middle of Paul's legs as he tried to sidestep and keep his gun on the men.

It was too late.

The three men leaped forward. Cawe and the young man grabbed Paul. The weasel grabbed her. Cawe and Paul wrestled for the automatic. She realized she held on to Cawe's gun.

Hitting behind her with it, she managed to land a telling blow to her captor's face. He let her go and grabbed his eye. She spun from him and brought the butt of the heavy forty-four down on his head. He went to his knees, then fell in the dust.

She whirled to help Paul, who was in a tight embrace with the other two thieves. Blood ran from his nose. She realized he'd been injured. Fury burst in her. She rushed forward to help.

A blood-chilling scream shook the forest.

Chapter Fourteen

The struggling men froze, a tableau of arrested motion. The younger man, who'd been trying to hold Paul's left arm, stumbled backward and looked wildly around. A snarl, close by and furious, sent him running down the road in the opposite direction.

In that moment, Paul brought his knee up into his opponent's abdomen. Cawe let go of Paul and the gun. He bent forward, then slowly toppled to the ground when Paul stepped back.

Dinah swung around in a circle, expecting the cougar to charge out of the woods at any moment and attack the humans who'd disturbed her. Behind her, she heard an engine start up and, whirling, spied the other two thieves in the truck.

She crossed the narrow distance between her and Paul, the pistol ready, her finger on the trigger in case Cawe tried anything, but he was through with the fight.

When there were no further snarls from the woods, Dinah drew a shaky breath. She looked at Cawe, who was glaring at Paul.

Looking around, she saw the other two men had the pickup turned and were heading down the track. Too late, she realized. A forest service fire truck was coming at them at a deadly speed.

The weasel stopped the pickup, jumped out and ran for the woods. He didn't get far before a forest ranger was upon him and clicking handcuffs into place. Another ranger had the younger man similarly in tow.

"Well," Paul said in his sardonic drawl, "looks like the cavalry has arrived."

Chris grinned over his shoulder at them. Leaving the older thief with the other ranger, he joined Dinah and Paul. "Well, look who it is." He nodded toward Cawe. "I went to school with him."

"He should have studied more," Paul remarked.

"Hmm." Chris looked toward the woods. "Was that our local mountain lion I saw heading up the ridge when we arrived?"

"I guess." Paul poked Cawe with a boot. "On your feet, man." He chuckled. "I wouldn't traipse around in these parts anymore, if I were you. Cats have long memories, and they're excellent at stalking." He turned to Chris. "I'm pretty sure Cawe's the one who shot her."

"I think so, too. Let's see—kidnapping forest service personnel, stealing valuable bark, harming the wildlife." He wrote in his notebook. "Looks like you're going to be put away for a good long rest," he said to Cawe.

The rangers took statements from her and Paul. They wrote it all down and had them sign the papers; then they had to scout out the area and take pictures of the stolen bark and the trees.

"You folks need a ride?" the other ranger asked when they were ready to leave with the thieves.

Dinah looked at Paul. His eyes met hers in a probing glance that shook her right to her bones. He was furious with her.

But why?

He declined for both of them. "We have horses we need to see to. We'll walk back to the cabin."

They said their farewells. The men left. Dinah and Paul watched them go. Then, "Ready?" Paul asked. "Or do you need to rest before we start back?"

He gave her another searching look, and a muscle twitched beside his mouth as if he held himself in rigid control.

"No," she said. "I'm fine." It took an effort to get the words out, she found.

She couldn't figure Paul out . . . and she was too tired to try. Her emotions had been through so much turmoil during the past hour, she wasn't sure what she felt. She had seesawed through fear for Paul and rage at the thieves so many times that her control was stretched to the limit.

"Dinah," Paul said behind her.

She pivoted slowly. "You could have been killed," she said, low and angry, a tremor running over her. "Three against one. Those men could have taken you apart—" She stopped, unable to think about all the things that could have happened to him.

He touched her chin, lifting her face to his. He glared at her with an equally fierce expression. "What about yourself?" he demanded. "Were you thinking about yourself when you put one man out of commission, then leaped forward, ready to take on the others as needed?"

There was no answer she could give to that without exposing all of her feelings for him. She couldn't do that.

She'd offered her love. He'd refused it. She wouldn't expose her soul, too.

"Let's not talk about it. Not now," she said, exhausted from the emotionally traumatic events. "If you're going to lecture me, it can wait. We have a long trip to the cabin."

Emotions, too fast and deep for her to interpret, crossed his face. She noticed a bruise at the side of his nose. Earlier, she recalled, she'd seen him holding a handkerchief to it.

"You're hurt," she said, unable to hold the worry in.

"Cawe punched me a time or two."

She touched the swelling. "It might be broken. We'll put a cold compress on it. That'll help."

"Will it mar my pretty face?" he asked. There was only a touch of irony in the question and no sign of his sardonic humor.

She supplied it for him. "Hardly. A slight imperfection in your looks would be even better. Women could exclaim over your daring and courage when you explained how you got it."

Whatever reaction she'd expected, it certainly wasn't the thoughtful study he gave her. He seemed to find her mocking answer a profound statement.

She turned and walked back up the trail toward the cabin. Forty minutes later, they arrived. The horses munched grass in the clearing. The scene looked bucolic and peaceful.

Still silent, he pumped well water onto his handkerchief, then folded it and placed it on his nose. "It's late," he said.

She noticed how tired he looked. "Yes."

They would have to stay at the cabin for the night. Then tomorrow... She'd face it when it came.

* * *

Dinah washed up, then prepared a simple meal for them. Paul seemed lost in thought. He sat on one of the stump chairs he'd made and said little.

"How much time do you have left here?" he asked after they'd eaten.

"Actually, none. I don't need to come back. My reports are ready to turn in. The yew trees that haven't been disturbed will need to be checked once or twice a year and the bark regrowth measured. The local ranger can do that."

She busied herself with their few dishes, not daring to look at her companion. She was too strung out. Her eyes burned with tears she wouldn't let fall. The world darkened outside the windows, and she felt the loss of light clear to her soul.

Such drama. Life was the way it was. She'd known that when she first came here and saw Paul again. That seemed eons ago. She'd been through so many changes since then . . .

Changes.

Life was full of changes . . . of choices made, of roads taken. And once taken, there was no going back. The Indians had a saying for it. *The pathway of life goes in one direction.* Her path was different from Paul's. She'd known it from the first.

"What will you be doing next?" he asked.

"We're starting a controlled-burn project in Yellowstone. After that, I'll study the Joshua trees in southern California."

"Sounds like you'll be moving around a lot."

"Yes." It was becoming difficult to talk. She swallowed hard, but it didn't relieve the tightness in her throat.

Paul shifted restlessly. "You like that?"

She met his eyes. "I don't mind. Working on various studies gives me a chance to learn new things."

"Yes," he said.

She couldn't read his thoughts, but he seemed lost in his own introspection, his gaze dark and withdrawn.

When night had fallen completely, she, too, sat in front of the stove, absorbing its banked heat as the air cooled.

Finally, it was time for bed.

She rose and went outside. Paul left when she returned. She brushed her teeth, then offered him her toothpaste when he came in and closed the door.

Glancing at him, a tremor rushed over her. She longed for his touch, but all evening, he'd seemed occupied and distant. Now she saw the hunger.

"Your nose looks better," she mentioned, nervous now that the time for bed had come. "The swelling has gone down."

He made a sound in his throat. He wasn't concerned about his injury. His eyes roamed over her restlessly. A fire burst into flames inside her. She was too vulnerable where he was concerned, but there was no point in telling him that.

"Well, I think I'll go to bed." But she stood there like some frightened animal mesmerized by a hawk's unblinking stare.

"Dinah," Paul said. "We need to talk."

She managed a smile. "Every time you say that, you lecture me—for my own good, of course—on something I don't want to hear."

He smiled reluctantly at her attempt at gallows humor. She licked her lips as he continued to stare at her. He clenched his hands, then opened them in a helpless gesture.

"I don't want you to go," he said hoarsely. He reached for her, his hands closing on her shoulders, and drew her close. His mouth was only inches from hers. She was acutely aware of that fact. One last time. They would make love one last time, then it would be over.

"Paul," she said. It might have been a protest. She wasn't sure. Her voice was reed-thin and breathless, her emotions going through several ups and downs without settling.

"Say you want to stay," he murmured. "Say you want me, too."

She saw the passion in his eyes and was consumed by it. He wanted her and, heaven help her, she wanted him. "No," she said suddenly. Her mouth trembled.

He tugged her closer. His lips were a whisper away.

She turned her head with an effort. If they made love, she would cry. "I want more than a casual affair—"

"So do I," he said fervently. "God, so do I."

She stared up at him. He smiled at her, then he went solemn and serious. He seemed hesitant... unsure. Paul... unsure?

"I want you," he continued after a tense moment.

She shook her head as sadness welled up in her. "Desire isn't enough," she told him. "You were right about that."

He leaned close. "I want everything," he said.

She searched his eyes, afraid to make any assumptions. The fire in him set off flames inside her. She shook her head slightly while her resolve slowly melted. When her legs trembled, she moved back a step. He released her. She sat on the bunk. With a shaky hand, she plucked at her sleeping bag.

He paced the room. "Dammit, pay attention," he suddenly barked.

She jerked her head up.

"Sorry," he muttered. "I'm trying to say something here that I haven't said in a long time. It's a lot harder when a man is thirty-one. It's more... serious."

Her heart nearly lurched out of her chest.

He paced some more. "I was going to give you time away from me—three or four months. I wanted to give you some space." He shrugged helplessly. "I can't do it. I can't take the chance you might meet someone else."

"Paul—"

"Listen," he said on a note of desperation. "I'm only going to say this once."

She closed her mouth, but she knew her eyes were starting to glow. The quiet seeped around them, filled with the increased beat of her heart. He paced and began anew.

"The chemistry is volatile between us. It has been since we first met. Neither of us can ignore it. Because of that . . . and what we've shared . . . you think you love me. I'm not going to argue with that."

"Thank you," she said, happiness starting to build rapidly when she gazed into his eyes. Men could make the simplest things so difficult. "Why don't you make love to me?" she suggested.

He stopped in midstride. "I'm not through."

"Sorry." She subsided.

"I want it all—the home, the family, the sharing. A woman who'll stand by me . . ."

Dinah leaped to her feet.

"Like you," he concluded. His tone went deeper, quieter. "You're the woman of my dreams. I don't think I could give you up if you met someone else. If later you discover you don't love me, that it was all passion and madness, it will be too late. If we marry—well, it's going to last. It has to last," he concluded grimly.

"It will." She walked toward him and laid her hands on his chest. "The first minute of forever is now."

He gave her a fierce stare, saw the glow in her eyes. She felt a tremor run through him; then he caught her to him and buried his face in her hair. She felt him pull air into his lungs like a drowning man coming to the surface.

"Dinah," he said.

She heard the need. "I love you," she told him. "I'll always love you. Nothing can ever change that." She slipped her hands around his neck and into his hair. "Make love to me."

"Yes," he said. "This has been the loneliest week of my life," he murmured hoarsely.

She held him close, grateful for the words, knowing they were hard for him. His arms tightened around her.

The tempest swept them into passion's vortex. Their clothing disappeared until there was no barrier between them. They lay together on the narrow bed, their bodies meshing perfectly.

"You were right," she said breathlessly at one point. "We fit . . . as if we were made for each other."

He nuzzled her neck, her ear, across her cheek until he found her mouth. He gave her ten, twenty quick kisses. "Yes."

She remembered something else. "You mentioned children then, too. The basketball team. Paul, did you—" She couldn't ask.

Raising his head, he gazed down at her. "Was I thinking about a family for us then?"

She nodded.

He paused, then shrugged. "I don't know. I only knew I wanted you in a way I hadn't wanted a woman in a long time. It scared the hell out of me. But I couldn't back off. I wanted to bother you the way you bothered me . . . the way you still bother me."

Without giving her time to think, he swooped down upon her mouth. Soon she wasn't able to think beyond the moment and the things his hands were doing to her.

"Such gentle hands," she said, kissing them.

"I'll never hurt you," he promised. "All you ever have to say is no. Just the word."

"I'll never say no to you," she told him fiercely.

He caressed her breasts, her waist, her hips and thighs. He became more demanding. She gave every response he wanted from her. The winds of passion roared through her, blocking out all sound but their labored breathing, the little sighs and murmurs they made as they touched each other passionately.

"Paul," she whispered.

"I love you," he said.

She heard the promises that came with the words. He wasn't a man to say them lightly. She knew now that his laughter had been as much a shield as her aloof attitude had been. The times he'd withdrawn from her were times when she'd gotten too close, when he'd felt threatened by his feelings for her.

She thought he might still be wary of trusting her love completely, but she'd be patient.

First man-first woman.

She smiled at her fantasy. Maybe they weren't the first couple to fall in love, maybe she wasn't his very first love, but from this moment forward, they would be first in each other's hearts. That was all that counted.

He moved over her. In his embrace, the connection was complete. Life flowed around her, through her, in her. Life touching life . . . making life . . . oh, yes!

* * * * *

Take 4 bestselling love stories FREE

Plus get a FREE surprise gift!

Silhouette

SPECIAL EDITION ™

WHAT EVER HAPPENED TO...?

Have you been wondering when a much-loved character will finally get their own story? Well, have we got a lineup for you! Silhouette Special Edition is proud to present a *Spin-off Spectacular!* Be sure to catch these exciting titles from some of your favorite authors.

FOREVER (SE #854, December) *Ginna Gray*'s THE BLAINES AND THE McCALLS OF CROCKETT, TEXAS are back! Outrageously flirtatious Reilly McCall is having the time of his life trying to win over the reluctant heart of Amanda Sutherland!

A DARING VOW (SE #855, December) You met Zelda Lane in KATE'S VOW (SE #823), and she's about to show her old flame she's as bold as ever in this spin-off of *Sherryl Woods*'s VOWS series.

MAGNOLIA DAWN (SE #857, December) *Erica Spindler* returns with a third story of BLOSSOMS OF THE SOUTH in this tale of one woman learning to love again as she struggles to preserve her heritage.

Don't miss these wonderful titles, only for our readers—only from Silhouette Special Edition!

SPIN2

by
Laurie Paige

Come meet the wild McPherson men and see how these three sexy bachelors are tamed!

In HOME FOR A WILD HEART (SE #828) you got to know Kerrigan McPherson.

In A PLACE FOR EAGLES (SE #839) Keegan McPherson got the surprise of his life.

And in THE WAY OF A MAN (SE #849, November 1993) Paul McPherson finally meets his match.

Don't miss any of these exciting titles, only for our readers—and only from Silhouette Special Edition!

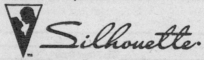

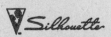